DATE DUE

FEB 1 8 2010	
APR 1 4 2010	
MAR 1 5 2011	
MAY 0 8 2011	
FEB 2 8 2013	
FEB 0 9 2014	
JUL 2 0 2017	

Something in the Water

CHARLOTTE MACLEOD
Something in the Water

THE MYSTERIOUS PRESS

Published by Warner Books

A Time Warner Company

Mysterious Press books are published by Warner Books, Inc.,
1271 Avenue of the Americas, New York, NY 10020.

A Time Warner Company

The Mysterious Press name and logo are trademarks of Warner Books, Inc.

Printed in the United States of America
First printing: April 1994

10 9 8 7 6 5 4 3 2 1

Library of Congress Cataloging-in-Publication Data

MacLeod, Charlotte.
    Something in the water / by Charlotte MacLeod.
        p.   cm.
    ISBN 0-89296-430-8
    1. Shandy, Peter (Fictitious character)—Fiction.   2. College
teachers—Maine—Fiction.   I. Title.
PS3563.A31865S59   1994
813'.54—dc20   93-32779
                                                        CIP

For
Lida Wentworth

Between the Great Glacier and the Mighty Atlantic, Maine's coast has been nibbled into so many picturesque points and inlets that it hardly needs somebody coming along and thinking up imaginary locales in which to commit skulduggeries. This being the only kind of waterfront property she'll ever be able to afford, however, the writer has conjured up Pickwance and Rondel's Head, along with Hocasquam and Sasquamahoc, and populated them with equally imaginary characters. The ocean, the rocks, and the clams are real; the rest of this yarn is straight off the liars' bench.

Something in the Water

Chapter 1

"How the flaming perdition does she get them to grow?"

Thus mused Professor Peter Shandy, horticultural hotshot of Balaclava Agricultural College in rural Massachusetts, temporarily transplanted to Bright's Inn at Pickwance, somewhere along the stern and rockbound coast of Maine. He was here for two reasons, the first being that his wife had taken it into her head to entertain certain friends of her youth at what sounded to Peter like an extended pajama party. Having made his token appearance as cock of the walk, he'd obliged Mrs. Shandy and her guests by taking himself out from underfoot and finding someplace else to roost pro tem.

The "she" in his unspoken question was the second reason for his being here. Helen's boon buddy, Catriona McBogle, first to arrive at the party complete with sleeping bag and fuzzy bedroom slippers with pussy-cat faces on the toes, had suggested that he take a ride up to see Miss Rondel's lupines while she herself made merry with his beloved though sometimes over-gregarious Helen and the rest of the quondam girls.

Frances Hodgson Rondel, to give the lupine expert her full

name, had been amenable to Professor Shandy's visit. He'd met her that morning, almost hidden among arrogant cone-shaped panicles of bloom that shot straight up, four, five, six feet and more from great mats of exquisitely cut, mysteriously green foliage. To have called their colors breathtaking would, Peter felt, have been like calling a Stradivarius a fiddle. They ranged from whites that he thought might look about right on an angel's wing through delicate pinks, innocent baby blues, from fugitive pale yellows like the feathers on a confusing spring warbler to suave apricot, to blatantly trumpeting burnished gold, to regal purples, to reds that Titian might have been able to paint if he'd had the northern lights to dip his brush into.

Peter had a keen and careful eye for color. He'd brought forth in his greenhouses hybrids that had won him much acclaim and quite a lot of money as a horticulturist. But he knew now, in his heart of hearts, that here on this starved, rocky fragment of Maine coast, Mother Nature had made a monkey of him.

No matter, he had not yet begun to show these unlikely giants who was who. He'd be here again tomorrow morning as soon as it was decent, his gathering bags at the ready. It was getting on into July now. Peter had noticed on the way up from Massachusetts that those stately legumes for which certain stretches of Maine roadsides are justly famed were starting to go by. Now was the time for action, and here surely was the place of all places. Miss Rondel couldn't quite see what he was so wrought up about but she'd been quite ready to grant him permission to take what he pleased, once she'd found out who he was, where he'd come from, and who'd sent him to her.

Peter had already taken a few soil samples, with Miss Rondel's amused permission. He would mail them off first thing tomorrow to his friend Professor Ames, for analysis in the college laboratory. He'd asked Miss Rondel what she used for fertilizer and received only an enigmatic smile by way of answer; he suspected a tea made of well-aged poultry manure. So far he'd spied no more than three hens at Rondel's Head, but those three were the size of young turkeys, with flaming scarlet combs, feathers that shone like the Golden Cockerel of legend, and expressions of smug self-satisfaction on their haughtily beaked faces. He'd be willing to bet they never laid anything less impressive than jumbo-sized eggs with double yolks.

Miss Rondel herself was no inferior specimen. She stood maybe five feet seven in her ragged sneakers without the hint of a stoop, although the deeply engraved lines in her face and the knotted veins on the backs of her hands gave evidence to the passage of years. Nor was corroboration lacking. After having checked in late the previous afternoon, he'd asked Elva Bright, the innkeeper, if she happened to know the lady who raised the lupines.

"I ought to," Mrs. Bright had replied. "She went to school with my grandmother."

Elva herself, as everybody but Peter seemed to call her, was a grandmother several times over. Peter had deduced this from sundry remarks he'd heard her exchange with some of the local people who'd come to supper last night and to breakfast this morning, from photographs stuck up around the cash register, and from the unblushing bud of sweet sixteen or thereabouts who waited on tables in shocking-pink stirrup pants and a demure flowered blouse and addressed the innkeeper as "Gram."

So Miss Rondel must be far advanced in years, despite her upright carriage and vigorous movements. Maybe couples mar-

3

ried young around here. Maybe this was the kind of place where families intermarried to the point where an infant could become another's great-uncle practically *in utero*. Maybe it was something in the water. Peter finished the last bite of his excellent chicken pot pie and looked around hopefully for the coffee and Indian pudding that he dimly recalled having ordered some while ago.

He'd been late getting back to the inn, having made a wide swing along the coast after leaving Miss Rondel and stopped to bird-watch. Dinner or supper, depending on where the eater came from, was just about over. Only two others were left in the dining room. One was the neatly dressed old man whom Peter had noticed last night at that same table over in the far corner; the other a big loudmouth who'd come in just after Peter; though a clutter of used china on the various tables indicated that business had been brisk enough earlier on.

The loudmouth had shot a hopeful glance at Peter, got no response, and settled for joshing the young waitress, whose name seemed to be Thurzella or something in that general vicinity. She'd endured his uncouth japeries without comment until she'd finished clearing a nearby table, then remarked that there was only one helping of chicken pot pie left and Mr. Flodge had better order fast if he wanted it because if he didn't, she sure did. It showed the sort of cad Flodge was, Peter decided, that he'd forthwith demanded the pot pie and was now wolfing it down as though he feared Thurzella might be scheming to snatch it away.

The old gent in the corner had set down his coffee and was watching in unconcealed awe as Flodge shoveled in the chicken and peas with the speed and efficiency of a well-oiled robot. Portions at Bright's Inn were generous to the point of overwhelming; Flodge was hardly more than halfway finished when, abruptly, without sound or sign, he pitched forward and landed face-down in his plate.

His hand jerked, smashing his water glass to the floor. Thurzella dropped a trayful of stacked plates, let out a shriek that no operatic soprano could have bettered, and made a grab for the stricken man's back hair. It came away in her hand.

"Granny! Granny, quick! Jasper Flodge fell in the gravy and his hair came off."

"Hush, Thurzella, it's only a toupee. Come on, Jasper, get up out of that before you drown yourself in the gravy. Don't just stand gawking, Thurzella. Go get something to clean up this mess."

Mrs. Bright threw the toupee disgustedly on an empty chair, took Flodge by the back of his shirt collar, hoisted him to a sitting position, and began swabbing at his face with a napkin. "Professor, I don't like to bother you—"

"It's no bother, Mrs. Bright." Peter was already out of his chair and at her side. "Let's have a look."

He'd brought along his own napkin and water glass, he wetted the napkin and sluiced it over the gravy-streaked face. The eyes were half open, the lids didn't flutter. Peter slapped the unconscious man between the shoulder blades, performed the Heimlich maneuver, finally picked up one of the stainless-steel table knives that Mrs. Bright kept polished to a mirror finish and held it close to the gaping mouth. Not a breath clouded the shiny surface. He glanced up at the innkeeper and she looked back at him.

"Better call the doctor, hadn't I, Professor?"

"And the constable, or whoever you've got for police around here."

As Peter stood by the lifeless body and wondered what in Sam Hill to do next, Mrs. Bright made a beeline for the front desk, where the telephone sat. Thurzella came in from the kitchen laden with a mop, a pail of water, a broom and dustpan, a roll of paper towels, and for some reason, a little pink-handled dishmop.

"Didn't the pie set right with you, Mr. Flodge?"

She reached for the messy plate. Peter stayed her hand.

"Leave it alone, Thurzella."

"But why? He won't want it now, all squished up like that."

"No. No, he won't want it now, Thurzella. Shouldn't you be doing something about that broken glass before somebody steps on it?"

The girl didn't seem to hear, she was staring down at the man who'd done her out of the chicken pot pie. "He's dead, isn't he?" she said at last. "I've never watched anybody die before. It's—scary, isn't it?"

"Yes, it's scary." She was only a kid, after all. "Here, why don't you go back to the kitchen and make yourself a cup of tea or something? I'll sweep up the glass. We ought to leave the table as it is until the police come."

"But why, Professor? It doesn't seem right just to—"

"I know," said Peter, "but that's the way they—watch it!"

He managed to catch the girl before she landed among the shards and ease her into a chair at the next table, where she wouldn't have to look at the frightening huddle that had so recently been Jasper Flodge. Then he called over to the silent man in the corner.

"Sir, could you come and keep an eye on this young lady while I pick up the broken glass? She's not feeling too well."

"Neither am I."

The man stood up, however, leaning heavily on a thick blackthorn cane, and labored himself across the room. Peter felt sorry that he'd bothered the poor old coot. Once the man managed to reach Thurzella, however, he proved competent enough. He lowered himself carefully into the chair next to her, pulled out, of all serendipitous objects, a dainty Victorian silver smelling bottle with a blue glass liner, and held it under the fainting youngster's nose.

"This was my mother's," he explained a trifle self-consciously, "and her mother's before her. Being somewhat subject to dizziness, for reasons I shan't bore you with, I find it a useful thing to carry around. Take a good sniff, Thurzella, it will clear your head."

She sniffed, coughed, sneezed and began to cry. The man handed her a fine linen handkerchief, ironed to a gloss, white as a snow goose's breast. "There, there, you'll be all right. Perhaps this kind gentleman might bring you a drink of water?"

An aluminum pitcher and a trayful of clean goblets had been left on a serving table over by the cash register. Peter went over and gave the pitcher an experimental slosh to see if there was still any water in it. There was, not much, but enough. He filled one of the goblets and carried it back to Thurzella.

She was still sobbing into the beautiful handkerchief. The elderly man was quite sensibly sitting silent and letting her cry. He took the goblet from Peter and offered it with the same Old World punctilio as he'd provided the handkerchief and the smelling salts. Thurzella gulped a few times, blew her nose, dried her eyes, and took the water, making a clumsy business of getting the goblet to her lips. It did the trick, though. By the time Elva Bright got back from her telephoning, the granddaughter was on her hands and knees under Flodge's table chasing stray chips with dustpan and brush while Peter wielded the broom.

The innkeeper was scandalized. "Give me that broom, Professor! You're not forking out good money to sweep my floor for me, not that I don't appreciate your helping. I've had the devil's own time getting hold of anybody, but it's finally fixed that they're sending the emergency wagon over from the Narrows to pick him up. Dr. Bee's promised to go take a look at him once he gets there. The doctor says it was most likely a heart attack, which wouldn't surprise me one iota, considering the way Jasper lived. So I guess it's all right to clean him up and make him halfway presentable, at least. He'd hate to be seen at the hospital with his face all gaumed up and green peas coming out of his ears."

"And his hair off," added the elderly man with a perfectly straight face. "Were you able to reach Flodge's—ah—housekeeper?"

"Oh, he hasn't had any for five months or better. The last one didn't find it lively enough around here in the wintertime, for which I suppose a person can't blame her. That's why Jasper's been eating here so regularly. He hasn't been able to strike it lucky again, if that's what you'd call luck. This is a fine way for me to be running on, I must say, with him sitting here dead. Thurzella, hadn't you better skite along home? Your mother'll be wondering what's happened to you."

"No, she won't. She and Dad are over at Aunt Sara Ann's. Uncle Ira's birthday's next week, you know, and Aunt Sara bought him a bunch of old Greta Garbo tapes for a present. Tonight's his bowling night with the crew from the mill, so she invited Mum and Dad over for a sneak preview. They'll be hopping when they find out what they've missed. Can't I stay with you tonight, Grammy?"

"Now, Thurzella. You know your father will have fourteen cat fits if you're not in bed when they get home."

"But I'm scared to walk home in the dark."

"Er—" Peter cleared his throat. "Does she have far to go? I could run her home in my car."

"Lord, no, Professor, it's just down the road. I'll take my flashlight and go with her if one of you men wouldn't mind waiting here till I get back, in case the wagon shows up."

"I can wait," said the elderly man. "Waiting's about all I'm good for these days. Perhaps Professor—I'm sorry, sir, but I don't know your name."

"It's Shandy. I teach at Balaclava Agricultural College down in Massachusetts. Go ahead, Mrs. Bright, I'll stick around and keep him company. Assuming you care for any, Mr.—"

"Withington. Claridge Withington. I've done some teaching myself, in years past. Am I right in thinking that you're the Shandy who hybridized the portulaca Purple Passion? Not to mention the famous Balaclava Buster rutabaga."

"M'well, yes, I suppose you could say so, though my friend Professor Ames did most of the work. You're not by any chance the Claridge Withington who writes for the *Lupine Ledger?*"

"Dear me, don't say you've actually read some of my pieces?"

"Oh yes, I always do. So does my wife, I believe you've quoted her once or twice. She's curator of the Buggins Collection at Balaclava and has written rather extensively on the Buggins family."

"Helen Marsh Shandy, of course! A lady I greatly admire, if I may say so. Well, well, this is indeed a small world. Your wife is not with you, by any fortunate chance?"

"No, she's entertaining a houseful of her old friends and I'm under orders to make myself scarce."

Peter found it odd to be making small talk in the presence of a possibly stiffening corpse, although he'd experienced a similar phenomenon often enough with some of his early-morning classes. He wondered whether Jasper Flodge hadn't

9

better be laid out on the serving table in order to prevent any awkwardness about getting him stowed into the emergency wagon. It would hardly do to voice his perturbation now, he wouldn't be able to manage the job alone unless Mr. Withington's cane turned out to be a collapsible gurney. Which wouldn't surprise Peter much, all things considered.

Anyway, the Narrows, in whatever direction it might lie, must not be any great distance from the inn if Mrs. Bright thought the wagon might arrive before she got back. Unless she was planning to drop over to Sara Ann's en route and watch the movie. Maine people, as Peter had learned on a previous visit, did tend to step to the music they heard, however remote and far away.

"And what brought you here, Professor Shandy?" Withington was asking. "Pickwance has its devotees, of whom I am one, but it's hardly a Mecca for tourists."

"That in itself would be reason enough," said Peter, "but in fact I came because our friend Catriona MacBogle suggested that I'd be interested in seeing Miss Rondel's lupines."

"Of course, the lupines! I haven't seen them in recent years myself, for obvious reasons, but I have vivid memories of how spectacular they used to be. Are they as gorgeous as ever?"

How in tunket was Peter Shandy supposed to know that? "They're the most impressive specimens I've ever run across. What does she use for fertilizer, do you know?"

"Sorry, I'm afraid I can't help you there. Fertilizers haven't happened to come within my frame of reference. It would be some kind of animal manure, I suppose; Frances Rondel hasn't much use for anything that doesn't come straight out of Mother Nature's cupboard. She used to keep a cow, I remember. Frederica, its name was, quite a pretty cow with a surprisingly melodious moo. I wrote a little piece about Frederica once but never thought to consider the—ah—end results, so to speak. I don't believe Wordsworth ever did, either. Ah well, each thing in its place is best, and what seems like idle show strengthens and supports the rest. Are you at all familiar with Wordsworth, Professor?"

Peter was well acquainted with Wordsworth. More to the point, he also knew his Longfellow. It would be cruel to explain that he and Helen read Withington's little pieces mainly for the fun of seeing which of them could pick out the larger number of unattributed and misapplied quotations.

"I've never danced with a daffodil, if that's what you mean. Then I take it you're a long-time resident of Pickwance, Mr. Withington?"

"Not precisely a resident. More a perennial summer complaint, to employ the pungent local terminology. I can't take the Maine winters nowadays, but I do stretch out my stays until the foliage season has gone by. Elva Bright is very good about making me comfortable, she's even sacrificed her back parlor so that I don't have to climb stairs. And I amuse myself absorbing the local gossip. I probably know more about Pickwance by now than most of its present inhabitants do. Not to be off-putting, Professor Shandy, but did you know that this building was once the regional pesthouse?"

Chapter 2

Peter suppressed a yawn. "You mean this is where they ducked the scolds and mured up the unruly schoolboys?"

Withington awarded this feeble sally a dry chuckle. "Not precisely. It's where they isolated their infected neighbors, back in the so-called good old days. Sailors would pick up exotic bugs in foreign ports, you know, and come home to infect their wives and sweethearts. Then there'd be outbreaks of mumps, measles, and so forth. Smallpox was the most dreaded, but tuberculosis was the chief killer. At one time, the pesthouse became a sanitarium, until vaccination put it out of business. The air around here was supposed to be particularly benefical to sufferers from lung disease; patients would come all the way from Boston and New York, hoping for miracles. And finding them too, sometimes, or so it's been claimed."

Withington eased his gammy leg and winced. "Now that some of the old diseases that we thought had been conquered are regaining their footholds, thanks largely to the fact that children no longer get trained to wash their hands before they eat and after they've performed their natural functions—thus

13

speaketh the schoolmaster—Elva might even find herself being asked to take in patients again. Not that she'd consider it, however, after what she went through with her late husband."

Peter supposed he ought to make some politely interrogative noise. He settled for cocking one eyebrow, which was enough. His fellow boarder didn't need to be coaxed.

"That was a sad affair. Jean-Luc was a Frenchman, a genuine hero of the Resistance who'd been caught and tortured by the Nazis but, it's said, never cracked. Somehow or other, his friends got him away and smuggled him aboard an American troopship that was bringing back a cargo of wounded and disabled servicemen. I'm not clear as to how he wound up at Pickwance; whether he was hoping to find relatives—as you know, there are many people of French descent in Maine—or whether he was just looking for a place to crawl into and lick his wounds."

The elderly man eased his leg again, using both hands to move it. "Well, to make a long story short, here he was. By that time, the Brights had been running the old pesthouse as an inn for quite a while. Elva is the third generation of innkeepers. She was about the age then that Thurzella is now, and doing much the same kind of work, helping out with the serving and flipping a dustcloth over the places that showed. She was quite a pretty girl, and Jean-Luc Mercier de L'Avestant-Portallier, if I've got it all in, was rather handsome in a gaunt and haggard sort of way. He was thirty-five and she was just out of high school, so it need hardly be said that they fell in love, notwithstanding the fact that Jean-Luc's experiences in the torture chamber had left him fit for nothing much except the begetting of children, which he proceeded to do in fairly short order."

14

"Too bad," said Peter, not knowing what else to say but not wishing to be churlish.

"Oh no, it wasn't bad at all. Jean-Luc had money of his own, either an inheritance or a pension of some sort. Presumably he had no entanglements back in France or else the Brights were careful not to inquire. Anyway, he and Elva were married before the situation got too far out of hand and lived as happily as most couples. Perhaps better than some, I wouldn't know. Jean-Luc had a nose for finance, he subscribed to the *Wall Street Journal* and played the market."

"Successfully?"

"Well enough. After a few years he was in a position to buy out the parents in cold cash, much to the chagrin of Elva's brother, who'd never raised a hand to help out but had confidently expected to inherit the inn after the old folks were gone. They did go, as a matter of fact, first to Florida to live it up on Jean-Luc's money, and thence in the fullness of time to the Pearly Gates, where I'm sure they had no trouble gaining admittance."

"Ungh. What about Jean-Luc?"

"He managed to sire a second daughter and pile up a comfortable nest egg for his wife and the girls before his infirmities caught up with him. He also left Elva the inn free and clear, which assured her a livelihood. I shouldn't suppose a small place like this would require much in the way of management and upkeep."

Like hell it wouldn't, but Peter saw no point in trying to say so when Withington still had a good head of steam up.

"I suppose it hasn't been a bad life for Elva, all things considered. Both the girls have married respectably and reared, as far as I can tell, reasonably civilized children. Michele, the elder, is the one who lives down the road. Her husband man-

15

ages a sawmill and she does hand-weaving, which I'm told she sells quite profitably through various craft shops, including her own. I expect Michele will take over the inn eventually, though one never knows. Therese, the younger, won't want it. She's a psychologist married to a prominent lawyer in Portland. They come up quite often. You may get to meet them if you stay through the weekend."

Withington speeded up his delivery, perhaps to keep Peter from saying no, he wouldn't. "Maybe Thurzella will take over, or possibly some of the other grandchildren. Whoever steps in will inevitably keep the Bright name, of course, as Elva has done. It goes with the job."

Peter was finding the Bright family saga less than enthralling. "I wonder what's keeping her?" he fretted. "I thought she was just going down the road."

"Please don't feel you have to stick around on my account."

The inflection in Withington's voice made it clear that Professor Shandy would be the rottenest of rotters to leave an infirm latter-day counterpart of the Ancient Mariner in the lurch with a cooling cadaver. Unfortunately, the old bore was right. Peter was greatly relieved when the front door opened and Mrs. Bright hurried into the dining room.

"Sorry I took so long. Thurzella was in kind of a taking, she's always been the sensitive one. I had to call up Sara Ann and tell her to send Michele and Bob home. Needless to say, that started a lot of backing and forthing about what happened and all that, you know how it is. It was real nice of you two to stay, you might as well go along and turn in now if you want to. Here's your smelling bottle, Claridge. Thurzella forgot to give it back. I'll wash your handkerchief tomorrow."

She dropped her flashlight into the drawer under the cash register and reached for the telephone. "I'm going to give those

16

gormless critters at the Narrows another ring and find out what's keeping the wagon. It's not as though Pickwance wasn't forking out good money every year for the service, such as it is. Would either of you care for a cup of cocoa, or maybe some ginger tea? It's a bit late for coffee."

"None for me, thanks," said Peter before Withington could get started on another oration. "But I'll go put the kettle on if you want something."

"No, Michele made me sit down and drink a cup of tea to steady my nerves, which it won't. I'll be tossing and turning all night, I expect. Oh, here they come now. All my ranting and raving for nothing, isn't that always the way? I'm sorry you two had to get dragged in like this, but I surely do appreciate your help."

"We didn't do anything," Peter demurred.

"Except to make ourselves better acquainted," Mr. Withington added with more grace. "Let's hope our next conversation occurs under less macabre circumstances, Professor Shandy."

Peter suppressed a mean hope that it wouldn't happen at all and guessed he might as well get out from underfoot. This was easier said than done. By now a stalwart young woman and a runty older man, both wearing clean white lab coats over dungarees and T-shirts, were blocking the dining-room door with a stretcher on wheels, an oxygen tank, and sundry other appurtenances for which there could be no earthly use. By now the late Jasper Flodge's fleshly integument was obviously beyond any hope of revival and his immortal self on the way to a better place. Or not, as the case might be.

The pair began nevertheless to put a blood-pressure cuff on his flaccid arm and an oxygen mask over his face, asking Mrs. Bright as they worked what had happened. She gave them the

17

particulars as best she could, with frequent interpolations from Claridge Withington. Having taken turnabout with their one stethoscope, watched the blood-pressure gauge, and failed to get either a breath or a pulse, the two paramedics at last removed the cuff and the oxygen mask and pronounced old Jas a goner.

"Nothing we can do but haul him along for Dr. Bee to take apart," said the man, whose name was Albert something. "Let's see now, wasn't Jas connected someway or other to the Rondels?"

"Not to my knowledge," Mrs. Bright answered, "though he might have liked to let on he was. You knew Jasper better than I did, he always laid it on pretty thick when he got the chance. Naturally he wouldn't try pulling any of his nonsense on me. Furthermore, there's none of the Rondels left but Miss Fran, and you can hardly expect her to help with the funeral, if that's what you're getting at."

"He looks awfully blue in the face," said the young woman, whose name was Cynthia something. "Don't you think so, Al? You don't suppose he strangled on his supper, Elva? You say he was eating awfully fast."

Claridge Withinton interrupted. "Elva was in the kitchen at the time. I was sitting where I could watch Mr. Flodge, however, and I can testify that he was gobbling at an astonishing rate of speed. So could Thurzella, if she were here and so, perhaps, can Professor Shandy, although he had a book with him and may have been reading."

"So Jas could have choked, then. Didn't you think to give him the Heimlich maneuver?"

"Professor Shandy did, but I believe Mr. Flodge was already dead by then."

"What about that, Professor? Was he?"

"He had no pulse and wasn't breathing. I did look up from my book, as a matter of fact, while Flodge was still eating, and saw him fall. I neither saw nor heard any sign that he'd choked, though he did jerk his hand and knock his water glass off the table. It happened in an instant."

"There, see," said Elva. "If Jasper had choked he'd at least have grabbed at his throat and made some kind of noise, wouldn't he? According to Thurzella, he just keeled over all of a sudden smack into his plate and never moved again. We had to wash the gravy off his face."

"Must have been an aneurism, then, or one of those sudden, massive coronaries," said Albert. "Been carrying a time bomb around in his chest, like as not, and never knew it. Well, there are worse ways to go than with a full belly and no fuss."

"You don't suppose he could have been poisoned?" Cynthia was obviously determined to extract the last ounce of drama, perhaps in compensation for not getting to use her oxygen tank to any good effect. "My husband and I were watching a spy movie on the "Late Show" the other night and this guy who got caught by the other guys chomped down on a cyanide pill that he'd had hidden behind his wisdom tooth and flopped down dead as a mackerel, just the way you say Jasper did."

"Jasper had no back teeth, and not many front ones. He'd lost them all from being scared of the dentist, fool that he was."

Peter was jolted by the surge of emotion in the innkeeper's voice. He wondered if Mrs. Bright was thinking about Jean-Luc in the torture chamber, and of what might have happened if her to-be lover and husband had had a lethal capsule parked behind his wisdom tooth then.

"Anyway," Mrs. Bright went on in a more temperate tone, "why should he poison himself, here or anyplace else?"

CHARLOTTE MACLEOD

"And furthermore," added Withington, ready like Cynthia
to keep the speculation going, "where would Jasper Flodge
have got the cyanide capsule? They're not the sort of things
people keep sitting around in their medicine chests. Don't you
agree, Elva?"

"I don't go prowling through my neighbors' medicine
chests, so I wouldn't know." The innkeeper was definitely on
a short fuse by now, and who could blame her? "Al, can't you
and Cynthia just put Jasper on that stretcher of yours and get
him out of here? I don't know about the rest of you, but I'm
all in but the toenails, and they're rattling. Do you have
everything you need for the night, Professor?"

"Yes, thank you. Good night, everyone."

Peter stood not upon the order of going, but went, hoping
that Withington would have the sense to do likewise before
this beleaguered woman hit the ceiling. He was developing a
partisan feeling toward Mrs. Bright. She reminded him a little
of his grandmother Shandy, though he knew better than to
tell her so. He was halfway up the stairs when a man with a
beer belly hanging out over his belt, wearing a dirty blue
lightweight nylon jacket and a feed-store cap that failed quite
to cover his bald spot, entered the lobby.

"You around, Elva?"

Peter felt it would be churlish not to say something. "Mrs.
Bright's—er—rather busy just now."

This man didn't look to him like somebody wanting a room
and could hardly be a presently registered guest. According to
Withington, Elva had just got rid of a party of six and wasn't
expecting anybody new until weekend after next. The rooms,
he'd said, were merely a sideline to the more popular and
lucrative dining room; Mrs. Bright didn't much care whether
she filled them or not. Making up beds and catering to the

20

divers needs of fretful tourists was almost more bother than it was worth. Or so had adduced the garrulous star boarder, during the latter part of their recent conversation, before Cynthia and Albert had shown up and he was running out of things to talk about.

The man in the feed cap was not accepting Peter's answer. "That so? I heard she was lookin' for me."

"Oh. Then you must be the sheriff. Or—er—"

"Constable. Where's she at?"

"In the dining room."

Just why Peter found himself impelled to go back downstairs and usher the constable to the scene of whatever action might still be going on was something he would wonder about afterward. The explanation, however, was clear enough. Several years ago, he'd found his most obnoxious neighbor stretched out dead behind his parlor sofa as the result of a horrendous practical joke that he himself had instigated. Adjured by Balaclava's even more horrendous President Thorkjeld Svenson to catch Jemima Ames's murderer without attracting unwanted publicity to the college or face the consequences, he had managed, by carrying out the President's order, to avoid being mangled and stomped on. Since then, he had somehow become Balaclava Junction's unofficial, unpaid, but too frequently overworked sleuth-for-all-seasons.

A sickening thought overtook him. Would Jasper Flodge's dramatic demise turn out to have been caused by a nice, tidy exploding aneurysm? Or was it the result of a skulduggerous plot in which P. Shandy himself would somehow become embroiled, simply because he'd waited for the Indian pudding that had never, come to think of it, got served to him.

As he steered the constable into the dining room, Peter began frantically running over the possible methods by which a presumably hale and hearty man in his middle years could suddenly be caused to expire into half a helping of excellent chicken pot pie. Vegetable poisons were out, he decided. Thanks to their snide way of lurking unnoticed in the digestive tract until all reasonable hope of recovery was past, these were usually reliable and hard to pin on the culprit. Before administering the coup de grâce, however, they generally put on a show of highly detectable and regrettably disgusting symptoms. Death, when it came, was the result of a slow paralysis rather than an abrupt thunk.

A knitting needle inserted through an eardrum or up a nostril into the brain might give the desired effect if deftly applied and quickly removed, but who could have managed it? Not the crippled Withington, who'd been sitting several tables away. Hardly the lissome but sensitive Thurzella. Not Shandy himself. Not Mrs. Bright, because she hadn't entered the dining room until after Flodge was dead.

An air gun shot through an open window nearest to where Flodge was sitting? Easy enough for a crack marksman, no doubt, but the bullet would certainly have left a hole in the screen and another in Flodge. A death ray, then? Most unlikely, although one could never be sure nowadays. An illwishing? Maybe Miss Rondel was the neighborhood witch and Flodge had been a hated relative trying to get his hands on the old homestead, not to mention those high-powered lupine seeds that Shandy himself was planning to obtain; though of course not unless he could come by them legitimately and with Miss Rondel's willing acquiescence. Here was indeed a puzzlement.

To which, no doubt, the often mentioned but as yet unseen Dr. Bee would give a tidy, unpuzzling answer as soon as he'd got around to examining the corpse. Then Mrs. Bright would be freed of all care, somebody or other would be stuck with administering Jasper Flodge's estate for better or for worse, and Peter Shandy would be wending his way back to Helen with a stash of lupine seeds in the glove compartment and a song in his heart. It was a consummation devoutly to be wished.

Chapter 3

Yet here Peter stood, trying to avoid looking at the blanket-covered heap on the stretcher while the constable, whose name was Frank something, heard the whole story from Elva Bright, with footnotes by Claridge Withington, embellishments from Cynthia and Albert, and a few words of corroboration from Peter himself. Frank greeted each utterance with a grunt, then pulled down the blanket and took a hard look at the corpse.

"Homely bahstid. Shame to waste the pie." He pulled the blanket back up. "He's yours, Al. Might as well take 'im along."

"Is that all you're going to do?" Cynthia clearly didn't think much of Frank's performance as contrasted to the one she'd seen on the "Late Show." "Aren't you going to look for clues?"

"What to?"

"How'm I supposed to know? All mysterious deaths have to be investigated. That's your job, isn't it?"

"Not if I can help it. Might have to get the state police in."

"And run up another bill for the town?" snorted Al. "You

25

know what happened when the last constable overspent his limit."

"Well, I don't care." Cynthia was still in there swinging. "You've got to do something, Frank."

"I'll know what to do when I find out what killed 'im."

"But by then the clues will be gone."

"If there ever was any in the first place." Albert was beginning to sound a bit testy, for which Peter didn't blame him a particle. "Cynthia's got it into her head that Jas chewed up a cyanide pill, like some bugger she seen in the movies."

"I didn't say that at all," his co-worker sputtered. "I just say I think it's mighty darned strange, him keeling over all of a sudden, just like that spy."

"One way to find out." Frank pulled away the blanket again and pried the dead man's mouth wide open. "Help yourself, Cynthia. Take a sniff."

"What, me?"

"You're the one that wants to know."

"He's right, Cynthia." Withington was all excited. "Cyanide smells like bitter almonds, at least that's what they always claim in the mystery novels. I was reading the other day—"

Nobody was listening. Peter, Elva, Albert, and Frank were all giving Cynthia the eagle eye. She flushed, tossed her head, and bent over the open mouth.

"My God!" She straightened up and backed away, her face now chalk white. "He does smell like almonds. Here, Al, you try."

"I think you're nuts." Nevertheless, Albert sniffed. "By jeezum, Frank, she's right. Go ahead, call me a liar."

"Never knew a time when you wasn't one." However, the constable knew his duty, up to a point, and he did it. "Ayuh. Anybody else want to give it a go?"

Claridge Withington was the only taker. He made heavy weather of it, fumbling with his cane and tripping over one of the stretcher wheels. The constable had to reach across the body and steady him with a massive hand; when he leaned over, he moved all of a piece, Peter noticed. He must have to wear some kind of body brace, poor devil. His sniff, when he'd at last got himself into position for it, was a halfhearted effort. When he straightened up, his face showed fastidious revulsion.

"I fear I'm not cut out for detection. It's almond, no question about that. Do you suppose you ought to—ugh—perhaps not."

"Not what?"

"Search behind his teeth for the remains of a capsule, I was going to say. I wish I hadn't thought of that."

"So do I." Cynthia had clearly lost interest in hunting for clues. "If"—she swallowed—"there's anything inside, Dr. Bee will find it. Right, Al?"

"Stands to reason. Jas sure as hell isn't going to swallow nothing now. Come on, let's not keep Elva standing here all night."

"Er—" Peter had no more desire to keep the party going than anybody else, but there was still one question that ought to be raised. "Not to strain your patience, ladies and gentlemen, but is there any chance that Mr. Flodge might have been drinking Amaretto or eating salted almonds before he got to the inn?"

It was Elva Bright who cracked up. Maybe her peals of laughter were mostly hysteria, she was entitled to a fit or two after the evening she'd put in; she showed no inclination to stop until Withington whipped out his grandmother's smelling salts again and held the open flask under her nose, throwing her into a choking spell.

"Take that fool thing away," she gasped once she'd got her breath back. "If you want to be helpful, go stick your hand in Jasper's pants pocket. You'd better do it, Frank, you're the constable."

"An' damn sorry I let myself in for gettin' elected. You won't catch me signin' on for another stretch."

"Oh, all right, then, if you're too finicky to search a dead man's britches."

She stepped over to the stretcher, paused to slip her hand under the late Flodge's chin and shut the gaping mouth, then began to rummage. It took her about thirty seconds to locate a small glass bottle and pull it out of his watch pocket. "There you are, folks. Here's your cyanide pill."

Cynthia was the first to catch on. "I'll be dipped! Almond extract, right? My mother puts it in her macaroon cookies. Are you telling us Jasper Flodge used to drink that stuff?"

"Why not? I understand back during Prohibition lots of men used to swill it down by the jugful. Women too, for that matter. Vanilla, lemon, peppermint, whatever they could get their hands on. Naturally Jasper would pick almond, he was crazy about anything that had a flavor of almonds to it."

The innkeeper's lips twitched in a grim smile. "After my husband passed on and Jasper found out that I wasn't likely to turn into the poor, starving widow some folks seemed to think I'd be, he tried to shine up to me a little. Not that he got any encouragement but an innkeeper can't be unneighborly. I remember one night he showed up on the doorstep with a box of marzipan candies shaped like different vegetables and colored accordingly, you know how they do. They were supposed to be for me and the girls, but Jasper plunked himself down on the sofa to watch some stupid television program and ate every one of those candies except a make-believe potato that old Rex managed to joggle out of his hand. Rex was an awful thief when he got the chance. But I still miss him, fool that I am."

This time, Peter sensed, Elva Bright's flicker of a smile was for her own human frailty and for a dog long gone to the Happy Hunting Ground.

"So, to make a long story short, after Jasper'd been arrested for drunk driving one time too many and the judge told him he could either stay sober or go to jail, he made a great show of going on the wagon."

"Still managed to keep a pretty good buzz on half the time, howsomever," Albert put in. "I often wondered how he got by with it."

"Simple enough. He'd keep his little bottle of almond extract handy in his pocket and sneak a nip every so often when he thought nobody was looking. I've noticed him doing it time and again, though of course I never said anything. I shouldn't be at all surprised if Jasper didn't take a swig tonight, while Thurzella was in the kitchen picking up his supper. I don't know why it didn't come to me sooner. Softening of the brain, I expect. The way I feel right now, you two might as well haul me away along with Jasper."

"But then who'd cook breakfast for Professor Shandy and me?" Withington's smile was not unattractive, his many wrinkles notwithstanding. "You're just worn out, Elva. Things will look different in the morning."

This dining room was going to look a damned sight emptier, Peter thought cynically, unless Dr. Bee brought in a verdict of death from natural causes. People did tend to turn skittish about eating in restaurants where patrons dropped dead in their plates for no apparent reason.

Well, it would be a crying shame if Mrs. Bright's business failed on account of Jasper Flodge, but there was nothing Peter

29

Shandy could do to help. This was not his territory, he was dratted if he'd let himself get involved. He said a last and final good night, and went upstairs.

Morning dawned clear as a bell, but Peter wasn't awake in time to take note of its matutinal blushes. By the time he'd roused himself out of bed and into the shower, shaved, got dressed in chino pants and a clean blue shirt, and wandered down to the dining room, it was close on to half-past eight. Judging from the clutter on some of the now-vacant tables, the place must have been jumping for the past two hours.

Thurzella was on deck again, wearing black stirrup pants, a demure white blouse, and a suitably decorous expression. The few patrons still present, all of them men wearing feed caps, kept bombarding her with questions. She would only reply "We feel real bad about it" and keep on refilling their coffee mugs and stacking up dirty dishes. When she brought Peter his pancakes and offered the syrup jug in reverential silence, he decided there was hope for the younger generation.

Contrariwise, her elders could have used a lesson or two in deportment. The participants in this impromptu wake, if that was what the gathering could be called, had clearly come to bury Jasper, not to praise him. Not being any too fluent in the picturesque vernacular of rural Maine, Peter was unable to catch all the nuances, but he got the general drift easily enough. Flodge could unload money faster than salts through a goose where his own pleasure and comfort were concerned but when it come to settling up for what he owed in honest wages or supplies, that was another and a sadder story. "Meaner than turkey-turd beer" was the general verdict on the so recently departed. By the time Peter finished his pancakes, he'd come to the conclusion that there couldn't be a single person in the village, except maybe the minister, who did not consider it his or her civic duty to hate Jasper Flodge's guts.

He particularly noticed two men who were either brothers or ought to have been. One of them was spouting off like a kettle at full boil, the other just sat scowling into his empty mug. It was the talker who threw money on the table and shoved his chair back.

"Come on, Ev, jawin' won't get us anywhere. Only thing to do now is sue the estate."

"Providin' he never figured out a way to take it all with 'im," said a third man who wasn't yet ready to leave. "Wouldn't put it past the bahstid to have it all stashed away in asbestos bags, ready to go. Well, see you boys at the funeral. Be a pretty fair turnout, I shouldn't be surprised."

"All comin' to make sure it's really him in the casket," said another.

"Huh! That twister won't need a casket. He was so crooked they might as well just screw 'im into the ground standin' up."

The parting shot had been fired, the funeral party melted away. Peter refused another refill of coffee and put his own breakfast money on the table. There was no nonsense here about signing the bill with his room number and letting the charges pile up until he was ready to check out; Elva Bright's rule was cash on the barrelhead, and very sensible of her. As Peter moved toward the door, Thurzella sidled up to him.

"Professor, I'm sorry you had to listen to them talking so free about somebody who's dead, even if it was Jasper Flodge. It's a good thing my grandmother was in the kitchen, she wouldn't have liked it much. Not that they weren't telling the plain truth."

31

Thurzella was coming out of her shock. She even started to giggle, then caught herself, grabbed up her tray and sped from the dining room. A nice kid, Peter thought again. He checked his pockets to make sure he hadn't left his wallet, his car keys, or his seed-collecting bags upstairs, and was all set to leave when Elva Bright hastened through the swinging door with a gallon-size glass jug in either hand.

"Professor, I hate to bother you, but as long as you're going out to Fran Rondel's place, would you mind taking these two jugs along? Ask her to fill them with spring water, she'll know. And—uh—before you leave, just kindly drop this envelope on the kitchen table or someplace where she'll be sure to see it. Don't try handing it over, she wouldn't let you. I'm not giving you too much trouble, am I?"

"Not at all, Mrs. Bright, I'll be glad to do it. I hadn't realized there was a spring on her property."

"You wouldn't notice it. The spring's sort of off beyond the house, hidden in the bushes. Miss Fran will insist on filling the jugs herself, so don't waste your breath trying to argue her into letting you help. She's awfully fussy about that spring, for which a person can't blame her, considering."

Whatever there was to consider, Elva Bright didn't pause to explain. "Thanks, Professor, I appreciate this. You won't forget to leave the envelope?"

"I won't forget, Mrs. Bright. My wife has me very well trained."

Peter took the empty jugs, wondering why the innkeeper was making such a point of getting two gallons of water from Miss Rondel's spring. She couldn't be planning to serve it to her customers, two jugfuls wouldn't be enough for even one go-round in the dining room. Maybe Mrs. Bright knew something about her own well that her patrons didn't, and wanted to be sure of good spring water for her personal use.

Maybe what she wanted wasn't water, and maybe that could explain why Miss Rondel was so all-fired persnickety about letting outsiders get too close to her alleged spring. There were coins as well as paper in the envelope, Peter couldn't mistake the feel of them. Well, it was no skin off his nose if two elderly countrywomen were running a little bootleg business on the side. He stowed the jugs in back so that they wouldn't rattle around when he got off the paved road and laid the envelope beside him on the passenger seat where he couldn't miss seeing it when he got out.

He was giving his car a second or two to warm up when his chatty acquaintance of the previous evening came limping out the inn door. Withington had mentioned that he hadn't seen Miss Rondel's lupines in years; Peter supposed it would be an act of kindness to take his fellow guest along for the ride but he was damned if he was going to. In the first place, that cow track Miss Rondel called her driveway was so rough and steep that he planned to leave his car down below the house and walk up rather than risk a broken spring or a banged-up fender. Withington wouldn't be able to make the grade and P. Shandy was not about to give that human squawk-box a piggyback.

Furthermore, Peter was on serious business. Collecting seed from the various shades of lupine, labeling the bags, and wheedling information out of Miss Rondel as to how in tunket she was able to grow such voluptuous specimens in so unpromising a location would take the whole morning, and maybe longer. He'd have a fine chance of getting Miss Rondel to talk with a gasbag like Withington monopolizing the conversation. He waved and drove off, solacing his conscience with the thought

33

that Miss Rondel might let him have a few of the blooms to bring back to the old man.

There was no sense in even thinking of taking a bunch to Helen, assuming Miss Rondel would let him. The lupines were all but ready to quit. They'd have dropped their blossoms, more than likely, before he could get them home, especially considering that he didn't yet know how long that all-female bacchanalia back home was likely to last. He'd taken a number of color photographs on yesterday's visit, he might take a few more today to give Helen an idea of what she'd missed.

Anyway, there would be other trips. He and Helen had begun coming to Maine fairly often now that they'd reestablished connections with her old friend Catriona McBogle and his college roommate, Guthrie Fingal. Pickwance wasn't all that much farther up the coast from Sasquamahoc. He'd telephone Helen after he got back and try to ascertain, tactfully if possible, how soon the party would be over. If the prognosis was not hopeful, he had a good notion to leave the inn tomorrow anyway and bum a bed from Guthrie for a night or two.

He didn't quite know what was bothering him. Maybe it was being away from Helen. Maybe it was having Jasper Flodge drop dead last night just after he himself had finished a helping of that same chicken pot pie. Maybe it was a little of both.

Peter was not a squeamish man. He'd grown up in farming country and seen animals slaughtered. He'd seen an uncle squashed to death under a fallen tractor and had crawled in to drag out the corpse while older and stronger men levered the heavy machine up enough to give him workroom. He'd ripped up his shirt for a tourniquet when a hired hand lost part of a leg to a gasoline saw that broke loose. Since getting stuck with being Balaclava Junction's unofficial man-about-the-trouble he'd seen corpses in various states of demise. Even counting

34

the chicken gravy, Jasper Flodge's was one of the less messy deaths, and more than likely an unassisted one.

Dr. Bee's verdict ought to be in by the time Peter got back to the inn. His diagnosis would be something like hobnail liver, clogged arteries, and general cussedness. Whatever it was, Peter Shandy wouldn't like the feel of it. He'd get his seeds, bring Elva Bright back her jugs, and maybe stay for supper and breakfast so she wouldn't think he was afraid of her cooking, but that would be all. He wasn't going to hang around Pickwance another day, not by a jugful he wasn't.

Chapter 4

It was as well that Peter had hardened his heart against bringing Withington along, the path up to the old Rondel place was even worse than he'd remembered it. Yesterday, he supposed, he'd been too pumped-up over these incredible lupines to notice. Today his chief interest lay in collecting the promised seed as expeditiously as possible and hightailing it off to Sasquamahoc and points south. He pulled off into the nearest excuse for a lay-by that presented itself in case somebody else might happen along with a jug to be filled, checked to make sure he had his seed bags, a marking pen, and his landlady's envelope, and picked up the canvas shoulder tote that had been his companion on many a seed-scrounging expedition.

What with mud stains, grass stains, and stains of various natures that he preferred not to think about, the bag was fairly disgusting by now. So what? A man of the turnip fields cared naught for such bagatelles. As Peter recalled, that sacklike garment Miss Rondel had been wearing yesterday hadn't been any too pristine either. He added Elva Bright's two jugs to his equipment and began the arduous clamber up the rock-strewn slope.

It was as well he'd pulled off where he did. Not much farther along he came upon a parked pickup truck, a biggish one, blue and silver with a cap on the back. This was really the kind of vehicle a person needed for such rugged terrain but Peter couldn't envision Miss Rondel driving it. Therefore, she must have company. He felt unreasonably put out at the prospect of not being given her full and undivided attention.

Quod erat absurdum. Grown men didn't wax petulant over such trifling disappointments. Or did they? Somewhere up above, either a basso profundo or a talking walrus was making the welkin ring.

"All right, I'll do it. And you won't like it!"

The roar was an affront to the lupines, to the buzzing of the bees among the blossoms, to the far-off susurrations of a receding tide on a day that should have been halcyon. Who was going to do what? And why wasn't Miss Rondel going to like it?

A shower of egg-sized pebbles rolled down the slope. Instinctively Peter dodged behind a boulder. He was just in time to avoid a whizzing pebble that might have hit him if he'd been a second slower to move. Instead, it hit a birch tree about twenty feet on with a thud that made him wince. More stones and more thuds followed in rapid-fire succession, then the bull-moose charge of a burly figure wearing a wildly stained feed cap that might once have been red. Peter recognized the cap. This was the surly cuss whom he'd seen a while ago leaving Elva Bright's dining room with the man who'd talked of clapping a lawsuit on Jasper Flodge's estate.

Not that it was any of his business, and not that he intended to get involved in anything related to the late Mr. Flodge's almond-flavored demise. Still, Peter couldn't help wondering. Was Frances Hodgson Rondel by any chance a family connection, in line to inherit Flodge's estate, assuming he'd had one? Had her disgruntled visitor been trying to talk her into settling Flodge's debt out of court instead of putting him to the expense of a lawsuit? And had she told him to take his threatened lawsuit and stuff it up his downspout?

Reminding himself again that none of this had anything to do with him, Peter clambered on, noting to his satisfaction that quite a number of the plants were ready to yield up their seeds, pausing now and then to take a soil sample. Lupines were supposed to crave a soil rich in leaf mold. He could not for the life of him figure out how luxury-loving plants the size of these could grow, much less thrive, in such meager footing. The logical explanation was that Miss Rondel fertilized the bejeepers out of them, but he could see no sign that such was the case. Drat, he wished Timothy Ames were here!

By the time Peter breasted the ledge, he felt like the youth who bore 'mid snow and ice a banner with a strange device; he had a sneaking urge to shout "Excelsior!"

He curbed it, however. In the first place, there was nowhere higher for him to climb. In the second, Miss Rondel was right here in the dooryard, pinning a towel to her clothesline. She might consider such behavior strange and rescind her permission to gather seeds. As he held his peace, she removed the weathered clothespin that she'd been holding between her lips—the way Peter's mother and grandmother had been wont to do, he recalled, surprised by a pang of nostalgia—and greeted him with the poise of a born aristocrat.

"Good morning, Professor. I see Elva's given you her jugs to be filled. Perhaps you'd be good enough to set them in on the kitchen table? I'll be done here in a minute or two."

39

She nodded toward the open back door and stooped to pick another damp wad out of her laundry basket. Pink plastic, Peter noted with inward disapproval. The basket ought to be of woven cane, stained dark by time and use and in none-too-good repair. He hooked his right-hand jug to a spare left-hand finger and fished in his pants pocket for Mrs. Bright's envelope.

Inside the house, he found nothing to disappoint him. Miss Rondel's kitchen was not laid out quite like his grandmother's, but the general impression was the same. Peter could have sworn he recognized the pattern that showed dimly through fifty years' buildup of varnish on the well-scrubbed linoleum. He knew exactly how those flat, hard sofa cushions stacked on the sagging iron cot in the corner would feel against his back, should he take the liberty of testing them. The granny afghan spread over the cot was the wrong mix of colors, though, and so was the money cat sprawled on the afghan, giving an occasional absentminded lick to its left hind leg.

Old Tige had been a brown tabby, his preferred lounging spot the braided mat in front of the black soapstone sink; he'd had the whole Shandy family trained to step around him. Peter hadn't thought of Tige since he couldn't remember when. Yet he'd loved the raggedy-eared old tyrant. Still did, he supposed, absurd as it was to be wasting sentiment on a critter who'd yielded up the last of its nine lives forty years ago or better.

The table was about right, standing plunk in the middle of the floor where a farm wife could work around it from whatever side was handiest. Its stumpy legs were enameled in once-glossy apple green with a few chips knocked off, its unpainted top scrubbed into humps and hollows with little rounded-off knots poking up through the grain here and there. The cast-iron stove was no more than Peter had expected. The electric toaster oven and teakettle sitting on a nearby shelf did give him a minor jolt, but it stood to reason that Miss Rondel wouldn't want to keep her stove fired up during the hot days of summer.

Peter set Mrs. Bright's jugs on the table as bidden, tucked one end of the envelope under the first one so that it couldn't be overlooked, and was about to go back outdoors when he noticed a new-looking stretched canvas that had been set on the seat of a green-painted pressed-wood chair drawn up to the table.

Peter Shandy was, in his way, a scholar. He knew a great deal about the kinds of culture that come with prefixes such as agri-, horti-, and silvi-. Culture without a prefix tended to leave him cold, particularly when it took the form of being herded around a gallery trying to pretend he liked what he saw. As a rule, Peter did not like what he saw: not minimalist, cubist, post-post-impressionist, or much of anything else with an -ist on it, not excluding realist. If he didn't know what the artists had been up to, he was bored. If he could identify what he saw, he was more apt than not to wonder why they'd bothered. He had thought well of Miss Rondel thus far, was his pleasant illusion to be shattered? Was she, then, a dabbler in art?

No, she wouldn't be the type to dabble. Peter knew full well that nice people didn't sneak peeks at other people's belongings that were none of their business, but the spirit of Rikki-Tikki-Tavi was too strong within him. If he were just to tilt back the chair very, very carefully so as not to risk smudging the—great balls of fire! All question of couth went by the board. He moved the chair far enough out to give him a good look, and stood transfixed. He was still numb with wonderment when Miss Rondel came looking for him.

"Professor, aren't you—oh."

41

She was angry, and trying not to show it. Peter didn't give a damn. Et in Arcadia Shandy. He too had been in Arcady, he still was. He hadn't been there long enough. He supposed he ought to say something.

"This—" No good. He tried again. "I—er—did you do this?"

"No." The anger was plainer now.

"Then who?"

"I am not at liberty to say."

"But it's—good God!"

"Are you trying to tell me you like it?"

"Yes." Peter was gathering his wits about him. "I apologize for taking the liberty, Miss Rondel, but I can't be sorry that I did. This picture—it's—I don't know what it's about, but it's—saying something I want to hear."

"You surprise me very much, Professor Shandy."

"I surprise myself. I'm not particularly inclined to notice paintings as a rule. What I know about art could be written on the head of a pin. Why this one gets to me the way it does is more than I can fathom. All I can say is, I wish it were mine."

"Do you really?" Miss Rondel had simmered down by now, she was studying the canvas herself. It took her a while to reply. "Yes, I suppose that would depend. Professor, I happen just now to have custody of some other paintings by the same artist. I haven't shown them to anybody else and didn't intend to, but you may see them if you wish. On one condition, that you say absolutely nothing about them to anybody at the inn or around the town."

"No problem, Miss Rondel. I'm planning to leave anyway, as soon as I've gathered the lupine seeds you've so kindly let me take."

42

"So soon? What a pity. Then you'd better see them now, if you want to. Come this way, please."

She opened the door leading into a small dining room that looked as if it didn't get used very often and raised the blinds that had been keeping out the strong sunlight off the water. "Here they are, what do you think of them?"

"I don't know."

In total bemusement, Peter stood before one, then another, and another of the unframed canvases that circled the walls. There were ten of them, all dealing with simple themes: sea, rocks, sky, fields, lupines. Not lupines. Something. Color. Form. Not form. He was damned if he knew what he was looking at, but he couldn't take his eyes away.

None of the paintings could be called pretty. Some of them made Peter feel uneasy, particularly one in which tall thrusts of color hurled themselves out of unrelenting granite. By some ocular magic, a few tawny-rose lupines growing in a small pocket of dirt up the sides of a rocky ledge had become a portrait of President Thorkjeld Svenson; not the way he'd looked but the way he must have been feeling a few weeks ago when he'd driven his prized Balaclava Blacks to yet another triumph at the Balaclava County Annual Workhorse Competition.

This was a young people's picture, Peter decided, one that ought to be hanging in the college. If any picture was worth a thousand words, this shape-changer should be good for many millions. Merely by passing by it day after day, students could learn a damn sight more than they would from the blether they got from some of their longer-winded instructors. He surprised both himself and Miss Rondel by bursting into joyous laughter.

If Miss Rondel had in fact gone to school with Elva Bright's grandmother, she might well be old enough to have imbibed the aura of Queen Victoria's day. Clearly, like the late Queen, she was not amused.

"I must say, Professor Shandy, that, while I can recognize a certain merit in some of these paintings, none of them has ever provoked me to hilarity. Obviously you see something here that I don't."

"Then it's remarkably kind of you to give them houseroom."

"Not really. It's just that I have the space, you see. It would have been a waste just to let them decay in a barn somewhere."

"It would be criminal. The artist has never considered taking them to a gallery?"

"Oh no, never in the world. It would be nice if they could be sold somehow, I suppose, but then the word might get out about who painted them, and that could lead to complications. You know how people are. Of course in your case, I don't suppose . . ."

Miss Rondel let her voice dwindle off. Peter wondered if he should have brought another envelope, he picked up his cue with alacrity.

"Er—assuming the artist did want to sell any of the pictures, what—er—price range do you think—er—"

"Goodness, I've never given that side of it a thought. I don't suppose the artist has, either. Perhaps you might care to make a suggestion?"

"M'well, say for instance that one out in the kitchen. Suppose for the sake of argument I opened with an offer of a thousand, and then we could dicker. I wouldn't mind going a little higher if . . ." He too knew when to dwindle.

In fact, Peter could go a good deal higher if he had to. His giant rutabaga, known in all cooler climates as the Balaclava

Buster, was still bringing in substantial royalties, as were the petunia Helen's Fancy, the viola Spritely Sieglinde, and various other horticultural triumphs, of which the Rondel lupine strain might yet become another. If his experiment worked out, Frances Rondel would of course get her share of the take. She looked as if she'd be around long enough to enjoy the extra income even if she was, as alleged by Elva Bright, well on her way toward the century mark.

As to that magical picture, Peter knew a decent amount of haggling would have to be gone through before a firm figure was arrived at. Furthermore, he was beginning to have feelings about some of the others and didn't want to price himself out of the market first crack off the bat. He must have struck a chord, though, Miss Rondel was looking at him through slightly narrowed eyelids.

"You did mean a thousand *dollars*, Professor? Would that be in American money?"

"Well, yes, that was what I had in mind. I've never bought a painting before, but I've been to a few exhibitions with my wife and somewhere between one and two thousand seems to be a—er—popular range. It's too bad to put you in the middle like this."

"Oh, I don't mind helping out, provided you're really serious. You're quite sure you want to do this?"

"Sure enough to give you a deposit right now, if you want one. I'd have to write you a check, but I can make it a counter check if you'll tell me where to find a bank. Or I could phone down to my wife and ask her to bring up a certified check, a money order, or even the cash if your—er—protégé would prefer it. You know our friend Catriona McBogle from Sasquamahoc. She's visiting at our house now, as I believe I mentioned to you yesterday. Helen can ride back to Maine with her. I'd want Helen to see the paintings anyway, if you don't mind showing them again."

"What if Mrs. Shandy doesn't care for them?"

"She will."

Gad, he'd done it now. What about all that garbage he'd been spouting to himself earlier about hightailing it away from Pickwance as soon as he'd finished looting the lupines of their seed? What had got into him, anyway? Peter wasn't an acquisitive man, by and large. Choosing adornments for the house had always been a job he preferred to weasel out of, whenever Helen would let him. But, dad-blang it, he was going to have that incredible painting and maybe a couple more even if, perish the thought, he had to hang around here for the rest of the summer while some neurotic genius was making up his or her mind to talk business.

Chapter 5

So on to the lupines and to hell with negative thinking. Peter slung his gathering bag over his shoulder, took out a few of his spillproof plastic envelopes, and buckled down to business. The range of color was greater than any he'd encountered before but the variations were often subtle; he had to invent a color code as he went from one magnificent stalk to another that was almost like it but not quite. He just hoped he'd be able to remember what his complex improvisations stood for when he got back to his greenhouses.

Some of the stalks had gone completely to seed, he labeled them with question marks and went on filling his little packets. He was in no great hurry, he paused now and then to settle a territorial dispute with a bee or a butterfly or to pass the time of day with Miss Rondel's overweight cat, who'd strolled out to see what was going on. A blue jay gave him hell for trespassing on its turf while keeping a wary distance, as a blue jay naturally would. A wren less than a third of the blue jay's size was far bolder, bouncing on the tip of a brier and carrying on a running commentary not six feet from the fat cat's nose. She put Peter in mind of his next-door neighbor back home.

He lost track of the hours and didn't care. Somewhere along the line he ate the sandwiches that Mrs. Bright had put up for him and washed them down with a big tumblerful of spring water that Miss Rondel brought out to him. It was in fact water, he was interested to note, and excellent water at that. Peter had drunk from many a spring, he was by now something of a connoisseur; he rated the Rondel's Head product grade A-plus and gave it five stars for good measure.

Somehow, the water had a relationship to his painting, the one that would be his forevermore even if, God forbid, he never got to lay eyes on it again. It carried that same hint of something far greater than excellence, something illusive but essential that he couldn't taste but was perfectly well able to recognize. He wished he'd brought a jug of his own to be filled, he had an instinctive feeling that Mrs. Bright was not going to let him have any of hers and he didn't blame her a whit.

His whistle thus transcendentally wetted and his vigor renewed, Peter went on gathering lupine seeds. He had seen Childe Hassam's idyllic painting of Celia Thaxter in her seaside garden, he'd thought this would be a nice, lazy way to pass a leisurely afternoon. Dropping down over a twenty-foot granite ledge with jagged rocks at the foot to reach a tiny pocket of soil that had managed to lodge in a crevice, hanging on more or less by the toenails while he broke off a few browned flower heads and tied them up in his shirttail for safekeeping so that his fingers could seek out handholds to climb back up by must have been a picture that Hassam would not have cared to paint.

The tide was rolling in by now, sending up great fans of spray as it hit the rocks. Peter's pant legs were half-soaked by the time he'd clambered along the cliff to where the going was less precipitous. He didn't care. He'd have gone back down for more seeds if there'd been any more to get. He still couldn't figure out how those plants could grow so phenomenally under what looked like such adverse conditions. He said as much to Miss Rondel as he was thanking her for letting him spend the day in her garden and bumming another drink of water for the road.

She only smiled and thanked Professor Shandy in turn for the several packets of mixed seed that he'd prepared for her. She'd told him not to bother sorting them out, she was only planning to chuck them along the roadsides as the by now legendary Hilda "Lupina" Hamlin had started doing down around Christmas Cove a good many years ago. Not that hers would ever do so well as Hilda's, she didn't suppose, but they'd be pretty in the springtime and she'd let him know about the paintings.

It was dismissal, courteous but definite. Peter hitched the strap of his gathering bag to a more comfortable parking place on his collarbone, took the two filled water jugs that Miss Rondel handed him—sure enough, he hadn't once set eyes on the spring—and hiked back to his car.

The blue-and-silver pickup wasn't there. He'd forgotten all about it until he noticed the empty spot where it had been parked, and also about that glowering oaf who'd come storming down the path, shouting back at Miss Rondel what had sounded like a threat.

Peter would have preferred to keep on forgetting. This had been too halcyon a day to clutter up the memory of it with some backwoods bully's melodramatic bellowings. He'd had enough melodrama last night at the inn, he wondered whether Mrs. Bright had had any word by now as to what Jasper Flodge had died from, and was annoyed with himself for wondering. Peter stowed his seeds in the trunk for safekeeping and set the jugs of water on the floor in back with a few sheets of last Friday's *Balaclava County Fane and Pennon* wadded up between them so that they wouldn't joggle together and crack on the way back down this deplorable excuse for a road.

He'd been wondering how he might recompense Miss Rondel for letting him raid her lupines. One thing she could really use would be a rented backhoe and a few loads of fill. On the other hand, maybe she preferred to keep her land the way it was. At least it must discourage gawkers from driving up to picnic in her garden. That wise old up-country axiom "If it ain't broke, don't fix it" might well apply here.

Peter remembered the first time he'd been in Maine, the real Maine that the tourists who came to shop in Kittery and Freeport never got to experience. He'd got a feeling then that this was a different place; he hadn't been able then to pin down the difference and he still couldn't put his finger on it, but he felt it nonetheless. His painting was part of the difference, so was the unknown genius who'd created it, so was the elixir that came from Miss Rondel's secret spring. He was in alien territory here. Not hostile territory, he hoped, but—he could think of no apter word—different. It behooved him to go canny, he steered a careful path around the rocks and over the ruts until his tires hit familiar, unlovely asphalt and he could follow the yellow line back to the inn.

Nobody was at the desk in the lobby. That didn't surprise Peter, it was coming up to the peak dinner hour, Mrs. Bright was no doubt busy in the kitchen. He wouldn't bother her now, he stepped around the counter and parked the jugs underneath, where nobody would stumble over them. His pant legs were stiffened from the dried-on salt spray, the day's activities must have left him looking and smelling like one of the early sea people. Strangely enough, he didn't feel the least bit tired, but comfort and common decency both demanded a shower and change before he showed himself in the dining room.

Peter took his time dressing. He'd lost, or at least temporarily mislaid that sensation of otherness. By the time he'd got himself sanitized and garbed in reasonably presentable slacks, a clean short-sleeved shirt, and a light jacket—no tie, of course, that would have been carrying gentility a step too far— he was feeling smug and contented. Now was the time to call Helen.

There was no telephone in the room but canny Mrs. Bright, or possibly the late Jean-Luc, had caused a pay phone to be installed in a booth at the far corner of the lobby for guests' convenience and, no doubt, to keep them from trying to charge calls on the telephone at the desk. Peter shut himself in the booth and fished out a handful of change. In a matter of moments, he was connected to his wife.

"Oh, Peter, I was hoping you'd call. Did you get to see the lupines?"

"I came, I saw, I conquered. Those lupines are even more overwhelming than Catriona said they were. And I took seed from every dratted one of them."

"You're a great man, darling."

"That I am. Nice of you to notice. By the way, O Psyche from the regions which are fairyland, would you care to stuff a couple of thousand dollars into your panty hose and ride up here with Catriona?"

"Peter, you don't mean right now?"

"Tomorrow would do. Or even the day after, if needs must."

"But why? Peter Shandy, don't tell me you're about to be arrested for stealing those lupine seeds and want me to bail you out?"

"Perish the thought, mine own. I am pure as the driven snow. Purer, in fact, considering how much air pollution goes into your average snowflake nowadays. Suffice it to say that I look the whole world in the face for I rob not any man. Or woman. Miss Rondel, according to information received, is somewhere in the midst of her nonage, but I got the impression that she could still lick me in a fair fight. We got on like a house afire, I'll have you know. She not only granted me carte blanche among her lupines, she also gave me a drink of water from her invisible spring and a private view of that which I need to raise the cash to buy you a present of."

"An antique buggy lamp?"

"No, nor yet an iron stag for the lawn. You'll know when you see it. Just do me a favor and don't say anything about this to Catriona or anybody else until you've had a chance to make up your mind. The deal is perfectly legitimate, to the best of my knowledge and belief, but the circumstances seem to be a trifle peculiar and I don't want to rock the boat."

"How deliciously enigmatic! But what shall I tell Cat, then?"

"Tell her I've wasted away from wifely neglect and am too weak to drive home alone. Alternatively, that I'm clamoring for you to see the lupines before all the color goes. The latter explanation might be the more plausible of the two."

"But the former is the more flattering to the female ego. All right, dear, I'll come as soon as I can. Audrey's already left, she got a call this morning that Maud Silver had taken one of her turns. Maud Silver's her cat, she suffers terribly from hair balls because she's always trying to give Audrey's husband's old bearskin rug a bath with her tongue. The rug molts terribly but Sam won't let Audrey junk it because his great-uncle Otis saved his great-aunt Margaret's life by shooting the bear while they were on a camping trip to Glacier Park with Mary Roberts Rinehart, which makes the beastly thing a family heirloom. Awfully hard on poor Maud, but you know how it is with families."

"The only family I don't know about is ours," Peter replied a trifle querulously. "Have you no thoughts on the matter that was under discussion before we got sidetracked to Maud Silver's hair balls?"

"Right. Sorry about that. As of this moment, Cat and Iduna Stott are out in the backyard hulling berries for the strawberry festival that Iduna's chairing for the Friends of the Library tomorrow, and I'm here in the kitchen getting our supper. Dan Stott will be back from giving his speech to the hog growers' association on Friday. I expect Iduna will be champing at the bit to start barbecuing the fatted calf for Dan's homecoming banquet as soon as she's done her stint at the festival. So would Thursday be soon enough?"

"Thursday will be fine."

A day in between should give Miss Rondel time enough to crank up her mysterious protégé's acquisitive instincts, Peter was thinking. She was probably eating her supper about now, he'd better leave her to it and phone in the morning. What he'd do with the rest of the day remained to be seen.

This chat about food reminded him that it was high time he got some; nevertheless he stayed on the line, giving Helen a brief rundown on the Jasper Flodge incident since she'd be bound to hear of it anyway once she got here, until a minor commotion at her end heralded the return of her friends and the strawberries. He sent them his hearty wishes for a fruitful fund-raising and hung up the inn's telephone.

The pay booth had been built by a carpenter who knew his stuff, Peter didn't recall having heard a sound from outside once he'd shut himself into it. What puzzled him was that he still wasn't hearing anything now that he was out of it. Surely this was not too early an hour for people to be arriving for dinner, could he possibly have frittered away so much time that they'd already come and gone? He quickened his step and entered the dining room.

There must be something wrong with his watch. It read ten minutes to seven, about the same time he'd come here on Sunday. The place had been packed. Last night he'd shown up almost an hour later, the patrons were gone but the uncleared tables had been proof enough that business had been at least equally brisk. Tonight, one diner was sitting at a corner table by himself; it was, of course, Withington. All the other tables were not only empty but tidily set for customers who must either have come surprisingly early or hadn't come at all. Thurzella rushed to meet Peter as though he'd been her long-lost rich uncle.

"Oh, Professor Shandy, we were afraid you weren't coming. And Grandma's made this terrific big roast of beef with Yorkshire pudding and—" She took a long deep breath. "And would you like yours rare or medium? Or would you rather look at the menu?"

"The roast beef sounds great to me. I haven't had Yorkshire pudding for ages. Rare to middling on the beef, if you can manage it."

"No problem," Thurzella assured him. "You can have it however you want it. There's the whole—I mean there's

54

plenty. And roast potatoes and fresh peas and what kind of dressing do you want on your salad and how about a bowl of chowder for starters? And we've got chocolate fudge cake for dessert and you can have ice cream on it if you want. I like mine plain."

"So do I."

Peter couldn't say that he was surprised but he was damned sorry for Thurzella and more so for Elva Bright. The word was out about last night. Patrons were understandably leery about eating in a restaurant where one of their neighbors had dropped dead in his plate.

They'd keep on feeling leery, moreover, until they got the official word on what Jasper Flodge had died of. Whether they'd accept the verdict was another matter. If the death had stemmed from natural causes there'd always be the few who claimed the report had been faked for sinister and underhanded reasons. If it was something other than natural, then, barring a miracle, Elva Bright might as well close the inn and move to Florida.

Peter supposed he might as well go down with the ship. "Shoot the works, Thurzella. Not a bowl of chowder, though, just a cup. Oil and vinegar dressing on the salad, please, and no ice cream on the cake. My wife says I'm too fat."

"No you're not, Professor. You're just right."

At least the young waitress wasn't looking quite so forlorn now. She popped into the kitchen and came back in a trice with the chowder and a basket of hot rolls, back in another trice with Peter's salad. By the time she bounced in a third time to clear away his empty chowder cup and fetch his roast beef with gravy on the side in a chipped but rather pretty old Bavarian gravy boat, she'd acquired another customer.

The man was not wearing his red cap this time. He'd smartened himself up to the extent of a wash and a clean flannel shirt in the Stuart Dress tartan. Nevertheless, Peter would have recognized that glower in the souks of Cairo or the howling wastes of Van Diemen's Land. He was not happy to see the surly one choose a seat at the next table, thus putting himself in perfect position to be glowered at. Thurzella, on the other hand, was delighted to see another table occupied.

"Hi, Evander. Where's your brother tonight?"

So he did have a name. Evander's answer was a shrug and a growl. "What you got?"

"Roast beef?"

"That'll do."

With no further question, Thurzella went and got her new customer a bowl of chowder and a basket of rolls. Nothing was said or done about a salad. Evander, whoever he might be, settled down to his chowder, bailing it in over his short but bushy beard efficiently but without undue zeal, pausing between spoonfuls to butter a roll, to pick a fishbone out of his teeth, or to glower at Peter Shandy. To give Evander his due, his table manners were almost dainty compared to the late Jasper Flodge's, although they might not have stacked up all that high against stiffer competition.

Peter had been aware ever since he'd entered the dining room that Claridge Withington was itching to bend his ear. They'd made eye contact once or twice, Peter had given the older man a reasonably cordial nod while selecting a table that was far away to discourage conversation; but clearly a nod was not enough. That was more than Evander, as Peter was now forced to think of him since Thurzella hadn't mentioned a last name, had done, however.

Evander was sitting with his back to the corner table, but the slight to Withington might not have been deliberate.

56

Perhaps he'd preferred to face the door into the restaurant because he was expecting his brother to show up looking for him. Perhaps he was glowering at Peter now simply because there was nobody else in the room conveniently situated to glower at. It was a mildly comforting thought.

The roast beef had been all that any carnivorous heart could desire. Peter speared his last bite of Yorkshire pudding and sent Thurzella for some black coffee to go with his chocolate cake. It was unlikely that he'd be able to swallow another bite of anything without something to wash it down. He supposed he could prepare himself for the cake by getting up and running a few laps around the table to joggle the roast beef into a less uneasy lie on his stomach, but that didn't seem quite the decorous thing to do.

Peter further supposed it would be only decent to take his coffee over to Withington's table. The insatiable old newshound might have some news, or at least an educated guess, as to how Jasper Flodge had met his demise. Anyway, since Peter had maneuvered himself into getting stuck here for another day or two, he might as well be sociable, within reasonable limits. Not that he was in any mood for trivia when there were those incredible paintings to think about; he kept toying with his cake to put off the moment of truth. Nevertheless, Peter experienced a pang of annoyance when he suddenly found himself redundant.

Chapter 6

A tall, broad-shouldered brunette somewhere between forty and fifty, Peter estimated, knowingly made up and smartly dressed in black with touches of scarlet, swept into the dining room. She was carrying a patent leather handbag the size of a briefcase, or maybe it was in fact a briefcase, and made a beeline for Withington's table.

"Hi, Claridge, long time no see. I was wondering if I'd find you here. What's good tonight?"

"I am, since I'm incapacitated from being otherwise. How are you, Lucivee. You look blooming as ever. Do sit down and keep me company, I'll call the waitress over."

"Ah, relax, she'll be along. I'm in no mad rush to eat, I stopped for coffee in Bangor. Where the heck is everybody tonight?"

"That's a good question. At least you shouldn't have any trouble getting a room."

"Who needs one? I've still got the key to my own house."

"Your—you don't mean Jasper's house?"

"I mean my house, and you'd better believe it. You don't

think I'd have been dumb enough to let that louse get away with not making it legal, do you? God knows what sort of condition the place is in by now. I figured I'd better get something substantial under my belt before I go to see."

The woman was making no effort to keep her voice down, she was staking her claim and she wanted the town to know. No fear. Peter noticed that the door into the kitchen was standing open a crack. Elva Bright wasn't about to miss a word. Even the dour Evander was forgetting to glower; when his brother did show up, he came perilously close to grinning.

This was turning into a real Old Home Week, the brother even went so far as to say "Evenin', Lucivee. Haven't seen you around here for a while."

"That's been my loss and your gain, Fred. Don't worry, you'll be seeing enough of me for a while yet. Once I get Jasper planted deep enough so that there's no chance of him digging his way up again, I'll have to begin settling the estate. Who's that kid? One of Elva's bunch?"

"Ayuh. Granddaughter. Name's Thurzella."

"That figures. Okay, Thurzy, if that's roast beef I smell, you can bring me the rarest you've got and whatever goes with it. Put it here on Claridge's table. Come on, Fred, join the party."

"I'll set here with Evander, thanks. Beef for me, Thurzella."

All of a sudden, business was booming. It couldn't have taken long for the word to get around a place the size of Pickwance. Faces appeared at the door. Noting that none of those at the tables had as yet keeled over, some of the snoopers ventured inside, asking for cake and coffee. A few even ordered a full dinner, Peter suspected that was to give them an excuse for staying longer. Lucivee Flodge, if that was in fact her legal name, was proving to be quite a draw.

Peter himself was interested to see how this small drama

would play itself out. He wished now that he hadn't frittered away his chance to sound out Withington as to whether the cause of Jasper's death had been established and whether the almond extract had anything to do with it. He allowed Thurzella to refill his coffee cup and sat back to let it cool. Lucivee was by no means a shy woman, she appeared not at all disconcerted by the breathless hush that hung over the dining room, or by the many sidelong glances being directed at the corner table. Withington was no shrinking violet either, he was playing up to the widow for all he was worth.

"So what have you been up to since we last met, Lucivee?"

"Oh, this and that. You know me, Claridge, I'm not the type to sit back and rest on my laurels, such as they are. A woman with a B.A. in business and a law degree on top of it doesn't have to, these days. One thing I'll say for Jasper, he did give me credit for being a damned sight sharper than he ever dared to be when it came down to business. He still came to me for advice, you know. I've got the whole kafoozle right in my lily-white hands, and you'd better believe it's going to stay there."

Since Elva Bright didn't have a liquor license, Peter surmised that Lucivee Flodge must have tanked up someplace else before she got to the inn. If she was in fact the clever lawyer she cracked herself up to be, she ought to know better than to go shooting her mouth off like this in public. Either she was drunker than she looked or else she was sending a message to somebody or other, he thought. If so, she needn't worry about its reaching the intended party, not with all these ears flapping in unison to catch every syllable she uttered, and all those toes twitching to rush off and spread the word to anybody who'd listen. There'd be a hot time in the old town tonight, that was for sure.

Ah, now came the big scene. The conversation had worked its way around to Jasper Flodge's last moments. Peter, having adjusted himself comfortably in his spectator's seat, was startled to hear Claridge Withington calling upon him to join the show.

"Ask Professor Shandy here, he saw the whole episode, from start to finish. He even wiped the gravy off Jasper's face. Didn't you, Professor? Wasn't that a shocking way for a man to go?"

"Er—" Damn it, why did Withington have to drag him into it? "I still don't know how he went. Has there been any— er—report?"

"There certainly has, and you're not going to believe it. Remember the odor of bitter almonds that you attributed to the almond extract found in Jasper's pocket after I'd suggested the possibility of cyanide poisoning? According to Dr. Bee, it was in fact cyanide poisoning that killed him."

And I win the chocolate-covered jelly bean. Smarmy old bastard. Peter felt a momentary urge to shove Withington's face down into his fudge cake. Such a death was hardly a thing to be smug about, no matter how big a bastard Flodge might have been.

Oh, what the hell? Let old Claridge have his moment of glory, if such it could be called. He probably didn't get many opportunities to shine. Peter said what he had to.

"How in Sam Hill did he get hold of cyanide?"

"Dr. Bee claims Jasper must have bitten into one of those capsules that spies used to keep tucked behind their back teeth in case they got captured. As to where the capsule came from, we can only surmise."

Sure they could, and Peter didn't have to be told what Withington was surmising. Not when the old snoop had that self-satisfied smirk on his face and his head cocked in the direction of Elva Bright's kitchen. So poor Jean-Luc was to be dragged from the grave and dusted off to keep the gossip mill running.

It was not an impossible scenario, the late hero of the Resistance hanging on to his cyanide capsule for auld lang syne the way too many soldiers had lugged home live hand grenades and parked them on the mantelpiece for their relatives to admire and their kids to play with. It even made sense, in a way, considering the shape Jean-Luc had been in, according to Withington, by the time he'd wooed and won the innkeeper's daughter. He must have accepted the fact that he was past mending. His suffering, both physical and mental, might often have been intense. He could have drawn some small comfort from knowing he had the means at hand to give himself a quick way out if the pain got beyond all bearing.

A man who had steeled himself to withstand unspeakable torture would not have been apt to reveal his deadly secret to outsiders. Peter found it less incredible that Elva Bright could have mentioned the capsule sometime during her widowhood when Withington happened to be the only other person around and she'd felt a desperate need for a sympathetic listener. If in fact such a capsule had even existed, the only really credible way for Withington to have known about it, Peter decided, was that he'd at some time taken it upon himself to do a little unauthorized prospecting. Having been a regular patron for years on end, the man must gradually have acquired something like the status of a visiting relative. The odds were that he'd often been left alone for a while when Elva was without an assistant and had gone off on some errand or other. A natural-born snoop like him could hardly have resisted an opportunity to go rummaging.

Nobody but Withington himself appeared to be much interested in how Jasper Flodge had come by his lethal dose. What they all wanted to know was why Jasper had chosen to commit suicide when and where he did. It was Fred who voiced what was probably the consensus of those present.

"Hell, if I'd known he was that anxious to kill himself, I'd have been glad to come and lend him a hand. Whatever possessed the bugger, do you suppose?"

"I'll tell you what!"

Lucivee Flodge was on her feet, her cheeks as red as her lapels, her eyes shooting sparks. "He did it to spite me, that's what. Him and his big deals! He gets himself tied up with a big-time mob, thinks he can outsmart them, pulls a fast one that backfires, and finally gets it through his thick head that he's about to be measured for a pair of concrete overshoes. So what does he do? He knows he's a dead duck no matter what, so he decides to go out with a big whoop and a holler right here where he knows there'll be witnesses around and there can't be any question about the verdict."

"But what's that got to do with you, Lucivee? Hell, it's been—what? Six or seven years since Jasper dumped you?"

"He never dumped me! Listen, Fred Wye, I'm the one who walked out when Jasper started bringing his floozies home for the night and expecting me to get up and cook their breakfasts in the morning. I told him to keep away from those crooks, but would he listen? Naturally once he got it through his fat head that he'd landed himself in big trouble, he claimed it was all my fault. So I had to suffer."

"Like how?"

"Like getting shafted the way that bastard's shafted me, you backwoods half-wit. The day we were married, I made Jasper take out a hundred-thousand-dollar life insurance policy. With me as the sole beneficiary, needless to say. Well, he paid the premiums once or twice, then love's young dream started to wear off and he quit. Not being quite so dumb as he thought I was, I kept on paying the premiums, figuring somebody was bound to kill him sooner or later for one reason or another. That's the only reason I never divorced him. And now, damn his hide, the bastard's gone and done me out of my hundred thousand because no insurance company will pay out on a verdict of death by suicide. God, I could spit!"

"Well, don't do it here." Elva Bright had come out of the kitchen, not pausing to take off her apron. "This is a respectable inn, as you ought to know by now, and I'll thank you to help me keep it that way. Jasper Flodge may not have been any great, shining light but I'd known him all my life, we went to school together, and I see no call to go ripping him up the back now that he's gone. I can't say I'm any too happy about Jasper's cashing in his checks at my table because it wouldn't be true, but if you're going to start running down a dead customer of mine, I'd rather you did it someplace else. Now if anybody wants anything more to eat, you'd better speak up. This dining room's going to close in fifteen minutes. Will you be wanting early breakfast, Professor Shandy? You said you'd be checking out in the morning."

"Er—yes, I did but now I'm not, unless you want to get rid of me. I spoke with my wife after I got back from Miss Rondel's. You were busy in the kitchen, I believe. Anyway, she wants to ride back with Catriona McBogle and spend a night here. They have something planned for tomorrow, so she'll have to come on Thursday, if it's all the same to you."

"Did you tell her about Jasper? I wouldn't want Mrs. Shandy coming up here and getting an earful from some stranger and starting to wonder what I've put in the food."

That was telling them. Peter didn't try to hide his smile.

"No fear, Mrs. Bright. Helen knows all about it. She sends her sympathy and looks forward to meeting you. So if you can stand having me around—"

"You're both welcome to stay as long as you like. I expect I sounded a mite snappish there a minute ago, but this has been a tough two days, in case you hadn't noticed. I guess I'm kind of frazzled around the edges. I don't know how I'd have managed without Thurzella here. She's a good little worker when she takes a mind to be, I'll say that for her."

"You goin' to be servin' breakfast tomorrow?" somebody wanted to know.

"Oh, I guess likely. Just don't expect anything fancy."

"Huh? No paper pants on the bacon or caviar stuffing in the doughnuts?" Fred pushed back his chair and gave the innkeeper a hearty thump on the shoulder. "I guess we can make do with what you've got for once. Come on, Evander, let's get out of her and let Elva rest her bunions. See you in the morning, Elva."

Fred Wye seemed like a decent sort of cuss, Peter thought, too bad his brother wasn't more like him. At least Evander wasn't glowering as he settled up for the meal and followed Fred out the door. He even managed a curt nod, though it was impossible to tell whom he was nodding at.

The brothers seemed to be persons of some consequence, others were getting up to follow their example. Elva moved up to the front desk, whipped off her apron in the name of propriety, and busied herself taking money and making change. Thurzella was clearing tables at top speed. The only ones not participating in the mass exodus were Claridge With-ington and Lucivee Flodge; she had sat down with him again and was swiveled around in her chair, demanding more coffee from the already overworked young waitress.

Had Peter been thirty years younger and unattached, he might have offered to give Thurzella a hand with the trays. Since he wasn't, he joined the queue at the cash register, paid his tab like the rest, then went on upstairs, carefully refraining from glancing back lest Withington nab him for another post-prandial chat.

Lucivee Flodge had been casting a few speculative glances his way, Peter had noticed while he was still at the table. He was glad he'd spoken out loud and clear about the impending arrival of his wife. God forbid that he should become in any way embroiled with a panther woman, particularly after his long day of cliff-scrambling and seed-sorting. Not that he'd ever met a panther woman, but the great P. G. Wodehouse had given one of his more beleaguered male characters a particularly rough time with a mate who, as Peter recalled, fitted Lucivee Flodge's description too closely for comfort.

He was quite willing to accept Wodehouse's negative verdict as to the wisdom of tangling with panther women. What failed to stir an acquiescent chord was Mrs. Flodge's yarn about Jasper bumping himself off in the midst of his chicken pot pie for the alleged purpose of canceling an insurance policy on which she claimed to have been keeping up the payments.

Nor did Peter put much stock in that knowing glance of Claridge Withington's, once he'd got up to his room and had leisure to think it over. It seemed crazy that a man with two small daughters whom he'd loved would have risked having anything so lethal around the house, but what if the late Jean-Luc had in fact hung on to his wartime souvenir? Peter had no idea what the shelf life of a cyanide capsule might be, but half a century did seem to him an excessive span of time for a pill to have retained so immediately effective a knockout punch.

He could understand why that romantic tale of the heroic

Frenchman could hold a special attraction for Withington. An intelligent semi-invalid must often draw on his imagination for entertainment. Jean-Luc would have been the ideal fantasy figure to appeal to a steady visitor with an active brain and a partially dysfunctional body. There was also, Peter supposed, the alternative possibility that Withington was simply a malicious old bastard who liked to stir up trouble. Infirmity did not necessarily convey instant sainthood, why should a handicapped person be any less human than his haler and often meaner fellow creatures?

Peter took off the shirt he'd worn to dinner and hung it up with reasonable care. It would have to do for tomorrow now that he was staying another day. Maybe he ought to take a run over to Sasquamahoc and bum a rag or two off Guthrie. It was less than a two-hour run, and would be something to do while he was waiting for Helen. He could take Guthrie to lunch at that place where they served fried-clam tacos, and be back at the inn in time for supper.

Before he took off, though, he ought to give Miss Rondel a buzz and let her know that his wife would be coming on Thursday afternoon to see the paintings. Better still, he could stop at Rondel's Head on his way to Guthrie's, take its doyenne a little present of some kind, and get another look at his special painting. Mrs. Bright could tell him what Miss Rondel would like and where to buy it, if she wasn't too busy with the breakfast orders to take the time. Between Lucivee's insistence that her husband had taken his own life and the backup Elva had got from her pal Fred Wye and his brother, not to mention Peter's own small contribution and the fact that nobody got poisoned last night, Elva's customers must surely have got the message that it was perfectly safe to eat at the inn.

He hoped. As Peter was tying the string of his pajama pants, he had a vision. It was not an agreeable vision. It was of a middle-aged woman in a restaurant kitchen, holding a small, roundish object very carefully between the points of a pair of tweezers. She was dabbing it with a cotton swab dunked in green food coloring, blowing on it to dry. Finally, she was tucking what now looked like a fresh pea under the crust of a large slice of chicken pot pie.

Chapter 7

It must have been the chicken pot pie. Peter gave his pillow an angry thump and got into bed. In the first place, the green food coloring most likely would have washed off in the gravy. And what if it had? What were the odds that Flodge would have noticed? The speed at which he'd been shoveling in his grub would hardly have allowed any pause for the analytical inspection of a single off-color pea.

Peter told himself not to be a blithering idiot, thumped his pillow some more, conjured up a mental picture of Dan Stott in his green porkpie hat driving an endless litter of piglets under a gate, counted up to four hundred and thirty-seven piglets, switched to sheep, got bored, tried cows and found himself milking them, filled two hundred and three imaginary milk pails, finally dropped into fitful slumber wondering what the flaming perdition he was going to do with all that milk, and dreamed he was an off-color pea making a tedious journey through the convoluted coils of Jasper Flodge's intestines.

About the time he'd intended to get up, Peter fell sound asleep. He woke an hour or so later, gummy-eyed and irritable.

A shower and shave helped some, but not enough. He was annoyed with himself for not having thought to bring an extra shirt. His left shoe eluded him for some time, it had perversely concealed itself under the patchwork quilt that he'd kicked off the foot of the bed sometime during his busy night. He went downstairs at last, fully expecting to be told that the dining room was closed and nobody would give him any coffee.

But it wasn't. Thurzella came charging down on him with the coffeepot in one hand and the juice pitcher in the other before he'd even got settled into his chair. For a moment, Peter resented the fact that she'd given him no excuse to glower. He began to perk up, though, once the coffee started warming his gullet, and decided he'd have a pancake or two with his ham and eggs. To hell with the calories, he'd park farther down the lane from Miss Rondel's and work them off climbing up to the house. Maybe he'd locate her magic spring on the way, he wouldn't mind another swig or two of that delicious water.

Breakfast was by no means over, there were still several tables occupied, he'd begun to recognize faces. A few of the patrons nodded to him, one or two vouchsafed the Mainer's formal greeting.

"Mornin'."

"Mornin'."

He got a fairly cordial "Mornin'" from Fred and a glower from Evander, who changed his seat in order to plant himself directly in Peter's line of sight. Peter gave their table an impartial nod to show he was amenable to being greeted but didn't give a hoot if he wasn't, and got down to business on his eggs. When Thurzella came back to refill his coffee cup, he asked whether her grandmother was too busy to give him a minute.

"Right now she's frying bacon with one hand and pancakes

with the other," was the girl's discouraging reply. "Is it something important?"

Peter shook his head. "Not really. I just thought it would be appropriate to take Miss Rondel a small present by way of thanks for her having let me collect lupine seeds yesterday, and I haven't the foggiest notion what she might like."

"Oh, then what you'd better do is stop in at my mother's shop. Mum will know, she's got lots of great stuff and she's a great friend of Miss Fran's. It was Miss Fran who taught her to weave. I'll go see if your pancakes are ready."

Thurzella was wearing plum-colored tights today, and a lavender sweatshirt that had pink and blue lupines embroidered on the front. The period of mourning was clearly over with; sic transit Jasper Flodge. Peter wondered whether the merry widow had stopped in for breakfast this morning. However, the only person he knew well enough to ask was Claridge Withington and he had no appetite for another lesson in local history so early in the day. Mrs. Flodge's eccentric doings were none of Peter Shandy's business anyway, he kept his eyes on his plate to avoid meeting Withington's, finished his breakfast rather quickly, and left the dining room.

Finding the shop took no time at all, there weren't many places to look in a town the size of Pickwance. "Michele Cluny, Master Weaver," as a modestly sized but elegantly calligraphed card in the window announced, was a good advertisement for her wares. Peter had seen plenty of hand-weaving in the Native Arts Department at Balaclava, he could recognize the quality of the handsome garment that Mrs. Cluny was wearing over a pair of stirrup pants like her daughter's. The tight pants looked just as good on her, she and Thurzella must be just about the same size and alike as two peas.

Drat it, why couldn't he get his mind off peas? Neither the

mother nor the daughter resembled a pea in any respect. Both were dark-haired, dark-eyed, red-cheeked without apparent resort to artifice, and as lissome as could reasonably be expected, considering that they'd both grown up on Elva Bright's cooking. Neither favored the innkeeper, though, they must take after Jean-Luc.

Peter wrenched his mind away from Jean-Luc's progeny and fell to wondering whether the tunic that looked so right on the weaver would go as well with his wife's blond hair, blue eyes, and peach-bloom complexion. He decided it wouldn't. However, it was dollars to doughnuts that Helen would manage to find something here that she did want. Lots of somethings. Expensive somethings. Far be it from him to begrudge the wife of his bosom a spree among the weavings when he already had his own shopping list pretty well made out. But what to buy for Miss Rondel? He stepped up to the counter.

"Er—my name is—"

"Professor Shandy! My daughter's been telling me about you, she says you're the nicest customer she's ever waited on."

Michele Cluny's smile was warm and welcoming. The one Peter gave in return was shy and modest. "Then she can't have been waitressing very long. She sent me here to have you help me—er—choose a present for a lady. Miss Rondel was kind enough to let me collect seeds from her lupines yesterday, as Thurzella's no doubt told you by now. I thought I'd like to take her something by way of thanks, but I have no idea what she'd like. Thurzella said you'd know."

There seemed to be much here to like and little to snoot. Handwoven garments, scarves, lap robes, tablecloths, and objects that Peter couldn't identify—though Helen would no doubt be able to—made up the bulk of the stock. There was also, however, a tasteful assortment of hand-crafted doodads and hand-thrown pottery geared to the well-heeled tourist's taste and credit card, along with a display of homemade jellies, jams, pickles, and cookies. These last must be a little sideline that Elva Bright turned out when business was slow at the inn. While Peter marveled at the prices, Michele pondered his request.

"There's no sense in giving Miss Fran anything handwoven, of course, she makes half this stuff herself. She's never been much for bric-a-brac and she's fussy about what she eats. She does like Mother's jams and cookies, though, I could make you up a nice basket. How much were you planning to spend?"

Peter shrugged. "Whatever it comes to. It occurs to me that yesterday, when I went into Miss Rondel's kitchen on a little— er—errand for your mother, I noticed a broken pitcher lying on the table. Do you think she might like a replacement? One of those you have sitting in the window, perhaps?"

"What kind of pitcher was it?"

Michele Cluny fairly snapped out the words, Peter wondered why so trifling a remark had elicited so sharp a reaction. He tried without much luck to recall what the shards had looked like.

"M'well, the pieces—er didn't appear to be anything out of the ordinary. Pottery, not china, not very big. Rather an unattractive yellowish color, as I recall with a dark-brown stripe. It's too bad my wife wasn't with me, she knows a lot more about such things than I do."

"Thurzella says Mrs. Shandy's coming tomorrow. That will be nice."

Mrs. Cluny was still smiling, but now she didn't mean it. She walked over to the window and picked out a pitcher about eight inches high, plump at the base, narrower at the neck, with a soft, brownish glaze and a delicately incised pattern of

75

lupine leaves and flowers. "Is this about the right size? It's one of Betsy Love's designs. Seventy-five dollars plus tax."

The shopkeeper's voice was almost accusing. Didn't she want to sell the piece? Peter refused to be daunted.

"Yes, that will do fine, if you think Miss Rondel will like it."

"She ought to, at this price. I suppose it's time Miss Fran had a new one. They do say a pitcher that goes too often to the well—" Mrs. Cluny shrugged. "Betsy Love does do beautiful work."

"Perhaps you wouldn't mind—er—wrapping it for me?"

"Not at all."

That was a lie, or at least an equivocation. Why was the woman so all-fired touchy about selling a pitcher? Couldn't Betsy Love make her another? A person might think a shop-keeper would be pleased to make a fairly good sale so early in the day. "Then you won't want the basket of jellies, Professor?"

"Why not?" Was she afraid he was going to stick her with a bum check? "Couldn't you use a bigger basket and just— er—bung the things all in together? If Miss Rondel doesn't care for the pitcher, at least she can eat the cookies."

"Oh, I expect she'll like it fine." Michele Cluny was getting her aplomb back, swathing the various items in sea-blue tissue paper and nesting them in the basket, the pitcher in the middle and the edibles fitted in around it. "I gave Miss Fran a couple of mugs in this same design for Christmas, she uses them all the time. How long are you and Mrs. Shandy planning to stay?"

"So far, just the one night. I can't say for sure. I expect my wife would enjoy visiting your shop sometime before we leave. Will you be open tomorrow?"

"Oh yes, we'll be here any time after nine in the morning

76

till half past five. We stay open till seven on Fridays and Saturdays, those are always our busiest days. We do close on Sunday because that's the only time my husband and I can have the whole day together. It used to be our family day, but now the kids are always off doing their own thing."

"Does the inn restaurant stay open?"

"Oh yes. That's Mother's biggest day, as a rule. She has a neighbor who's a widow in to help with the cooking Sunday, Monday and Tuesday; she takes a day or two off the first of the week to catch her breath and do the marketing. Normally Mother has a couple of waitresses she can call on, but one's off on her second or third honeymoon, I forget which, and the other broke her wrist last week trying to start her lawn mower. So poor Thurzella's working double shifts and no time off till we can get one of her cousins up from Portland to pinch-hit. You can't have just anybody waiting on tables at a country inn, you know. People around here don't take much to strangers handling their food."

That was a bad slip. She buttoned her lips, got very busy tying a fancy green bow to the handle of the basket, then shoved it across the counter. "That'll be ninety-eight dollars and fourteen cents, counting the tax."

Peter liked to carry a hundred-dollar bill folded into a secret pocket of his wallet in case of emergencies. Slightly irked by this off-and-on treatment, he fished out his hidden hoard and handed it over. Michele counted $1.86 in silence, then dredged up a last ounce of courtesy.

"Thank you for coming in, Professor. Enjoy the rest of your stay and give Miss Fran my love."

"I will. Thanks for your help."

Peter felt a bit like the Easter Bunny carrying Miss Rondel's present out to his car. He set the beribboned basket on the

77

floor beside him and started the engine, still puzzling over why Michele Cluny had reacted so oddly when he'd mentioned that broken pitcher. Well, it was no skin off his nose, he just hoped the old lady would like the replacement. People did get attached to objects they'd lived with for a long time.

Michele had learned her weaving from Miss Rondel, the former teacher supplied merchandise for the shop. it stood to reason there must be a strong bond between them. Maybe the pitcher was an heirloom that the last member of the family had cherished. Maybe she'd promised to pass it on to Michele. Maybe Michele saw the breakage as a sign that her old friend was beginning to lose her grip. Or maybe she was afraid the damage had come from another source.

Peter hadn't forgotten what that fellow Evander had shouted yesterday morning; "I'll do it. And you won't like it." The surly cuss couldn't have helped realizing that Peter had heard what sounded far too much like a threat. Was that why he'd been so glowery in the restaurant? Could those yellowish shards have signaled a warning of more serious damage to come? Peter found himself stamping down on the gas pedal, worrying about what he might find at the end of his ride.

What he found was Miss Fran Rondel, seated on the wellhead coping, having a sociable morning chat with three of the biggest, handsomest hens he'd ever been privileged to lay eyes on. Their combs and wattles were fiery scarlet, their plumage shone red-gold in the sunshine. Their eyes sparkled like cabochon-cut jewels, their expressions were amiable. Peter had been pecked on the ankles too often as a farm boy gathering eggs to have worked up any great fellow feeling for the species; but here, he felt, were fowl he wouldn't mind getting to know.

78

Miss Rondel had three eggs gathered together in the lap of her apron, all of them pretty much the same color as the pitcher he'd brought her and about the same size Peter fancied eagles' eggs might be, albeit he'd probably never get around to dropping in on an aerie for comparison's sake. It was a pity Dan Stott wasn't here. Dan wasn't much of a poultry man as a rule but even a dedicated hog fancier wouldn't be able to resist taking a shine to these three. Now that he'd had such luck with the lupine seeds, Peter wondered whether he might try to negotiate a setting of eggs. He saw no sign of a rooster around so perhaps Miss Rondel's flock weren't that kind of girls. Anyway, this was hardly the time to ask; there was still the burning question of the paintings to be addressed.

Ah, Miss Rondel had spied him and not recoiled in revulsion. As a matter of fact, he thought she looked rather pleased.

"Good morning, Professor Shandy."

"Good morning, Miss Rondel. I just dropped by to bring you a—er—small thank-you for your great kindness yesterday, and to say that my wife will be coming tomorrow. She's very interested to see the paintings."

The elderly woman accepted Peter's offering with a slight inclination of her head. "I spoke to the artist last evening. It took some time for your message to sink in, but I'm fairly confident that a purchase can be arranged if you're still of a mind to go through with it. What time do you think would be convenient for Mrs. Shandy?"

"She and Catriona are planning an early-morning start, they should be able to reach Sasquamahoc sometime between noon and one o'clock. I'll drive over in the morning, be there to pick Helen up when they arrive, and bring her here. Shall we say half past three or so to be on the safe side?"

79

"That will do nicely, I have no other special plans for the afternoon. You do understand that I also have no authority to negotiate any sale until I've conveyed your offer and obtained the artist's consent?"

"Oh yes, no problem. We're planning to stay the night in any event, so there ought to be time enough to get squared away."

"One day is much like another to me, Professor. Thank you for this tempting basket, I shall save it to enjoy as my suppertime treat."

Miss Rondel hadn't so much as lifted a corner of the tissue paper, it was obvious to Peter that the interview was over. He said good-bye, walked back down to his car, and turned it in the direction of Sasquamahoc.

This wasn't a bad day for a drive, there were enough mares' tails in the sky to keep the sun from being too glary. He'd be pleased to see Guthrie, he was even more pleased that the unknown genius sounded willing to talk turkey. Peter did feel a slight sense of chagrin at not having got to take a second look at his painting, but tomorrow was another day and it would have been impolitic as well as discourteous to pester Miss Rondel for extra favors this time around.

There was no special reason why Peter couldn't have brought his toothbrush along and stayed overnight with Guthrie instead of driving there and back two days in a row, but he didn't want to. Guthrie's housekeeping was less than magnificent; his house looked not only tacky but also barren without the mass of kitsch that Guthrie had chucked out after his marriage, if such it could be called, had broken up with a resounding crash. Catriona had been nagging him to get a woman in to clean once or twice a week but Guthrie was not yet ready to let a female foot cross his doorstep, for which he could hardly be blamed, all things considered.

Peter would cheerfully have bunked at Catriona's but she wouldn't be there to cook him a sumptuous breakfast of eggs and home fries, so back to Elva Bright's cuisine he would go. And a far, far better thing it would be, provided nobody else dropped dead in the dining room and he managed to elude the clutching claws of Claridge Withington, though that might not be a hazard now that Lucivee Flodge was back in town.

Peter made good time, his mood was pleasantly anticipatory. He and Guthrie Fingal had roomed together all through agricultural college. By graduation time, Peter had become thoroughly convinced that Guthrie had Ent blood on some limb or other of his family tree. Guthrie had majored in silviculture, had come home to Maine and taken a teaching fellowship at Sasquamahoc Forestry College. He'd liked it at Sasquamahoc, he'd refused offers from several more allegedly prestigious institutions. He was now, and had been for some time, president of the venerable college. He would remain so, no doubt, until the Great Forester in the Sky hauled him up by the roots and replanted him on a higher plane.

It was barely noon and this morning's breakfast had just about worn off when he rolled into the college yard, figuring that Guthrie would be either in his office or out communing with some tree or other. He was right the first time. Guthrie sprang from his presidential chair, the padded arms of which had been reupholstered with duct tape since Peter's last visit, and leaped to extend a welcome.

"What the hell are you doing here, you old blot on the landscape? I thought you wouldn't be infesting the premises till tomorrow. Where's Helen? Where's Cat?"

"Don't ask me. Helen was burbling about their planning to take the bus to Boston and visit some den of depravity like Filene's Basement or the Aquarium, or possibly both. Or neither. The ways of womankind are beyond comprehension."

Peter refrained from adding "As you ought to know," but Guthrie filled in the blank for him. "Look who's telling who. How come Helen let you off the chain?"

"I'm here on business, drat it. I spent all day yesterday deseeding lupines at Rondel's Head. Know where it is?"

"How the hell could I keep from knowing? Cat bends my ear often enough about this mysterious woman who's lived all by herself with three French hens and a partridge in a pear tree for the past two hundred years and never gets a day older. She's asked me to go up there with her when the lupines are in bloom but I never seem to find the time. I suppose Cat's the one who set you on to Miss Rondel?"

"She is and I went and you don't know what you've missed. The fact that this occurred just at the time Helen was beginning to give me strong hints about betaking myself elsewhere before the eaglesses gathered may or may not be coincidental. I'm staying at a pleasant little place called Bright's Inn. Have you been there?"

"I've heard of it. They're supposed to have a great restaurant. Say, somebody mentioned something about that place last night, it was in the newspaper. I didn't have time to listen because we're running a summer evening program and I had to give a seminar on our friends the earwigs or some damn-fool thing. I've done so many that half the time I forget what I'm supposed to be talking about. You want to give a program tonight?"

"Not on your life, comrade. I'm going back to the inn for

supper. Speaking of food, how would you feel about going to that fried-clam taco place for lunch?"

"You paying?"

"I am, and proud and happy to have the privilege."

"What's the matter, you got religion or something?"

"Cease the schoolboy persiflage, oaf. You've been spending too much time among the earwigs. Your car or mine?"

Chapter 8

Having gone through the formalities, the two erudite scholars knuckled down to talking their own highly specialized kind of shop. President Fingal became fairly impassioned with regard to the spruce budworm, Professor Shandy waxed eloquent on the nematode. Neither of them had a good word to say about the carpenter ant or the Japanese beetle, much less the curculio weevil.

This feast of reason naturally whetted their appetites for more tangible fare. Once arrived at Edna's Diner, a quaint little bistro in Squamasas that sat out on a wharf over the water, they both ordered lavishly of Edna's fried-clam tacos with home-brewed root beer and extra coleslaw on the side.

Edna had her own idea of what a taco ought to be. She laced the batter with tartar sauce to save the patron the bother of lathering it on the clams, and ignored all that outlandish nonsense about chopped-up hunks of lettuce and tomato. Clams were what her customers came for and clams were what they got: fresh-dug, fresh-shucked, succulent bivalves, tenderly enrobed in corn meal, fried in good, clear cooking oil just long enough but not too long, and served hot from the basket. Guthrie and Peter suspended their learned discourse until the inner man had in each case been satisfied and a pushy herring gull had made off with their scanty leavings. They then ordered coffee and took it out on the rocks, where they could stretch their legs and be comfortable.

Perhaps not everybody thinks of rocks in terms of comfort, but New England Coast rocks are friendly rocks, at least to New Englanders' buttocks. Dumped by the Great Glacier, eroded and scoured by ages of battering from waves and weather, cracked and creased and warmed by the sun, they were, by Peter's and Guthrie's standards, just the ticket for a postprandial loll. The rocks wouldn't be offering much in the way of hospitality a while from now, though, if those clouds that had chased Peter all the way here kept on thickening.

"Drat!" Peter crushed his coffee cup, weighted it with a pebble and lobbed it expertly into a trash can about fifteen feet away. "I hope we're not in for a rainy day tomorrow. Helen and Cat are planning to start out sometime around the first crack of dawn, they say."

"That so? Cat hasn't called me. I've been dropping over now and then to make sure Andrew's doing right by the monsters."

Guthrie was referring to Carlyle and Emerson, two Maine coon cats approximately the size of Maine bobcats but looking larger because of their luxuriant ruffs, long fur, and plumy tails. Catriona's cantankerous old hired man affected to despise the critters as he did most people, things, and circumstances on general principles; in fact, Andrew was devoted to the cats. He would have resented anybody else's muscling in on what he considered his territory, but he made an exception of President Fingal, who never put on airs and was quite ready to hunker down and swap gossip when Andrew's alleged boss wasn't around.

Andrew's relationship with the woman who paid his wages could perhaps be described as feudal; in fact they feuded quite often, nor did the alleged Mistress of the Manor always triumph over the Old Retainer.

As for Guthrie Fingal's relationship with Catriona, Peter and Helen were both wondering what, if anything, was going to happen now that Guthrie was back to being a bachelor. At the moment, Guthrie seemed to be both pleased to hear that his friend was coming home sooner than he'd expected and piqued that she hadn't bothered to let him know. Whatever happened, the Shandys had agreed, it wasn't going to be all roses.

As her reputation in the field of mystery writing had grown, Catriona had become accustomed to alternating periods of semi-solitude in the old brick house where she parked her typewriter and pecked out her tales with spurts of travel urged upon her by her publishers in the interests of generating ever greater sales. About once a year, sometimes twice, she attended one of the burgeoning assortment of mystery conventions, to greet her fans and hang out with other practitioners of her odd profession. Lately she'd taken to slipping off on private junkets with particular friends such as Helen Shandy, Iduna Stott, and a few others whom she'd known and cherished over the years.

Guthrie Fingal, on the other hand, was a confirmed stick-in-the-mud. He seldom went anywhere he didn't have to go, except in his professional capacity, and then only when he couldn't find a way to weasel out of the trip. The paradoxical result of their contrasting life-styles was that Catriona never knew what was going on in her own home town while Guthrie's bush telegraph kept him up to the minute on everything that happened over a well-nigh incredible range of territory. Peter was, therefore, suprised to find himself the conveyor rather than the recipient of the startling news from Pickwance.

He had barely uttered the dead man's name, however, when Guthrie interrupted. "Jasper Flodge? Great big piss-cutter dressed to the nines, with patent-leather hair and squinchy little eyes the size of granny's shoe buttons? Won every pie-eating contest in the county for the past thirty-seven years or so."

"That sounds like him," said Peter. "He was shoveling in Mrs. Bright's chicken pot pie as if he'd been a fireman on a Mississippi steamboat when all of a sudden he flopped over into his plate and that was the end of him."

"And damned good riddance!" snorted his friend. "I'm not a vindictive man as a rule, Pete, but there's one bastard I'm glad to know got what was coming to him. Flodge was the skunk who got me and the college into that god-awful mess over the woodlot that was bequeathed to us by the founder's daughter's niece, I believe she was. Nice old soul, she lived to be almost a hundred. I used to drop by now and then and take her little doodads and whatnots: magazines, fruit off the college trees, maybe a box of candy or a bottle of port for what ailed her. Sit and visit awhile, clip the burdocks out of the cat's tail, maybe do a chore or two around the place. You know how it is with an old house, there's always something."

Guthrie fell to contemplating a lineup of shags perched on a spit of rock that hadn't yet been covered by the incoming tide. Peter waited for him to get on with the story.

"So anyway, she died. When it came time to settle the estate, didn't that goddamn Flodge horn in with a faked-up family tree claiming he was her cousin's great-nephew and the legal heir, which he damned well wasn't. He claimed I'd been using undue influence, getting the old lady drunk while she was of unsound mind, which she sure as hell wasn't, and tricking her into signing the will. He bad-mouthed me from here to hell and gone, even went to the college board of trustees and tried to get me kicked out of my job. Of course there wasn't a word of truth in any of the things he said. He got turned down flat at the hearing but the judge happened to be a third cousin of mine twice removed or some damned thing— I'm related to half the county, as you know—so naturally there was talk over that. Needless to say, it didn't help the college any, nor me, either."

"You should have sued the bastard for defamation of character."

"Huh. Do you think that would have made any difference? You know as well as I do, Pete, you can't touch pitch without getting smirched. And we weren't the only ones he tried his tricks on, not by a long shot. The hell of it is, sometimes he won."

"Flodge must have made plenty of enemies, then."

"You bet he did. To know him was to hate his guts. Don't be surprised if they have cheerleaders at the funeral. I might take a run up there myself and help with the yelling, if I thought he was worth wasting the gas on. If somebody wanted to rent an excursion bus, you can bet there wouldn't be any trouble filling the seats."

Guthrie was really wound up by now. He went on to regale Peter with some of Flodge's other perfidies, some of them verging on the ridiculous, others downright evil, all of them adding to the roster of persons who had reason to hold the name of Jasper Flodge in obloquy. As far as Guthrie knew, Elva Bright and her late husband weren't on the list, nor was any member of their family; perhaps Flodge had been smart enough not to inflict his shady deals on his near neighbors. Catriona had given Guthrie the impression that Miss Frances Rondel, though relatively unblessed with worldly goods, had always wielded a good deal of power locally and that Flodge or anybody else would have known better than to risk tangling with her. Peter wondered.

"Maybe you know something about a couple of—I think they might be brothers—who seem to have some kind of standing in the town. I've seen them in the inn dining room, they seem to be regular patrons. I don't recall their last name, but one's called Fred and the other's Evander."

"I've heard of them. Wye, their name is. They own a tourmaline mine. You probably know there's a lot of first-rate tourmaline in Maine. Fred's the brains of the outfit, I believe, and a pretty big gun in Maine politics, though you mightn't think so to look at him. I've never heard of anybody saying a word against Fred Wye, which is going some, I can tell you. The other one, I don't know much about him. Works in the mine some, I guess. He seems to be on close terms with his brother but that's about it. Everybody seems to like Fred but, when Evander's name comes up, they just shrug and pass him off. One fellow from up that way did tell me that Evander was a handy cuss in a row and it didn't do to provoke him because you wouldn't know what he might do. I don't suppose you're likely to run afoul of him."

Peter shook his head. "Apparently I already have, though I don't know why. When he comes into the restaurant, he seems to make a point of sitting where I can't help seeing his face, and glowers at me all the time I'm eating."

"I'll be damned. You haven't said anything to turn him ugly?"

"Not a yip. The only thing I can think of is that when I was walking up the path to Miss Rondel's house yesterday morning, Wye came charging down, yelling back over his shoulder about something he was going to do that she wouldn't like. He could be angry that I overheard him, though I've no idea what he was talking about."

"Um. You never can tell with somebody like that. Maybe you ought to stay here for the night. I might have a pair of clean sheets around somewhere."

"Thanks, but I told Mrs. Bright I'd be back for dinner. I'm coming over tomorrow to collect Helen, I thought we might all have lunch together before I take her to the inn. She wants to see the lupines, what's left of them. And we have a couple of other things planned," Peter replied somewhat evasively.

He couldn't quite bring himself to let Guthrie know he'd fallen in love with a painting. Furthermore, he had a superstitious fear that if he so much as mentioned their existence, the whole roomful might have vanished into thin air by the time he got back to Pickwance.

"Helen and I are only planning to stay the one night," he went on. "I expect we'll stop at Catriona's on our way home, though. You going to be around?"

"Oh, I expect likely I'll be able to spare you a few minutes of my valuable time." Guthrie glanced at his watch and leaped up as if the rock had suddenly turned to molten lava. "Sorry, Pete, but we've got to head back. I'm supposed to be doing some damn thing or other exactly twelve and a half minutes from now. So when do we meet tomorrow?"

"I don't know, it depends on how early Helen and Catriona start out and how many pit stops they make on the way. I'll probably be here by noontime. Miss Rondel's expecting us out at her place around half past three, so I may have to just stuff

Helen into our car and whomp her on up there. I shouldn't be surprised if we stayed a night in Sasquamahoc on the way back, though, unless Catriona sics Carlyle and Emerson on us. We could come to your seminar and root for the earwigs."

"Like hell you could. I don't tolerate any coarse ribaldry in my classroom. Added to which, this crowd will have pulled out by then and I don't have another lot coming till week after next, thank God."

They made it back to the college with half a minute to spare. Peter got into his own car and headed for Pickwance. He was in no great rush to get there, he stopped at a barn that had a "Used Books" sign nailed to the front, and treated himself to a browse. Peter liked some of the early-twentieth-century novels, he wasn't much for modern poetry but he did have a penchant for old-fashioned narrative verse, the cornier the better. An hour or so later and sixty-seven dollars poorer, he emerged from the barn triumphant with a paper bag full of treasures.

Along with Holman Day's *King Spruce* and *The Go-Getter*, the collected Mr. Glencannon stories of Guy Gilpatric, and a few more priceless tomes, he'd unearthed a scrapbook that some noble soul had pieced together out of the poetry pages that used to appear on the back page of the magazine section of the *Boston Sunday Globe* when Boston was still the cultural hub of the universe and New Englanders could gloat over such deathless epics as "The Deacon's Masterpiece" and "Some Little Bug Is Going to Find You Some Day." Peter's grandmother Shandy had collected a shoe box full of these pages but she'd never got around to pasting them in a scrapbook. When the farm had to be sold and the house cleaned out, some officious bastard had chucked out the shoe box before Peter could get to it. He'd always suspected his great-aunt Bedelia, a fanatical housekeeper who'd never picked up a newspaper except for the purpose of starting a fire in the wood stove or spreading the pages over her freshly scrubbed linoleum to keep anybody from tracking it up. He wondered where Great-Aunt Bedelia was spreading newspapers now. Probably on the road that was paved with good intentions, he decided.

By the time Peter left the bookshop, the clouds that had begun threatening while he and Guthrie were warming their behinds on the sun-heated rocks were assembled in full force. He barely had time to stash his trove in the car's trunk alongside the lupine seeds before it started to rain. This wasn't going to be one of the summer thunderstorms that pelt awhile, let up awhile, and then pelt some more; this was a down-to-business rain that set Peter to worrying about whether farmers in the area had got their hay in.

It was a long time since Peter himself had been engaged in any of those desperate races against the elements that used to lend extra pep and ginger to life on a small farm. He felt a stirring to be out in somebody's field with a pitchfork, doing the neighborly thing; but either the early crop of hay was already in around these parts or else nobody had got around to cutting any as yet. Anyway, they wouldn't be using pitchforks these days. He flipped on his windshield wipers and headed for Pickwance, grateful not to be lurching along some dirt road behind a truck piled high with logs destined for some pulp mill and a scary great log-lifter on behind looking like the leftovers from a *Tyrannosaurus rex.*

Peter rather liked driving in the rain, particularly on a secondary route when he had the road pretty much to himself. He didn't see another car for quite a stretch. When he did come upon one, it was pulled over to the side of the road with its hood up and a denim-covered backside protruding from underneath. This wasn't the greatest place to break down, he hadn't passed a house since shortly after he'd left the book barn and there didn't look to be another up ahead. He drew up and opened his window.

"Need a hand?"

The stranded driver straightened up and shook the rain out of his eyes. "Don't suppose you'd have a spare fuel pump with you?"

"No, but I might be able to get you one, if you'll tell me where."

"Don't want to put you to the trouble."

That was a typical Mainer's reaction, Peter thought. What the man really didn't want was having to feel beholden. He could understand that well enough, he didn't like having to feel beholden either. He put on the raincoat and shapeless tweed hat that he'd thrown into the back seat just in case, got out of the car, and leaned over the engine as protocol required. "Mind if I take a look?"

"She's all yours, mister." The man was looking at Peter's own car with mingled scorn and awe. "You a mechanic?"

"No, but I've doctored plenty of ailing tractors."

This crate could certainly stand some doctoring. Peter spotted at least four potential causes for a breakdown without even trying, no doubt there were more. The car hadn't been neglected, it wasn't more than reasonably dirty inside, it was just plumb worn out. He had a repair kit in his own car but he wouldn't dare go fiddling around with this one for fear the whole shebang would collapse in a heap of rust. He straightened up and wiped his hands on one of the bandanna handkerchiefs that he always carried from force of habit, even to weddings and funerals if Helen didn't frisk him and make him take a white one instead.

94

"I see your problem, but we can't do much in this rain. Where were you heading?"

"Up the coast a ways. Place called Pickwance."

"Oh, well then, we're in business. I'm staying at Bright's Inn. I was just on my way back from seeing a friend in Sasquamahoc."

"You don't say. I figured you was just a tourist, with them Massachusetts number plates. Got folks in Sasquamahoc, have you?"

Peter decided his old roommate could count as a folk. "You know Guthrie Fingal at the forestry school?"

"I've met him. Had a nephew went there. Seems to be doing all right. Name's Tilkey."

"Mine's Shandy. You wouldn't be related to Eustace Tilkey who runs the *Ethelbert Nevin* out of Hocasquam?"

"Yes, but I ain't proud of it. You know Eustace?"

"I suppose you could say so. My wife went on one of his whale-watching trips." And damned near didn't make it back, Peter winced at the memory.* "Look, hadn't we better tow your car someplace where it will be safe? Have you anything we can use for a towrope?"

"Nope, but I've got a cousin with a tow truck. If you'll drive me to a telephone, I can give him a call. He'll come and pick up the pieces when he finds the time. Just let me get my good clothes out of the back, there's nothing else worth stealing. Including the car. It's just a piece of junk my boy cobbled together. Didn't want to leave my wife stranded, so she's got the pickup. She could have come but she didn't want to. Can't say's I blame her, considering, but I wouldn't miss this for all the tea in China."

*Vane Pursuit, 1989

"You're on your way to some—er—function?"

"You could call it that. And I'm going to enjoy every minute of it. Say, I don't want to get your upholstery wet."

"Don't worry, my wife always keeps a few old towels in the car. I tend to get pretty grubby myself often as not. Here, spread this one under you. What's the big excitement at Pickwance?"

As if Peter didn't know. The excursion bus that Guthrie Fingal had hypothesized might turn out to be not such a bad idea after all. After Jasper Flodge was safely planted and the cheering had died down, Mr. Tilkey could book a seat and ride the bus home.

Chapter 9

It was lucky for the stranded one that Peter had stopped. They were almost four miles up the road before they managed to locate a gas station that had a pay phone in working order. Tilkey didn't waste many words because he only had one quarter, he was naturally reluctant to bum another off his rescuer and the manager didn't look like the type to break a bill for a non-customer. Peter then decided he'd put some gas that he didn't really need into his tank not only to demonstrate that they weren't pikers, but also to drag the surly lout into the rain, where he obviously didn't want to go. Their mission accomplished thus far, Shandy and his new acquaintance set off again.

Tilkey wasn't a bad companion in his way, sociable enough to relieve the monotony of a longish drive but no ear-bender. When he did talk, it was mainly about tractors and root vegetables. Both subjects were, of course, entirely congenial to Peter. By the time they got near to Pickwance, he himself had waxed almost magniloquent on the cultivation of turnips.

It was only then that Tilkey realized he was in the presence of greatness.

"Gorry mighty! You wouldn't happen to be that Professor Shandy from Balaclava Aggie? I've heard of you."

Peter hunched his shoulders. "Whatever you've heard, don't believe a word of it. Were you planning to put up at Bright's Inn for the night?"

"Not when I can sponge on my relatives. I've got a couple of second cousins baching it out at their folks' old place. You happened to run into the Wye brothers?"

"Yes, though I didn't know they were brothers until Guthrie Fingal told me this noontime. Fred and Evander, would they be the ones you mean? I've seen them in the dining room, they seem to be regular customers of Mrs. Bright's."

"That doesn't surprise me any. I expect I'll be eating there tonight myself, it's either that or starve to death. What them two boys need is a woman in the house. My wife keeps telling them to hire a housekeeper, but Evander's scared to death she might want to marry him, though God knows why any woman in her right mind would want to. And Fred's still pretty bitter about the way his wife walked out on him. She took him for everything but his hernia truss, and all for that conniving son-of-a—Godfrey, I'm gabbing away like some old hen at a tea party. I ought to watch my mouth for saying that, my wife always claims men gossip a damn sight worse than women do."

"So does mine," said Peter. "Do you want to go along to your cousins' place and get settled, or would you rather come straight to the inn and wait for them there?"

"Seeing as how they don't know I'm coming because I forgot to call and let them know, I expect I'd better try 'em at the house."

"What if they're not around?"

"Won't matter a particle, I know where they hide the key. Anywhere along here'll be fine, Professor. I've put you to enough trouble already. I can hoof it the rest of the way."

"It's no trouble at all, Mr. Tilkey. I have nothing special to do, I'm just killing time waiting for my wife, and she won't be coming till tomorrow. There's no sense in your walking in the rain and getting all soaked. Which way?"

"Well, if you're sure I'm not putting you out any. Keep on the way we're heading till you come to the church, then take a right up the hill and it's the big yellow house with the cupalow. The road's paved, in case you're wondering."

Peter nodded. A big yellow house with a cupola, not that any Mainer would pronounce it as it was spelled, meant that there must have been money in the Wye family for quite a while. Nobody was building that kind of house anymore, and not many could have afforded to build them back when those great wooden arks were fashionable among the elite. In earlier times, much of Maine's wealth had come from lumber or shipping, Peter didn't know what kind of money there was in tourmaline mining and he didn't think it was any of his business to ask.

The rain still showed no sign of slacking off as they dipped down into Pickwance. There was more traffic here than they'd been seeing along the way. Pedestrians hunched over under umbrellas were crossing the main street, more concerned about avoiding the puddles than getting run down by some motorist temporarily blinded by a fan of muddy water thrown up from a vehicle going the opposite way. Peter crawled along with his windshield wipers going at high speed until he spied the church, a typical white-painted clapboard building with a modest steeple that contained a bell and provided parking space for a black-faced clock with gilded numerals and a weather vane in the shape of a banner.

"Here's where we turn," Tilkey's reminder came a bit late, Peter was already slowing down, waiting for a very wet spaniel to make up its mind whether or not to risk the puddles in the road. At last the disgruntled person at the other end of the leash picked up the dog and lugged it across, squirming and yapping, Peter was free to turn.

Down at the business end, houses were set close together. As they climbed the steeply snaking road, the dwellings sat farther apart. Finally they got to the big yellow house with the cupola, standing snobbishly alone on the crest of the hill, surrounded by a couple of acres of lawn, or what passed for one, made up of anything green that could be kept mown short and interrupted here and there by ornamental shrubs that were overdue for pruning and not getting any.

The Wye place might not quite attain the status of a mansion, but it didn't miss by much. Previous owners must have kept the place up the way it ought to be, but now signs of neglect were beginning to show. Damned shame to let it go this way. Peter could see no evidence that the Wye brothers were around, but that didn't appear to bother Tilkey. He thanked Peter for the lift, took his plastic-covered Sunday suit out of the back seat, jerked his chin in farewell, and walked around to a side door. This must be where they hid the key, Peter waited long enough to make sure his erstwhile passenger had got in out of the rain, and drove back to the inn.

The temperature had dipped, not a great deal but enough for somebody, most likely Mrs. Bright herself, to have lighted a wood fire in the small front room that served as lobby, registration area and sitting room. Wicker chairs drawn up around the fireplace offered a warm welcome to guests who might not feel like holing up in probably chilly bedrooms. Peter went upstairs to get rid of his raincoat, freshen up a little, and take a therapeutic sip or two from the pint of Scotch that he'd brought along for medicinal purposes. As he'd expected, the bedroom that he'd thus far found pleasant and comfortable was now definitely on the dank and gloomy side. He picked up a book he'd brought along because he thought he ought to read it and hadn't yet opened because he had a premonition that it would be duller than ditch water, and went back down to the lobby.

He might have known. He'd no more than made his choice of the armchairs, switched on the one puny table lamp, and adjusted its shade so that he could see to read when he was addressed by what he'd taken for an afghan thrown down in a heap at the far end of the one sofa.

"Good afternoon, Professor Shandy. Elva tells me you've been off to visit some friends in Sasquamahoc. I hope this rain didn't spoil your ride."

This was no more than Peter should have expected, but what the hell? He might as well be bored stiff by Claridge Withington as by an author who could convolute a sentence more intricately than any of those whom Mark Twain lampooned so wickedly in "The Awful German Language." He put down his barely opened book, steeled himself for the lesser evil, and responded as cordially as he could manage without undue strain.

"No, the rain didn't start until I was on my way back. I'd had lunch with an old friend who's connected with the forestry school."

Withington's eyes lit up. He flung off the afghan and dragged himself to a proper sitting position. "That wouldn't have been President Fingal, by any chance? I had the privilege of chatting with him a few years back, at a colloquium on the uses and abuses of Maine's forests, in which a friend of mine participated. I myself, needless to say, was merely an interested member of the audience but there was coffee and so forth afterward, which gave me a chance to let the president know how impressed I was by his incisive and pertinent remarks."

Which would have been short, snappy and maybe somewhat acerbic in spots, Peter surmised. He admitted that the friend he'd visited was in fact Guthrie Fingal and was thereupon treated to a playback of what Withington had said to Fingal and what the president had said in reply, which must surely have been a damn sight less than Withington remembered. Withington wound up with a fervently expressed hope that Professor Shandy would convey greetings from a grateful admirer at his next meeting with President Fingal and followed up with in-depth questions as to whether the two learned gentlemen had enjoyed their luncheon and if they would be meeting again in the not-too-distant future.

"I expect so." Peter decided he might as well volunteer the information rather than put Withington to the bother of wringing it out of him. "I may see him tomorrow, as a matter of fact. My wife will be riding up to Sasquamahoc with her friend Catriona McBogle. I'm going to meet her at Catriona's sometime around noon and bring her here. Mrs. Bright may have mentioned to you that Mrs. Shandy will be staying at the inn overnight."

"For the purpose of seeing Frances Rondel's lupines," Withington filled in neatly. "I hope for Mrs. Shandy's sake that this storm hasn't already battered them all down. According to the NOAA weather forecast, however, this storm is supposed to have blown itself out to sea by morning, so you ought to have fine weather for your drive tomorrow. As should Mrs. Shandy and her illustrious friend."

Withington smiled as benevolently as though he'd taken personal charge of the weather and custom-tailored it to his new acquaintance's particular needs. "I had the privilege of hearing Miss McBogle speak last summer in Orono at a symposium to which a fellow guest from the inn here drove me. Rather a distinguished guest, I may say. Perhaps you and Mrs. Shandy may have had the good fortune to see Alexandria Baxter in her starring role as Lizzie Borden in *Forty Whacks*. Will you ever forget that breathtaking moment when she picked up the ax and just touched the tip of her finger to its freshly sharpened blade? I still get the shivers thinking of her tiny, secret smile. Miss Baxter went to Orono incognita, of course, not wishing to steal the spotlight from Miss McBogle, although the long black widow's veil that she'd donned to hide her face did attract a good many curious glances."

"I can see where it might have," said Peter. "Er—I don't suppose Miss Baxter brought along her ax?"

Mrs. Bright's star boarder thought that one over, then decided on a tiny, secret chuckle. "No she didn't, somewhat to my disappointment. I shouldn't be at all surprised if one or two axes showed up at our big event tomorrow morning, however."

"Oh?" Peter didn't try to hide his yawn. The long drive, the drumming of the rain on the lobby windows, the hypnotic effect of the burning logs in the fireplace were conspiring together to put him to sleep. "What big event?"

Not that he gave a damn, but Withington flew into a tizzy. "Good heavens, Professor, don't tell me you've escaped hearing about Jasper Flodge's funeral? His lawfully wedded wife, as

Lucivee has in fact turned out to be, hasn't lost a moment getting him safely tucked away. I understand she's already ordered a tombstone half the size of Cadillac Mountain to make sure he's well weighted down, and set the funeral for nine o'clock sharp tomorrow morning. Seeing that you were in at the death, so to speak, you may wish to witness the obsequies before starting back to Sasquamahoc."

Peter was wondering why in tunket he'd thought a fireside chat with this garrulous old ghoul would be preferable to sitting alone in a cold, lonesome upstairs bedroom. He found the notion of popping in on the obsequies altogether repugnant. While the very little he'd seen of Jasper Flodge alive had not predisposed him in the man's favor, watching him die had been a shock and the aftermath a nightmare.

The earful that Peter had got from Guthrie this noontime had suggested a multitude of reasons why some one of Flodge's victims might have thought it a good idea to drop a cyanide pill into his gravy, but who except Elva Bright or her pretty granddaughter could have managed to get hold of one? And why would either of them have been dumb enough to do it on their own family premises?

That Flodge had killed himself for the purpose of ruining the plans his wife had made for collecting his life insurance was more than Peter could swallow. Unless Flodge knew he was at death's door anyway, which he certainly hadn't looked to be, or was so far around the bend as to think he could kill himself with cyanide and come to life again. The possibility that he was indeed loopy to the nth degree could not be counted out. Peter remembered an incident from his own college days, when a fellow student had gulped down a handful of barbiturates, then made a movie date for the following afternoon.

Maybe Flodge had had that same inability to relate actions

to consequences, which could explain his propensity for pulling dirty deals without caring who got hurt in the process, himself apparently included. If he'd really got himself into bad trouble, as his wife averred, he might have had some kind of Tom Sawyerish wish to die *temporarily*. Or, Peter supposed, Flodge could have got the clever idea of slipping some noxious dose into his own food in a scheme to make himself sick enough so that he could sue Elva Bright for all she had, and got hold of the wrong poison.

The hell with it. What was the sense in speculating about a situation that was none of Peter Shandy's business? Bad enough to have that pestiferous Withington jiggling Flodge's funeral in front of his nose like a ribbon in front of a kitten. If Withington was merely angling for a lift to the obsequies, let somebody else take him.

"Sorry, Mr. Withington." Peter knew he sounded snappish and didn't care. "My plans are all made, I'll have to be on the road by then."

If he left the inn before nine o'clock, he'd be kicking his heels in Sasquamahoc by half past ten or thereabout, but one excuse was as good as another. At least he understood now why yesterday's stranded motorist had been so elated at the prospect of getting the last laugh on a dead man. Tilkey must have been another of Jasper Flodge's victims. Guthrie would know, maybe Peter could ask. Then again, maybe he wouldn't. He was getting sick and tired of Flodge and his rotten schemes.

It was high time for a change of subject. Because he couldn't think of anything else to say, Peter began relating the details of yesterday's drive to Sasquamahoc and back, making as long a yarn of it as he could just to keep from having to listen to Withington's voice instead of his own, starting with his brief visit to Miss Rondel, going on to the clam tacos, working his way back via the book barn to the meeting with Tilkey, thence to the Wye house and at long last to Bright's Inn.

Had any chance-met acquaintance tried to bend Peter's ear like this for so long a stretch, he'd either have fallen into a stupor or taken decisive action two chapters ago. Withington, however, hung upon every word, rapt and eager, now and then emitting an excited whimper like a terrier after a barn rat, torn between fear lest he miss a syllable and frustration at not getting the chance to put in his own two cents' worth at every turn of the tale.

Accustomed to lecturing in his classroom, Peter was able to keep it up for quite a stretch. But all things must have an end; the moment he'd uttered his final syllable, Withington pounced.

"That must have been Schuyler Tilkey you picked up. He's eaten here at the inn on various occasions with the Wye brothers. They're cousins of his."

"Second cousins," Peter corrected smartly.

"Really? That does surprise me. I hadn't realized. Second cousins, eh?"

Just why Withington should look so almighty flabbergasted by so trivial a piece of information about a casual acquaintance was beyond Peter's comprehension. He drew himself a mental picture of Withington writing down the particulars on a pink card, or maybe a green one, and filing it neatly away in some pigeonhole of his subconscious mind, to be hauled up and read off to some other luckless wight during some other wearisome talkathon. Peter felt a stab of pity for Withington's next victim, whoever that might be.

His incubus was not ready to yield the floor. "I gather that Sky, as they call him, must have come for the funeral. Naturally he wouldn't want to miss the happy event, after what Jasper did to his second cousin. Fred, that is to say."

"Not Evander?" Peter only mentioned the other brother's name to keep himself from falling asleep. He wished he hadn't, now Withington was off and running again.

"Oh, even Jasper Flodge wouldn't have had the moxie to pull anything on Evander. Perhaps I should caution you, Professor Shandy, that Evander Wye is not a man to be trifled with. I don't know whether President Guthrie happened to mention—"

"Yes, he did."

That was another false step. If Peter Shandy thought he could get away with interrupting another spiel about a man to whom he'd never yet spoken a single word and had no intention of ever addressing, he might as well think again. Was he in truth collared by Coleridge's Ancient Mariner, or had he got permanently stuck with the albatross? Peter wished the chap with the loud bassoon would happen along; at least it would be a change of annoyances.

Chapter 10

"Oh, then you do know about the time Evander tried to run Jasper down with the brush cutter?"

"Well, you could hardly blame him, could you?"

Peter wished he knew what he and Withington were talking about. He did see why chasing somebody with a brush hog might not be such a bad idea under certain circumstances. His companion evidently viewed the incident from a different angle.

"Just because Jasper had called him a sissy? Not to be quarrelsome, Professor, but quite frankly I myself can't help feeling that Evander's reaction was somewhat excessive."

"Everyone to his own opinion," said Peter. "I might point out that you can't get any great burst of speed out of a brush hog unless you're on a steep downhill grade, which isn't the best place to be if you're the one driving it. Not to be contumacious, Mr. Withington, but it appears to me that Mr. Wye's little prank might be taken as no more than a—er—symbolic gesture."

That got Withington where the wool was short. He didn't

utter a sound for fully thirty seconds. The best he could do then was "Is that what President Fingal thinks?"

"I'll see if I can't get an official statement from Guthrie tomorrow. Good Lord, is that the time?" Peter jerked himself out of the wicker armchair. "I'd better go and telephone my wife before she starts wondering what I'm up to."

Helen was not at home, which didn't surprise Peter any. He tried the Stotts' number and there she was, helping Iduna to serve high tea for Catriona and a couple of hundred others, judging from the volume of sound in the background. Helen reassured him that what he heard were just a few of the big, broad, forward-thinking women from the neighborhood and that the revels would be over early enough for her and Catriona to get a good night's sleep and be on the road by the time the lark was on the thorn. "And if you decide to go tarryhooting after more clam tacos," she added, "be sure to leave a note on Cat's door so that we'll know where to find you."

Peter said he would, tacked on a few husbandly kindnesses, and hung up the phone. While he'd been in the phone booth, customers had begun trickling into the restaurant. His stomach suggested that it might be time to think of joining them. He carried the book that he still hadn't opened back to his room, mixed a small preprandial libation in the tooth glass from the tiny bathroom, and sipped it slowly to make sure Withington had plenty of time to get stowed away in his usual corner.

It had been Peter's intention to sit alone at one of the smaller tables. Somewhat to his dismay, however, he found Schuyler Tilkey already there with the Wye brothers, motioning for Peter to take the fourth seat. It would have been uncivil for him not to do so, and perhaps even dangerous; he'd better not rile Evander by any act that might be considered hostile. He went.

"Evening, Professor, haul up and set," was Tilkey's greeting. "I guess you've seen my cousins. I'm Sky, in case I forgot to mention it before. This here's Fred and that's Evander."

"Evening," said Peter. "My name's Peter Shandy."

"Teaches farming at Balaclava Aggie," Tilkey supplemented.

"That so?" Fred Wye seemed willing enough to hear more, but Thurzella popped over with her order blank at the ready and gave a dramatic rendering of tonight's specialties, which consisted chiefly of fresh-caught haddock broiled, baked with cheese and tomato, deep-fat fried, or cut up in chowder. Peter opted for broiled, Fred for baked, Schuyler for fried because his wife wasn't around to tell him he was too fat already. All three decided they might as well try the chowder for starters.

Evander didn't say anything, but Thurzella brought him a thick white cup of chowder with a blue stripe around the top, the same as the other men were having. She then went scooting back for a basket of hot corn bread and a huge bowl of tossed salad from which they could help themselves ad lib, and assured them that their real food would be along soon. The still-silent Evander ate what was put in front of him, pausing now and then to give Peter a sideways glower, but neither shying away from him nor showing any sign of getting set to attack. After a while, Peter decided it would be safe to venture an opening conversational gambit.

"I understand that you two operate a tourmaline mine."

Evander scowled again but Fred was quite ready to talk about the family's unusual business. His information was so clear and succinct that Peter wondered whether he sometimes gave guided tours to schoolchildren. Fred admitted that he sometimes did, and went so far as to suggest that the professor might care to go over and mosey around a little sometime

111

when he had nothing better to do, not that there was much to see.

Peter replied with a careful balancing of enthusiasm and regret that it was nice of Fred to offer but he didn't know how much time there'd be for visiting the mine because he'd already promised to take his wife to meet Miss Rondel and to Michele Cluny's hand-weaving shop, and they were only going to be here through tomorrow night.

"Too bad." Fred Wye bore the disappointment bravely, he turned to his cousin. "Run into Ed Whitbread from the county coroner's office a while back at the gas pump. He says it was cyanide, all right."

"That so? Did Ed say where it come from?"

"Hell, no. Ed Whitbread wouldn't know, an' wouldn't tell you if he did. Jeezum, look at that!"

A bolt of lightning had flashed through the dining room. At least this was the first impression Peter got, he sensed that every other person in the restaurant was feeling the same as he. Lucivee Flodge hurled herself into their midst with a spring in her step, a gleam in her eye, and a bottle of champagne under each arm. She was dressed all in black, but there are blacks and blacks; hers was the other kind. Black lace stretch tights, a black satin top ablaze with sequins, slashed down the front far beyond the bounds of probability, and a huge black bow studded with fake diamonds riding atop her titian hair made a clear statement that here was the merriest widow of them all.

Peter's second impression was that any woman as broad in the beam as Lucivee must have had to do a good deal of positive thinking or else avoided looking in the mirror when she'd stuffed herself into those tights. That was her affair, definitely not his. He averted his eyes and got to work on the salad.

"Doesn't look as if there'd be much sense in wasting a

sympathy card on that one," Sky grunted. "I take it she's the weeping widow?"

"So she claims," said Fred. "Her story is that they were never divorced, though they hadn't lived together for six years and Jasper had had a few more women after her. Mine included, damn him." He reddened, cast an apologetic glance at Peter, and stabbed his fork into a chunk of cucumber.

While Bright's Inn did not have a liquor license, it was apparently not illegal for patrons to bring along their own wine or beer. Lucivee Flodge had by now come to light at Claridge Withington's table and was making a great to-do over ordering ice for her champagne and enough glasses for everybody in the restaurant. The green plastic bucket and the squatty little juice glasses provided by a young girl who must be the granddaughter from Portland because she looked just like Thurzella and was wearing pink stirrup pants, seemed not to be what Lucivee had envisioned but were all that Lucivee was going to get.

From the look of things, her party was turning out to be more fizzle than fizz. It was pretty obvious that most people there were of the opinion that throwing a champagne hootenanny in the same room where the man they were going to bury tomorrow morning had met his death two nights previously was not in the best of taste. When the new girl circled the room with a trayful of filled glasses, she found few takers. The Wye brothers shook their heads, so did Peter. Sky Tilkey might have taken some, if he'd been alone, Peter thought, but he wouldn't go against his relatives. However much ill will Jasper Flodge had managed to generate, and whatever the grounds for celebration might be, to stomp on his grave before he'd even been put into it was carrying things too far. When the new girl carried the tray of champagne back to the table in the corner, there were almost as many full glasses on it as when she'd started.

Peter happened to be sitting where he got a good view of the people coming in. He was at first indifferent, then mildly interested to spot a woman of indeterminate age who might once have been pretty, wearing a blue suit that had also seen its best days. She'd stepped diffidently inside the dining room and was looking around for a waitress to seat her.

"Good Lord," he exclaimed. "I know that woman. She keeps house for some neighbors of mine at Balaclava."

"That so? What else does she do?"

It was Fred Wye who'd spoken. He was watching the woman too. There was an intensity in his voice and his look that made Peter feel somehow uneasy.

"I believe she was one of the dormitory maids at the college and did some housecleaning for faculty people in her spare time, the Enderbles among them. They're a couple well along in years who live across from Helen and me on what's called the Crescent. When Mary broke her wrist some months ago, and needed somebody to cope full-time, Mrs. Howard moved in with them. Very quiet woman but a good worker, Mary and John think the world of her. She's good with their animals—John's field is local fauna—they have a number of pets including a very old rabbit who needs special care. I understand she also has a part-time job at a kennel, washing and clipping dogs, and has even helped our president's wife to braid the manes and tails of the college's Balaclava Blacks for the Annual Workhorse Competition, which is Balaclava County's big event of the year. I suppose I ought to speak to her."

"Tell her Fred said hello."

The mine owner's words came out as a snarl. Thurzella was now leading Mrs. Howard over to a small table not far from where the four men were sitting. Peter noted that the woman kept her head bowed, that her face was pale and her mouth set tight as though she might be trying not to cry. He wondered whether he ought to leave her alone, but that seemed a caddish thing to do. He got up and went over to her table.

"Good evening, Mrs. Howard."

"Why, Professor Shandy, what a surprise. Are you staying at the inn?"

"Yes, I came to see the famous lupines. I've been here since Sunday night. My wife's driving up tomorrow with Catriona McBogle, a friend who's been visiting her. I don't know if you've had a chance to meet Catriona?"

"Just to say hello to, she seems very nice. I've been very busy at the kennel lately. Flea time, you know."

Her voice was light and rather sweet, but her short gust of laughter came out harsh as a raven's call. Peter began to wonder if he'd overstayed his welcome, then recalled that he had a message to deliver. "Er—Fred Wye told me to say hello. He's sitting over there."

"Yes, I noticed. Would you tell him—" Oh God, was she going to cry? "Tell him—tell him I've forgiven him for what he—he—oh, Lord be merciful! Why did I come here?"

The woman looked ready either to faint or fall into hysterics, Peter decided he'd better leave her alone. As he went back to his table, Fred Wye gave him a look that could not be ignored. Peter said what he had to.

"She—er—told me to say she's forgiven you."

"The hell she did!" Fred started up from his chair, eyes blazing. "Well, you can tell her for me—"

"Er—I seem somehow to have put us all in an awkward position. May I suggest that I just step aside and let you and Mrs. Howard—er—"

115

"You stay right here. Whatever lie she's trying to pass off, that bitch can come over here and say it to my face. Scooch over, Evander, and set another chair. We might as well try to act decent, even if she's forgotten how. Go get her, Professor."

God, what a mess! It dawned on Peter that this shabby little mouse must be Fred Wye's errant wife, the one who'd taken everything that wasn't nailed down except his hernia truss and run off with Jasper Flodge. How the flaming perdition had she wound up de-fleaing the spaniels and setters of Balaclava Junction and cleaning up after the Enderbles' elderly, incontinent pet rabbit? Well, it served him right for trying to be a gentleman. He went back to Mrs. Howard and delivered an expurgated version of her husband's invitation to join the party.

Mrs. Howard, if that was her real name now, neither swooned nor sobbed. Her face dead white and stiff as stone, she marched like an automaton over to the chair that Evander had set for her. Nobody spoke, nobody moved until Thurzella, bless her, zoomed over to recite the specials yet once more.

"Just chowder, please."

That was all she said, and probably more than she'd be able to eat. Peter wished he'd thought to bring his pint of whiskey to the table, he suggested that perhaps Mrs. Howard would like some tea or coffee right away. She said tea, which he hoped might be a small step in the right direction.

Fred might have a little spark of love still burning. At least he was humane enough to let her get a few swallows of hot tea into her before he attacked. "Okay, Iolanthe, suppose you tell me what it is you've forgiven me for since you cleaned out my bank account and ran off with Jasper Flodge?"

"How dare you!"

She was alive now, all right. Her cheeks were ablaze, her

eyes boring into his like a pair of laser beams. "You know perfectly well what you did to me, you—you whited sepulchre!"

"What are you talking about?"

"I'm talking about those nine teenage girls you seduced and abandoned."

"Are you out of your mind? What nine girls?"

"The ones who bore your children out of wedlock and you wouldn't even send them enough money to put food in the poor little babies' mouths. Don't try to lie out of it, Fred Wye. Father showed me the letters he got, and then the woman from the Department of Human Services came looking to put the law on you because you hadn't paid."

"Look, Iolanthe, this isn't making any sense at all. Let's go back and start from the beginning. All I know is, Evander and I and Sky here went up to the camp for a few days' fishing, and when we got back you were nowhere to be found. I might have known that jeezly old lunatic of a father of yours would have had a hand in it somewhere. What were these letters you're talking about?"

Iolanthe took another sip of tea and drew a deep breath. "It was the day after you left for camp. I was watering the houseplants. That gardenia I'd been nursing along was finally just about to bloom, and I was glad there'd be a new blossom to show you when you got back. I remember it all very well, you see, because that was the last truly happy moment of my life."

She was twisting the teacup around in the saucer, struggling for what little composure she could scrape together. "I was just going back to refill the water pot when Father barged in without knocking, as he always did, absolutely beside himself with rage."

117

"As he generally was. So what?"

"He—I don't know if I can—he—he read me this letter. It was from a girl you'd been seeing—a girl seventeen years old, who'd sung in a church choir where Father had preached once. She pleaded for Father to intercede for her with you because she was sick and penniless and her parents had thrown her out of the house and she had nowhere to turn, and her baby—your baby, Fred—would die if it didn't get food and shelter soon. It was the most heartrending—"

"Pack of lies anybody ever thought up! And that old bastard believed every word of it because he'd been dead set against me from the day we met, as you very well know. I wouldn't be surprised if he'd written the damned thing himself."

"Well, he didn't, because about ten minutes later a woman from the Department of Human Services drove up to the house looking for you with a warrant. Father read her all those letters, one after the other, as if he were Moses reading the tablets. Then he began praying at the top of his lungs, exhorting me to get down on my knees and repent for having spurned my father's teaching and married a whoremaster. That's what he called you, and that's what you are. He said I must leave you at once and never set eyes on you again because the sins of the husband were visited upon the wife and I'd burn in hell forever if I stayed in that house one more night. And that woman standing right there taking it all in and nodding her head. I wanted to slap her."

"Why the hell didn't you? What names were on those so-called letters?"

"None that I recognized. The only one I remember is Muriel Flodge. She was the one who wrote to Father."

"Flodge, eh?" Fred snorted. "You know, that doesn't surprise me a bit. So then all of a sudden in gallops Jasper Flodge on his white horse, saying he's come to rescue you from the foul clutches of your rotten whoremaster of a husband and carry you away to some tropical paradise where you and he can live happily ever after on my money."

"No, Fred. It wasn't like that at all. Jasper did come, after that awful woman had left and after Father had finally quit praying over me and told me I could come home and keep house for him, but not until I'd atoned for my terrible sin by meekly bowing my head under the yoke and ridding my heart of any wifely feeling I'd ever had for you and signing over my inheritance to him. So I said that would be never, because I loved you and always would, no matter what you'd done and even if I never saw you again this side of the grave."

She broke down then, hiding her face in her napkin, shaking like a poplar in a windstorm. Peter had been thinking of Mrs. Howard, as he'd known her, as being vaguely middle-aged; it suddenly dawned on him that this woman must be still in her twenties, and Fred Wye not many years older. Without that bushy beard, he'd probably be quite a good-looker. Evander, then, must be the elder brother, and Schuyler Tilkey an old relic of forty-five or so. They must think Professor Shandy was Methuselah in disguise.

Nobody was making a sound, just sitting there trying not to watch her cry. It was a relief when she mopped her face, sniffed a final sniffle, and went on with her story. "So then Father said I was no daughter of his and I needn't think I'd ever see one red cent of the money Aunt Prunella left me, and stormed off hurling anathemas right and left. I felt as if I'd been torn to ribbons. I didn't know what to do or where to go. My legs buckled under me, I fell down on the floor still holding that silly watering pot, and started to cry. The way I'm doing now."

"Can't blame her for that."

Of all people, it was Evander who spoke. He must have surprised himself, he buttoned his lips tight together and concentrated on searching for bones in his haddock. Perhaps those few kind words had helped a little, Iolanthe's voice was a trifle steadier as she went on.

"I don't know how long I stayed there like that. All I remember is Jasper Flodge sticking his head in at the door and saying 'Anybody home?' I couldn't let him see me like that, I got up and pulled myself together as best I could and told him to come in. All I could think of was that poor little Muriel Flodge; I believe the first thing I said was "Is she your sister?"

"Jasper knew right away what I meant. He told me Muriel was only a distant cousin whom he didn't know very well, which was why he hadn't thought to warn her about Fred Wye in time. You can imagine how I felt about that! He showed me the letter she'd sent him, he told me he'd cried when he read it."

"I'll bet he did."

Fred wasn't giving up without a struggle. Iolanthe must be wishing she were back at the Enderbles', changing the old rabbit's diaper. Peter would as soon have been there himself about now, he hadn't reckoned on another soap opera with his dinner. If he'd thought a little bit faster, he could have found some excuse to leave the table when the fur began to fly. It was too late now to do anything but pretend he wasn't among those present and finish his meal, though it did cost him a pang not to drop a word about that letter Flodge had allegedly got from his alleged cousin.

Fred was close to exploding by now. "What the hell was he up to?"

Iolanthe still had spunk enough in her to snap back. "Well,

he didn't yell at me, and you needn't either. Jasper said pretty much the same as Father had, only more nicely and without any praying. He said the sooner I left, the better, and he'd help me. I forget what all he said, I just knew I had to go because it wasn't my house any longer. He told me to go upstairs and pack a suitcase and he'd run me down to Portland. He knew of a respectable boardinghouse where I could stay. All I had to do was give him my bankbook and sign a paper, he'd get a power of attorney and take care of everything. So I gave him the bankbook that had both our names in it—"

"My God! Didn't you know any better than that?"

"How could I? I'd never handled a cent of money in my life except what you gave me to buy the groceries. Father always said females' brains were inferior to men's and we must submit to their higher knowledge. And you handled everything after we were married, Fred, you know that. Jasper said that since my name was on the bankbook, it was perfectly legal for me to draw on the account. I didn't want to, but Jasper made me realize that I must have something to live on. I didn't even know how to get the money out, he had to do it for me. We stopped on the way to Portland, he went into the bank and came out with some blank checks. He asked if I wanted to stop someplace and eat, but I didn't want to so we went on to this big old house and a woman came to the door and Jasper carried my suitcase upstairs and showed me how to fill out the check for my rent and said when I needed more money all I had to do was write another check and take it to the bank. Then he went away. He said he'd be back in a week or so to see how things were going with me, but he never came."

"What did you do?"

"Sat in my room and cried, mostly. It was so hard, Fred. I wanted to write you a letter, to call you up, not to talk, just to hear your voice and know you were there. But I knew that if I once weakened, I'd come running back and be damned forever. When it got too bad, I'd go out and walk till I was too exhausted even to think."

"Did you eat?"

"I don't know, Fred. I suppose I must have, sometimes, or I'd have starved to death. All I remember is trying to force myself to swallow and feeling this big lump in my chest. I think what brought me to my senses was when it came time to write another check for the room rent and the bank sent it back saying there was no money in the account. At first I thought I'd gone crazy, then I realized that Department of Human Services woman must have got hold of the money and was using it to help those poor girls. I knew they must deserve it more than I—at least that's what I thought then—but it put me in a terrible position. I had to sell my engagement ring, or the landlady would have thrown me out."

"What do you mean, sell your engagement ring? For God's sake, Iolanthe, you took plenty of jewelry with you when you left. Where did that go?"

"I didn't take it! I might be a fool but I'm not a thief. I left everything but my engagement ring and my wedding ring right in the top left-hand dresser drawer, where I always kept it. I did take some clothes. That didn't seem so much like stealing, and I had to have something to wear. I wasn't trained for anything but being a wife, and when Jasper told me I had to go—"

"Oh hell, Iolanthe," Fred was still struggling. "So what it boils down to is that Jasper broke into the house and stole the jewelry as well as the money?"

Chapter 11

"I suppose it must have been Jasper who took the jewelry, if you didn't find it. I remember he took my door key when he came to get my suitcases and made as if to throw it away, but he may have been only pretending. I wrote to him after that rent check came back, and all I got was a letter from somebody I'd never heard of before, saying that Mr. Flodge was away on business and they didn't know when he'd be back. That's the last I ever heard of Jasper till I got this week's *County Record* and saw that he was dead. I started subscribing a year or so ago, I'd got so homesick. I suppose the funeral was really just an excuse to come back in hopes of seeing you. I thought I was resigned enough not to make a fool of myself."

Iolanthe picked up her napkin again and dabbed at her face. "But anyway, once I realized I had nothing to fall back on, I knew I'd have to fend for myself somehow, and that sort of pulled me around. Not being trained for anything, of course, I had to take what I could get, jobs like working in a doughnut shop, and bundling groceries in a supermarket, that didn't pay me more than barely enough to get by on."

"God damn it!" The struggle between rage and compassion was all but over. "If I'd known you were having it so rough—"

"I survived, didn't I? At least it taught me a few things. After a while, I happened to remember a cousin of my mother's who lived in Balaclava County. She'd always hated Father, so I thought maybe she'd be willing to help me a little. I went down on the bus and she found me a job working in a candy factory. It was awfully monotonous work and my back ached so badly all the time from bending over the conveyor belt that I had to quit. So I went back to doing housework, and that's what's kept me alive ever since. It's quite pleasant working for the Enderbles, they're lovely people and the animals are cute, even if they do mess up the floor. But when I think of the beautiful home we had—oh, Fred, I've missed you so terribly! And all this time I've felt like a sinner for even daring to think about you."

"Why the hell shouldn't you think of me? You're still my wife, Iolanthe. That goddamned lying son of a bitch! Putting us both through three years of hell for one of his cute tricks. If Jasper Flodge wasn't already dead, I'd kill him myself. Here, you'd better eat something. Want Elva to heat up that chowder? How about a piece of pie? You always used to like Elva's pie."

"Oh, Fred!"

Now was the moment for the hero to fold his heroine to his manly bosom. Fred was showing every inclination to do so, despite the fact that by now almost every eye in the room was upon them, when Iolanthe froze.

"Fred, look!" she whispered. "That's the woman!"

"What woman?"

Fred needn't have asked. Lucivee Flodge wasn't wearing her spangled hairbow now, she was trying to sneak out of the dining room without attracting attention, which was about the silliest trick she'd pulled yet.

"You mean she was the one who claimed to be from the Department of Human Services? Iolanthe, are you sure?"

"As sure as I can be. How could I forget that face, leering and grinning and nodding at me while Father raved on about iniquity and damnation? Who is she, Fred?"

"She calls herself Lucivee Flodge, and claims to be Jasper's wife. God damn it! Nine little teenage girls with nine of Fred Wye's bye-blows. Of all the rotten, filthy lies—let go of me, Iolanthe, I've got a few things to say to that bitch."

"Please, Fred, not here. You could get arrested."

Peter couldn't stay out of it any longer. "Er—not to butt in on what's none of my business, but if I were in your shoes, I wouldn't try to tackle that woman by myself. She's too tough and too slick, she'd slap you with a lawsuit on some pretext or other and you'd be lucky not to wind up either broke or in jail. I'd say the smart thing to do is get hold of a good lawyer before you're a day older."

"Oh yes, Fred, do," begged Iolanthe. "I couldn't bear it if you got into any more trouble on account of me."

Fred thought a moment, then shrugged his shoulders. "Okay, honey, if you say so. I guess what we'd better do is stop at Matt Barrett's on our way home."

"While we're there, you might ask him about that money Aunt Prunella willed to me, that Father's still not letting me have. At least it would make up a little for what Jasper stole."

"I'll ask him, all right. Come on, finish your chowder and let's get moving. Sky, would you and Evander mind if we take the car and go on ahead?"

"I'll run them back when they're ready to leave," said Peter. "My wife's coming tomorrow, Mrs. Wye, I'll phone her right away and ask her to bring up whatever you want from the Enderbles's. I'll also ask her to call Mrs. Lomax about finding somebody to take over their housekeeping if you'd like."

"Oh, that would be wonderful of you." Iolanthe was looking about twenty years younger. She was clinging to her husband with one hand, dutifully spooning up the last of her chowder with the other. "There, Fred, all finished. Have we any food in the house, or shall I ask Elva to wrap us up a loaf of bread and some eggs for breakfast?"

"Got your old job back, eh? God, it's good to see you, Iolanthe. We got anything to eat, Evander?"

"Half a jar of instant coffee and a few stale crackers. General store's still open. I'll go if you tell me what to get."

That was quite a speech for Evander. Iolanthe gave her brother-in-law a smile and shook her head.

"That's all right Evander. I can do the shopping while Fred talks to Mr. Barrett."

"Need any money?"

"Thanks, but I got paid yesterday. That must sound funny, coming from me. Please don't get up, Professor Shandy. I do hope you and Mrs. Shandy will drop by for a cup of tea before you start back to Balaclava. Is the house a dreadful mess, Fred?"

"Not too bad, considering. We shovel out every six months or so."

"Well, we can have our tea on the porch if it isn't raining. Come along then, darling. I want to go home."

Hand in hand into the sunset. Just like the cowboy and the rancher's daughter in those mushy endings Peter and his buddies used to groan over from the peanut gallery at the old movie house. He could almost smell the popcorn. Evander and his cousin weren't making any move to stir their stumps.

126

They'd give Fred and Iolanthe time enough to get home and settle in, as was only decent.

While Evander and Sky waited for their coffee, Peter told Thurzella to save him a piece of her grandmother's pie and went to give his own wife the latest installment in the serial. He was feeling right at home in the antique telephone booth by now, he reversed the charges and chatted on with Helen for upward of fifteen minutes. Then he remembered the pie and left her to let the Enderbles know they were about to suffer a switch in housekeepers. He hoped Mrs. Lomax wouldn't have too tough a time finding somebody who didn't mind scooping up bunny balls off the living-room rug.

The pie was rhubarb, as would naturally be expected at this time of year, a bit thick in the crust for Peter's taste but otherwise well up to standard. The company wasn't too bad, Evander didn't say anything, but at least he wasn't glowering. Schuyler Tilkey talked about potato farming and a hypochondriacal hay baler he'd once owned, sensible topics that Peter could relate to instead of those interminable screeds that Withington would have been reeling off if he'd got the chance.

When Peter and the others at last stood up to go, Withington was still sitting alone in his corner. Nobody had come to his table since that scene Lucivee Flodge had made, those untasted glasses of champagne had sat losing their fizz until he'd motioned for Thurzella to take them away. It seemed discourteous to walk out on him without a word, but what was there to say? Peter gave him a nod of farewell, and left with his new acquaintances.

One amenity of Pickwance that Peter hadn't known about was a small, shabby, but evidently well-patronized poolroom situated on a side road that ran up from the corner where the weaving shop stood. Schuyler Tilkey had talked himself out by now, Evander still wasn't uttering, but it was still a bit early for Fred and Iolanthe to have their reunion broken in upon. Peter had no objection to stopping in with the cousins and whiling away an hour or so knocking the balls around.

Peter and Tilkey were both pretty good, but Evander was a wizard. He skunked them both, he skunked a few more. When nobody else would play with him, he put on a bravura solo performance that left all present rapt in awe and reverence. At last, in a spirit of mutual bonhomie, Peter delivered his human cargo to the big yellow house on the hill, went back to the inn, and sneaked up to his room atiptoe lest Withington might again be lurking under the lobby afghan, ready to pounce.

All was well that ended well. Peter slept the sleep of the agreeably pooped and awoke to a morning upon which he would not have been at all surprised to see Pippa passing. Thurzella's equally pretty cousin was helping out again this morning, both girls were wearing pink stirrup pants and rose-printed tops, Pippa herself could not have chosen more appropriate garb. They were recommending the waffles and maple syrup. Who was P. Shandy to say them nay?

The waffles were crisp, the bacon was crisper, the orange juice well-chilled, the coffee just short of scalding. The lark was probably on the wing by now and the hillside no doubt dew-pearled. He must remember to go out and check, but first things first. Peter savored each mouthful, said yes to more coffee and a regretful no to a third waffle because his pants were beginning to feel uncomfortably snug around the waist. He ought to go out and walk a brisk mile or two before girding his loins for the ride to Sasquamahoc.

But what if Helen and Catriona came back early and he wasn't there to greet them? He'd better get to Sasquamahoc first and take his brisk walk after he got there. Feeling compe-

128

tent, decisive, and let off the hook, Peter wiped the syrup from his lips, paid his score, and asked Thurzella to wish her grandmother good morning for him as she was no doubt too fully employed with the mysteries of her culinary art to exchange small talk with her paying guests.

Now to be up and doing with a heart for whatever Fate might dish out to him, which might well be more fried-clam tacos unless Helen happened to notice that slight bulge above his belt. He might, he supposed, stop somewhere along the way and buy himself a wider belt; but such artifice would be a touch unmanly and Helen wouldn't be fooled by it anyway.

So what? Elva Bright's cooking must inevitably have had its effect on Fred Wye during those years when husband and wife were parted and the inn his only source of edible provender, yet Iolanthe hadn't seemed to notice anything about him to complain of. Her man was her man for a' that, and it was to be hoped that Helen Marsh Shandy would feel the same when she realized how much money her own man was prepared to fork over for a few square inches of painted canvas just because he wanted it and could not explain why. He was in the same sort of relationship with that picture as Sir Percival (or was it Sir Galahad?) had been with the Holy Grail, he could see it as a vision drawing him and his checkbook ever onward to Rondel's Head. Peter wished it were half past three already, and that he and Helen were climbing that awful path to Miss Rondel's enchanted dining room.

He'd arranged last night to drop Schuyler Tilkey off on the way back to Sasquamahoc. They'd left it that, if Tilkey wasn't at the inn by eight o'clock, that would mean he was having breakfast at the Wyes's so as not to hurt Iolanthe's feelings and would wait for Peter to swing by the house whenever he took the notion. It seemed a bit early to interrupt the family reunion. What he'd really like to do would be to run out to Rondel's Head for a few minutes but Miss Rondel might take umbrage if he did and call off the negotiations. He settled for a leisurely exploration of the back roads, of which there weren't very many, and found his way by accident back to the Wyes' house.

Already the big old house looked less forlorn than it had the day before. Windows were open, the big front door standing ajar, rugs thrown over the porch railings to air, a bunch of field flowers in a pottery jug on a windowsill. Evander was out weeding around some perennials that had been too long neglected but had bravely kept up the struggle. Peter wouldn't have minded stopping to pull a few weeds as a neighborly gesture but those inside must have heard the car drive up and were coming out to meet him.

Schuyler Tilkey was back in his traveling costume of elderly denims and a flannel shirt, his funeral suit in its plastic bag hung over his arm. Fred was carrying Sky's overnight bag and an old cast-iron apple corer evidently intended as a present to Mrs. Tilkey. Iolanthe was wondering whether Professor Shandy wouldn't like to stop in for a cup of coffee before they got on the road. Peter said he'd already had too much coffee, thanks, and he and Tilkey had better get started because Helen had said she and Catriona were planning to be on the road by sunup, which they probably hadn't stuck to, but one never knew.

He then delivered sundry messages from the Enderbles and Mrs. Lomax, all of whom had been flabbergasted but delighted to learn that Mrs. Howard had so romantically turned out to be Mrs. Wye. They hoped she wouldn't forget them, that they'd get to meet Mr. Wye in the not-too-distant future and that Mrs. Wye, as they now knew her to be, wouldn't worry about the animals because Mrs. Lomax's late husband's cousin's niece was studying veterinary medicine and anxious to make some tuition money this summer. She was quite willing to houseclean and not a bit fazed by the elderly rabbit's little problem.

Mary Enderble had packed some of Mrs. Wye's things and was sending them along with Mrs. Shandy. The rest would be coming as soon as Mary could get them boxed up, which she was able to do now that her wrist was so much better thanks to all the help she'd got from dear Mrs. Wye. What with one thing and another, half an hour passed before Peter, his passenger, and the apple corer got on the road. Even Evander made a gesture that might be interpreted as a farewell wave. At least Peter chose that hypothesis over the less attractive one that Evander might in fact be hauling off to heave a rock through his windshield.

The ride down was, fortunately, uneventful. Tilkey was less chatty this morning. He didn't say much that hadn't been covered last night, although he did have a few interesting expletives saved up for Iolanthe's father. Peter was ready to say "Amen" to them all even though he'd never met the old Bible thumper and didn't want to.

On the brighter side, Tilkey informed Peter that he'd phoned home before leaving Fred's house and been given the joyful tidings that the agglomeration of junk which his son was so deluded as to call a car was, by some miracle, back in running order, waiting to be picked up and paid for at the garage to which the cousin with the tow truck had taken it. This was indeed good news. It meant that Peter need only stop at the right spot along the highway where he'd picked up the stranded Tilkey and wish him bon voyage instead of having to deliver him to some outlying farm and waste an hour or two maundering along a maze of country lanes that were supposed to be shortcuts back to the highway and would have turned out to be anything but.

In due time, they reached the garage and exchanged a typical rural New England farewell. Sky Tilkey picked up his overnight bag and his funeral suit and said "Thanks for the lift." Peter handed out the apple corer that Sky had forgotten to take and said "Don't mention it." Sky replied "Don't worry, I won't," and they parted the best of buddies.

While his former passenger strode bravely forward to face whatever dire tidings might await him regarding the mechanic's bill, Peter flipped his ignition switch back on and pulled out to the highway. Now that he had no passenger to scare the bejesus out of, he let his foot rest more heavily on the gas pedal; he was perturbed lest Helen and her friend had in fact beaten the sun to its rising. What if they were already sitting in Catriona's two-hundred-year-old kitchen, eating crullers and wondering what in Sam Hill was keeping him?

Chapter 12

The natural result of Peter's fretting was that he got to Sasqua-mahoc much too early. Guthrie was tied up at the college until noontime. Rather than sit in on the class and make Guthrie nervous or sit on Catriona's doorstep twiddling his thumbs, Peter found her mattock and began rooting up burdocks. His benevolent, though most likely vain, hope was that getting rid of the pesky plants might assist the two resident Maine coon cats to keep their bushy tails and trousers free of burs when autumn rolled around.

Once the first frost hit, those pink-and-green globules that could look so pretty in late summer would dry out to an ugly brown. Their myriad tiny rays would stiffen into vicious little fishhooks, ready to tangle themselves in long, silky cat fur and have to be cut out with a pair of embroidery scissors to the accompaniment of loud curses, both feline and human.

Whether or not Carlyle and Emerson linked cause to effect in the same way as their erudite namesakes had done, they did pay Peter the courtesy of sauntering along every so often to see how he was getting on with the work. Perhaps they were just being sociable; more likely they were hoping he'd dig up some small creature they could chase. If so, they were wasting their time; all he heaved out were roots that had apparently been intending to keep on growing straight down to a far hotter place than Sasquamahoc.

This was sweaty, dirty work on a summer day. Peter was in a sad state of dishevelment by the time Catriona's energy-efficient puddle jumper chugged into the yard, but Helen kissed him anyway.

"What's the matter, dear, couldn't you find anything else to play with? Go put away that mattock like a good boy, and wash your face and hands. Where are you and Guthrie taking us for lunch, or don't we have time? When is Miss Rondel expecting us?"

"Not till half past three. That gives us approximately one hour, thirty-seven minutes and fourteen seconds to loiter, unless that sundial over there has its gnomon on backward."

"Are you quite sure about the fourteen seconds? We don't want to keep her waiting."

"Trust me, mavourneen. We're supposed to alert Guthrie that the expedition is about to get under way. Do you want to give him a ring while I wash up, Catriona?"

Catriona's long, auburn hair had come down, as it generally did. She was trying to twist it back up and spoke through a walrus mustache of hairpins. "How about if we just go over to the college and beat on cooking pots? Or is that only done during solar eclipses, to keep the Giant Pipsissewa from swallowing the sun?" She spat out the last hairpin and rammed it firmly into her bun. "All right, I'll call him. Did you feed the cats, Peter?"

"Of course not. They were already licking their whiskers and belching discreetly behind their paws when I got here. I assumed that either Guthrie or that hired man of yours must have fed them. Or possibly both."

"I shouldn't be surprised, they're awful scroungers. Rotten critters, I'll bet you haven't missed me a bit."

Scooping up an armload of cat, the alleged mistress of the house headed for the telephone. Peter retired to the downstairs bathroom, which had a wonderful old porcelain washbowl spacious enough to give a coon cat a flea bath in, if anybody should ever be fool enough to try. He emerged damp but recognizable, just in time to catch Guthrie Fingal hugging his wife.

"Aha! They do say the husband's always the last to know. Were you planning to unhand my woman any time soon?"

"Oh, you here, Pete? Okay, if you insist. Come on, let's get this show on the road. I phoned for reservations, Millie's saving us a rock."

"Good thinking," said Catriona. "Did you feed the cats this morning?"

"Ayup. Gave 'em their breakfast at half past six and their elevenses at a quarter to ten. What's the matter, are they yammering for their supper already?"

"Yes, but they're not getting it. Shut up, you monsters. Be good little kitties and Mommy will bring you each a clam. Ready, Helen?"

"As ready as I intend to be. Whose car are we going in?"

"Ours," said Peter in a tone that brooked no denial.

Neither Guthrie's banged-up old four-wheeler nor Catriona's little dingbat held any appeal for a son of the soil who'd been waging war on burdocks for the past aeon or two. Peter suspected that both his wife and her friend were feeling much the same as he was after their long morning's ride in a popcorn wagon, although he knew Helen would be too polite and

135

Catriona too stubborn to admit the battering they must have got.

So the four of them climbed into the Shandys' comfortably upholstered car and went and got their clam tacos and took them out on the rocks by the water and ate them and were happy withal. Then Peter happened to glance at his watch and said a rude word, whereupon they all rushed back to the car and returned Catriona and Guthrie to the waiting paws of Carlyle and Emerson so that Peter and Helen could make a beeline for Rondel's Head.

They got there almost to the dot. Frances Rondel must have been listening for the sound of their car. She came halfway down the slope to meet them, regretting that Mrs. Shandy hadn't been able to come earlier, before the rainstorm that had beaten down the last of the lupines. Helen made the proper sort of conversation for the proper length of time, then they got down to business.

"You won't mind if we go in through the kitchen?"

The question was purely rhetorical. Miss Rondel didn't wait for an answer but led them through the dark, narrow entryway into the bright kitchen. Peter experienced a moment's panic when he caught sight of the empty kitchen chair on which his painting had sat earlier, but it was all right. They went on into the dining room and there, strung all round the walls, were the wondrous paintings. And on the mantelpiece, next to a funerary wreath of human hair under a glass dome, stood his own true love.

"Oh, Peter!"

What else could Helen say? Peter took his wife's hand. The two of them stood rapt, until Miss Rondel broke the spell.

"As you requested, Professor Shandy, I delivered your mes-

136

sage. I must say that I had some difficulty in convincing the artist that you are seriously interested in buying one, or possibly more of the paintings. The sum you offered seemed to be quite acceptable, I trust you haven't changed your mind?"

"Oh, no. No, not at all. What do you think is right, Helen?"

Helen shook her head. "I don't know what would be enough. It's like trying to pin a price tag on a moonbeam. Let me buy this one for you, Peter. I still have that money I got from my book on Praxiteles Lumpkin's weather vanes, and I can't think of a better way to invest it."

Miss Rondel was looking by now somewhat bewildered. "Professor, it was my understanding that you were offering a thousand dollars."

"Peter, you cheapskate!" cried Helen.

"Well, how was I to know? I'd never bought a painting in my life, I only meant that as an—er—opening bid. It's what Dan Stott paid for that big oil portrait of Balaclava's Belinda and her nineteen piglets."

"Dearest, one does not rate a work of art by the number of piglets it contains. What Dan and Iduna got is a very accurate and attractive depiction by a competent craftsman of a prize sow and her brood. These are genuine works of art. Miss Rondel, Peter claims they've never been shown in public. Is that possible?"

"Why, yes. Then you really believe the artist has promise?"

"Promise is hardly the word. Would you mind if we take a little time to get acquainted?"

"No, indeed, take all the time you want. I have bread dough rising, so if you'll excuse me I'd better go and punch it down. I'll be right in the kitchen if you have any further questions."

"My further question is how many of these marvelous things

we can afford to buy," Helen remarked once she and Peter were alone. "I don't want to be grabby, but you must surely realize that this is the opportunity of a lifetime."

"M'yes, the thought had crossed my mind," said Peter. "See anything you particularly like? I was thinking we could put my landscape, if that's what it is, in the living room, unless you see something you like better. On second thought, let's buy two. It would be nice to have something cheerful in the bedroom, don't you think?"

"Definitely. And another in the dining room, and that little one there would be just right to hang over the kitty box." Helen was laughing now for sheer joy. "I'd gladly take them all, but where could we hang them? Anyway, it wouldn't be fair to snatch the lot before anyone else even gets a peek at them. They ought to be shown, Peter, it's just not right for an artist of this caliber not to be recognized. Didn't Miss Rondel give you any clue at all as to who it is? You don't suppose she paints them herself?"

"The thought did cross my mind, but I'm inclined to think not. I don't believe she even cares much for them. The impression I got when we talked was that she's playing fairy godmother to somebody who's too emotionally unstable to risk possible rejection or else is in a position of extreme vulnerability."

"Vulnerable to what?"

"Who knows? My first guess would be that the artist lives among a pack of yahoos who'd find it amusing to deride, deface, or destroy what they're unable to understand."

"Yes, that would make sense. People who couldn't see beyond the piglets, poor things. Their loss is our gain. So what else do you see that you can't live without?"

"I got first pick, it's your turn now. How do those pink lupines strike you?"

"Lovely, but—I don't know. A bit on the bland side for my taste. Ah, now here's something I could live with."

"What is it, a sunset?"

"Of course not, silly. It's a hen laying an egg."

"You could have fooled me. Where's the egg?"

"Still in the hen, of course. Do you really hate it?"

"No, come to think of it, I don't hate it at all."

Peter was getting the gist of the business. Here was not just a barnyard fowl performing her usual office, this was how a hen *felt* when she laid an egg. Now he was beginning to understand why hens made such a fuss over their achievements. This must surely be painted from one of Miss Rondel's splendid, golden flock, not one of those wretched creatures crowded into too-small cages at poultry factories with nothing to crow about and nothing to peck at except each other.

It was a joyous picture, a triumphant picture. It reminded Peter of the farmer who'd displayed an ostrich egg in his hen coop, and hung a sign below it that read "Keep your eyes on this and do your best." This was a shining apotheosis of hendom, a hen who was doing her best.

"You've chosen well, Helen," he said. "By all means let's have the hen."

So that made one apiece. Then Helen found the lupine painting she wanted most of all. "How about this, Peter? Doesn't it remind you of Thorkjeld Svenson?"

"Do we want to be reminded of Thorkjeld Svenson?" Peter took another long look. "As a matter of fact, I'd already decided when I was here before that this would be my second choice. But I'm damned if I'll have it hanging over our bed."

"Perish the thought. I was thinking of the dining room."

"If you say so." Peter had already gone on to a new love, the biggest painting of the lot. "Here's Oliver Wendell Holmes's description of a Turner, Helen. 'Foreground golden dirt, the sunlight painted with a squirt.' Makes me want to get in there and mow the hay."

"I know, darling, it's beautiful. But do bear in mind that it's also at least twice too big to hang anywhere in our little house."

"Who wants to? My thought was that we might donate it to the college."

"Oh. Then why don't we? It could hang over the library mantelpiece in place of that ghastly daub some itinerant sign painter did of President Simms back in 1927 or thereabout."

"Alternatively, it could hang in my classroom and give me something to look at besides students' tonsils. Early-morning classes can get a trifle unaesthetic when the whole damn pack of them stagger in looking like the morning after the night before and start yawning in perfect unison. Would five thousand be too plebeian an offer for a painting this size?"

"I'd call it rather aristocratic, myself. Let's see what Miss Rondel thinks, if she's finished punching down her bread."

Miss Rondel might have been keeping an ear cocked, she appeared in the doorway as if on cue. "Were you wanting to ask me something?"

"Yes," said Peter. "We were wondering whether you'd consider five thousand dollars an adequate price for this big oil of the hayfield."

"Would I—Professor Shandy, are you serious?"

"Yes, of course. We're thinking we'd like to present it to Balaclava Agricultural College, where we both work. My wife is curator of the Buggins Collection."

"Yes, I know. I have your history of the Buggins family, Mrs. Shandy, and also your delightful little book on Praxiteles Lumpkin, thanks to my young friend Catriona McBogle. I suppose you know what you're doing, but I must say five thousand dollars sounds to me like a great deal of money to put out on a piece of canvas that wouldn't even cover a hayrick."

"Don't worry," said Helen. "I can assure you that it will prove to have been a great bargain. I do wish, though, that your friend could be talked into signing his or her work. People always want to know the artist's name, and you can imagine how embarrassing it's going to be for a librarian, having to keep saying 'I can't tell you.' "

This was a facer for Miss Rondel. "Oh dear, I hadn't thought of that. But didn't that Mr. Whistler from Lowell, Massachusetts, sign his paintings with a butterfly? Perhaps some similar device might be worked out in lieu of a signature?"

"Why not?" said Peter. "A potato bug, do you think? Or how about a quahog with its neck sticking out?"

Helen gave him a look. "Don't pay any attention to my husband, Miss Rondel. You'd only encourage him."

"Actually I've always considered potato bugs handsome, as insects go," Miss Rondel replied quite seriously, "though I can't say as much for the quahog. I'd be quite willing to suggest the potato bug, if that's what you want. I shouldn't think it would be much of a job to have them painted on, if you wouldn't mind coming by again to pick up the paintings after they're done. The only problem is, I'm not sure how long potato bugs take to dry."

"I shouldn't think it would be long, Miss Rondel. We only want very little ones, you know. If the artist prefers some other symbol, or perhaps his or her initials, that's perfectly all right with us. Why don't we give you a ring tomorrow morning from the inn and see what time you'd like us to show up?"

"That would be fine. I'll be here, I'm pretty much a homebody these days. Now, you're quite sure which of the paintings you've decided to buy?"

"Yes, we've decided." Peter took out his checkbook. "Er—how shall I make out the check?"

"Oh, my, another dilemma. May I let you know about that tomorrow?"

"Of course. Here, I'm going to jot down the descriptions of the paintings we've picked and the amounts we're prepared to give, so that there won't be any confusion."

"That's very thoughtful of you, Professor, I don't seem to be much of a businesswoman. Now can I offer you a glass of water?"

"You certainly can, thank you. We'd like that very much."

Peter knew Helen must be wondering why he was waxing so eloquent over a drink of water. She wondered even more when, having got her company seated at the kitchen table, Miss Rondel picked up the pitcher that Peter had given her and went out the back door.

"Where's she going?" Helen murmured. "Doesn't she have running water in the house?"

"Judging from those shiny brass faucets on the sink, I assume she does; but her drinking water comes from a spring out there someplace that she never lets anybody go near. I've had some, it's remarkably good."

"That's interesting. I suppose she keeps the spring a secret so that she won't have outsiders tramping around making pests of themselves."

"M'yes, but I suspect it's also because she uses the spring as

142

a source of income. The day I came to gather seed, the innkeeper gave me two jugs to be filled and an envelope that clanked, which I was supposed to leave discreetly on the table here. That's how I happened to spy my painting, perched on that chair you're sitting in now. When Miss Rondel saw me taking it seriously, she asked if I'd like to see some more. And that, my love, is how history's made."

"I shouldn't be surprised if you're right, dear," Helen agreed. "Darn, I wish she'd tell us who the artist is. I'd love to do a monograph on the paintings now that the Lumpkin book is going so well, but how can I when I don't even know his name? Or hers. I suppose 'The Potato Bug Painter' would have a certain cachet, though. What'll you bet that Catriona gets a mystery plot out of this? We probably shouldn't say anything, even to her or Guthrie, until we've at least got our paintings safely home. You do realize, darling, that you've started something that isn't going to be stopped."

"Seems to me it was the potato bug who started it. Ah, here comes Miss Rondel. Look thirsty."

Chapter 13

Miss Rondel must like her new pitcher, she was smiling as she brought it to the table. "You see I'm making good use of your gift, Professor Shandy. I thought I was going to miss the old one, which was my great-grandmother's, but perhaps it was time for a change."

If Frances Rondel was the age of Elva Bright's grandmother, then her family must surely have had their good out of that pitcher by now, Peter thought. He was interested to notice her making a little ceremony out of pouring the water. Having set the pitcher in the exact center of the table, she stepped into her pantry and brought out three heavy old glass goblets, three worn but perfectly ironed tea napkins, and three wedding-band porcelain tea plates with the gold all but worn off from generations of use. She set the three goblets in a precise row in front of the pitcher, gave each of her guests a plate and a napkin and laid a place for herself, then went back to the pantry, brought out another porcelain plate with four oversized cookies on it, passed them first to Helen, and then to Peter. Finally, she poured the water and handed around the goblets.

Peter wondered if Miss Rondel was about to say grace or embark on some mystic ritual; but all she said was, "I made these this morning, I hope you like ginger and molasses. And now, Professor Shandy, do please tell me what's going on at the inn. All I've heard is that Jasper Flodge died of cyanide poisoning with his nose in a plateful of Elva's chicken pot pie, and that he was actually married to that woman from Portland who's been making such an exhibition of herself. You're going to think me an awful old gossip, but a person does like to know what's going on in her own home town and you're my best hope of a dispassionate account."

How could a man refuse? Peter took a sip of his water and groped for a beginning. "Of course the inn has been the— er—focal point of the action and, as a guest, I could hardly have escaped being in it. Some of it, anyway."

"The big ruckus started just about the time you arrived, didn't it?" Miss Rondel prompted.

"Pretty much. As you doubtless remember, I'd called on you last Monday, asking permission to take soil samples and gather lupine seeds, which you most graciously granted. After I left you—good Lord, was it only four days ago?—I went directly to the inn. By that time, it was later than I'd realized. Nobody was left in the dining room but a chap named Claridge Withington."

"Yes, I know Claridge. He's been coming to Bright's Inn for years."

"So he told me. Anyway, I ordered the chicken pot pie and had started to eat when this great hulk in a business suit and a loud necktie surged in with fanfare of trumpets and beating of drums. Once he found out there was only one piece of chicken pie left, which the waitress wanted herself, he demanded that and began shoveling it in as if he were scared she

146

might snatch the plate away. Then, all of a sudden, he pitched forward, dropped his fork, made a sort of clawing motion with his right hand, and was dead before the rest of us fully realized what was happening. It was a dreadful thing to watch. I felt sorry for that nice child who was waiting on us."

"Thurzella Cluny, Elva's youngest granddaughter. She is a dear, isn't she. They're a fine family, Jean-Luc must be proud of them, wherever he is. So great a spirit and so little time. But I mustn't digress. So Jasper was dead. And then what happened?"

Helen hadn't heard the story either, Peter went whole hog. He repeated what he'd got from Withington, though in less tedious detail. He described that grim scene in the dining room while they'd waited for the body to be taken away. He told of Lucivee Flodge's first appearance in the dining room, her rage at her husband's having, as she insisted, committed suicide, her wild insistence that Flodge had killed himself on purpose to cheat her out of his insurance. Evidently she'd been keeping up the premiums on the chance that Jasper would oblige her by walking in front of a truck carrying a full load of logs.

By the time Peter had finished with a full account of Lucivee's tasteless failed attempt to throw a champagne gala in celebration of her widowhood, his goblet was empty and his throat was dry. Miss Rondel picked up the new pitcher and refilled Peter's goblet.

"Silly woman. According to Elva, her real name is Lucy Veronica, though the nickname seems the more appropriate. Lucivee is what we call a lynx around here. From the French *loup cervier*, you know. I'm told she assisted Jasper in that unconscionable swindle he pulled on poor little Iolanthe Wye. Is that true, Professor?"

"Apparently so. Iolanthe recognized her going out of the inn dining room as the woman who'd passed herself off as having come from the Department of Human Services. It might be as well not to repeat this, Miss Rondel, I believe the Wyes are going to take legal action against her."

"Good for them. At least something positive seems to be coming out of that debacle. Were you on hand for the Wyes' reunion, Professor?"

"Front-row center. I played an insignificant role in that one, myself."

Peter explained how, on his way back from Sasquamahoc yesterday, he'd picked up a stranded motorist who'd turned out to be a cousin of the Wye brothers on his way to the funeral, not to mourn but to make sure that the bastard who'd wrecked Fred's marriage got his final comeuppance. Peter described the confrontation between the estranged pair, trying to keep it from sounding too much like a soap opera and thus winding up with a Victorian melodrama. This must have been more to Miss Rondel's taste because she offered him the last cookie and another drink of water.

"What I can't get over," Helen put in, "is that Mrs. Wye, whom we knew as Mrs. Howard, has been working for several months as housekeeper to our dear friends and near neighbors, the Enderbles. Talk about serendipity!"

"Some people might call it guidance," Miss Rondel suggested gently.

Helen accepted the correction with grace. "And they might be right. We don't know, do we? She's been a wonderful help to John and Mary, but she's always looked—bereft, is the only word I can think of. I thought she must be a widow."

"And everybody thinking all this time that she'd run off with Jasper Flodge and gone to the bad." This was the first

148

time Peter had heard Miss Rondel come anywhere near raising her voice. "What a dreadful, dreadful shame! Anyone with half an eye should have seen it coming, what with that awful old Bible thumper dinning it into her from the day she was born that women are all born sinful and brainless. Between a sanctimonious know-it-all like Absalom Bliven and a scoundrel like Jasper Flodge, poor little Iolanthe never stood a chance. How true it is that the letter killeth. At least she hasn't had to stand on her head in a river for twenty years like the fairy she was named for. I suppose one must be grateful for small mercies."

Helen awarded that last comment a well-merited smile. "Tell me, Miss Rondel, if Mr. Bliven is so righteously religious, how did he allow his daughter to be named after a comic-opera fairy? Was it his wife's doing?"

"Oh, heavens, no. That poor woman never got a chance to call her soul her own, much less express an opinion. She died of a ruptured spleen, and it's easy to see why. But to answer your question, Absalom Bliven had an aunt Prunella, who'd married a lumber baron and inherited a good deal of money. She was a lovely woman. When she got too far along in years to drive herself, she'd have her hired man bring her over to Pickwance every so often in a great big old Packard that had been her husband's. I was always glad to see her come, everybody was. She had the most delightful laugh, like a gurgling freshet in mud season, when the sun's getting higher and the snow begins to melt. Prunella was the one who got to name the Blivens' baby. She was a great Gilbert and Sullivan fan, as you must have guessed, though I think she did it partly to get a rise out of Absalom. She wasn't any too stuck on him either as a minister or as a nephew, but her husband was gone and their only son had been killed in the war so there really wasn't anybody else. And family's family, after all. Absalom Bliven wasn't about to cross a rich aunt over a mere infant daughter. He naturally assumed he was going to inherit Prunella's money. It was a dreadful blow when she finally died and he found out she'd left the lot to Iolanthe, tied up so tight that he could never lay his hand on a penny of it."

"He's managed so far to keep his daughter from getting any, however," said Peter.

Miss Rondel was surprised. "But how can he? Unless Absalom's been working a fiddle, which I must say I wouldn't put past him. Of course he'd think up some kind of sanctimonious twaddle to justify his cussedness, which is what it boils down to."

"M'well, I suspect Mr. Bliven's about to get a lawyer's letter that he won't forget in a hurry. Fred Wye was waxing pretty wroth about that inheritance by the time he and his wife had got their various misunderstandings sorted out last night at the inn."

"Good for Fred. I've worried a good deal about that marriage. Iolanthe was such an innocent, and so desperately in love with Fred. Fred's a fine, decent fellow, but he's always had a tendency to fly off the handle and then wish he hadn't. Poor boy, he's learned a hard lesson. And she's found out how to stand on her own two feet, which is something she'd probably never have known if she hadn't had to get out and fend for herself. Perhaps it's all for the best. They're still young enough to start a family, I hope they do. He'll spend the rest of his life making it up to her, and she'll be the happiest wife in the State of Maine. Please remind them when you see them that I'm expecting a visit."

"Glad to. Mrs. Howard—er—Mrs. Wye's asked us to drop by the house for a cup of tea before we leave. She seemed anxious to get back to keeping house for Fred. Will the brother stay on with them, do you think?"

"One never knows what Evander will do, but I don't see why he shouldn't. There are just the two brothers, they own both the house and the mine jointly and they've always been close. I don't know what Fred would have done these past few years without Evander to keep him on an even keel."

"You surprise me, Miss Rondel. I'd got the impression that Fred was the strong one."

"You're not the first to think so, but they're neither of them weaklings. Evander is by far the more self-sufficient of the two, Fred needs very much to love and be loved. Iolanthe's apparent defection took a dreadful toll of him, I very much doubt whether he could ever have brought himself to trust another woman. That anyone should have tried to link him with Lucivee Flodge is simply bizarre."

"This whole affair seems totally bizarre to me," said Helen. "It's hard to believe that one small-town shyster could have wrought such havoc just by forging a marriage license."

"Jasper never forged that license, nor the power of attorney either." Miss Rondel's voice carried total conviction. "He was a bad one all right, I found that out by the time I had him in my third-grade class, but he was no great thinker. He'd never have had the subtlety of mind to hatch up such a scheme on his own. And even if he had, he couldn't have forged the papers for the plain and simple reason that he never learned to read or write. Jasper Flodge was completely illiterate. He couldn't even sign his own name properly, he just made a meaningless scrawl."

"Good Lord!" said Peter. "How did he get by?"

"The same way lots of other folks do. Being illiterate doesn't necessarily mean being stupid, you know. With Jasper, I

believe it was a mixture of dyslexia and laziness. He did understand figures; he had a retentive memory and a good deal of
cleverness, though cunning might be the more appropriate
word. Most people never caught on to his disability. He'd
pretend to have mislaid his eyeglasses or something of the sort
and ask somebody else to read for him. But it's hard to fool a
schoolteacher."

"As many a pupil has learned to his sorrow," Peter agreed.
"Then you think Lucivee managed the whole affair?"

"No, I don't think so at all. Perhaps I underrate her, but
in my opinion Lucivee lacks the insight, the logical mind, and
the self-control to have organized so complicated and drawn-
out a swindle. We must realize, Professor, that its success
rested entirely on the psychological pressure that had been
brought to bear on Iolanthe by her father's constant preaching
about the hideous doom that awaited any woman who trans-
gressed against what he called God's law."

"Which I suppose translated into Absalom Bliven's law,"
Helen put in.

"Precisely. Absalom was very much against Iolanthe's mar-
rying Fred Wye. Nobody could understand why because Fred
was, and remains, a man of good family and sound principles,
able and willing to give her a far better life than she'd been used
to. Whether or not Absalom's disapprobation had anything to
do with the fact that Fred's too good a businessman to have
let him play games with his daughter's inheritance should be
left open to question, I suppose, but I wasn't the only person
around these parts who had a rather cynical view of what the
answer ought to be. Anyway, Iolanthe defied her father for the
first time in her life and married the man she loved. It's quite
likely, however, that she suffered a good deal of guilt, if only

at a subconscious level, in going against what she'd always been taught. Don't you agree, Mrs. Shandy?"

"Please call me Helen. Certainly I agree. Iolanthe wouldn't be human if she hadn't felt some guilt. And naturally that would have predisposed her to put credence in Jasper Flodge's dirty story. It's a plot straight out of a gothic novel. Who around here reads Sheridan Le Fanu?"

Miss Rondel shrugged. "Surely not Lucivee Flodge."

"Then what it comes down to," said Peter, "is that we've got to start looking for a third person who masterminded the swindle but took no active role in carrying it out."

His hostess looked slightly amused. "I take it that 'we' is to be taken as rhetoric, Professor. It does seem a shame that you won't be here to lend your expert assistance. Catriona's told me about some of your exploits, particularly that remarkable affair of the Lumpkin weather vanes.*"

"Never believe what a fiction writer tells you. It's just a matter of getting all the data and sorting it out. For the sake of argument, let's see where the matter stands so far. Fred Wye mentioned last night—this was before Iolanthe showed up— that his friend Ed Whitbread, whoever that is—"

"Assistant to the county medical examiner."

"Thank you. Anyway, Whitbread's report was that the verdict on Jasper Flodge so far is death by cyanide poisoning, as we already knew, with no decision as to how it was adminis- tered. There was some talk about Elva Bright's being the only one who'd had an opportunity to poison the chicken pie, but nobody could come up with a motive. Besides, Mrs. Bright's reputation is such that nobody would believe it if they did."

*Vane Pursuit

153

"I should hope not! And that's as far as they've got?"

"No, it appears that they're taking Lucivee Flodge's allegation of suicide seriously. They've checked into Flodge's bank statements plus some business records that she's supplied them. It looks as if his credit was in fact shot to perdition and he had every reason to be despondent. They're even prepared to swallow Mrs. Flodge's yarn about his killing himself to spite her out of collecting his insurance. She's got receipts to show she had in fact been keeping up the premiums. By the time she'd finished making her case in her own sweet way, the consensus seems to have been that anybody fool enough to tie himself to that besom would naturally have preferred a quick and merciful ending to the prospect of crawling to her to bail him out."

"Which doesn't surprise me any."

Miss Rondel's hands were lightly folded, resting on the table. Peter noted that the fingers showed not a sign of the arthritic bumps and gnarling to which people of her age were generally prone. "They'd rather it was suicide, you see. We do have murders in this county as elsewhere, but they're usually the obvious kind. A drunken brawl gets out of hand and somebody grabs a hunting knife. A man finds his wife in bed with someone else, picks up his hunting rifle, and blazes away. Simple, brutal crimes of passion, horrible enough when they happen, but easy to understand."

She refolded her napkin and began drawing her fingers through its fringe, comforting herself with the familiar touch of weaving thread. "Poison is silent, treacherous. A person can die from it and never know why, or how, or who put it where it could be swallowed unbeknownst. We don't even want to think of such things, much less find them happening to people we know in a place we've always before found safe and respectable. I don't suppose Lucivee meant to do Elva a favor when she made that scene about Jasper's having poisoned himself, but the fact remains that her doing so probably saved the inn from having to shut down."

"There's no question about it."

Peter described the pathetic scene he'd walked into the night after Flodge's dramatic end. He told of Elva's magnificent roast going begging, of young Thurzella almost in tears, of the sudden rush of business once Lucivee began insisting that Jasper Flodge had killed himself to spite her, his wife. The simple fact that nobody died from the roast beef had become proof enough that the food at the inn was wholesome as usual. Last night's melodrama had been played to a full house; it was safe to bet that there'd be no dearth of customers tonight.

"The Wyes won't be there, though," Helen predicted. "She'll want to cook him the best meal she can think of."

"And he'll want to tell her all about the lawsuit they're going to bring against Absalom Bliven for cheating on her inheritance," Peter added. "The way Fred was talking last night, he's also fixing to slap a lien on Jasper Flodge's estate just in case there might be a chance to salvage some of the money and jewelry that Flodge stole. I shouldn't be surprised if Fred went a step further and laid a charge of criminal conspiracy against Lucivee."

"But none of that is going to tell us who organized the operation," Miss Rondel fretted. "That's what concerns me more than anything else. I've lived in this town all my life, I thought I knew the history of just about everybody in it and had a fairly sound idea of what they were capable of and what they weren't. Now along comes a situation like this, and I feel myself standing on foreign soil. Jasper Flodge was a nasty little boy and he didn't get any nicer as he grew up. I can believe

155

him only too ready to join a scheme to fleece Fred Wye of his money and destroy Iolanthe simply because she was an easy target. What I cannot believe is that Jasper committed suicide. He was too cocksure of his ability to lie his way out of any jam he got into. As for that cyanide pill, he wouldn't even have known where to look for one. Such things aren't sold over drugstore counters, you know."

"Er—a suggestion has been made that Elva Bright's husband might have kept one as a souvenir of his wartime experiences."

"Ah, yes, and I can imagine who put him up to it. Poor Claridge Withington never had an original thought in his life, he just parrots what he hears without stopping to consider how it might sound to the next one. Lucivee Flodge seems determined to make herself as obnoxious as possible. I can't help wondering whether she's simply enraged because Jasper died insolvent or if she's playing some kind of game to divert attention from his hidden assets. I believe it's not unheard of for an entrepreneur to keep more than one set of books. I can readily see Jasper pulling such a stunt, but he'd have needed somebody else to write them up, just as he needed someone to write those preposterous letters about Fred Wye. I suspect that was the real bond between him and his wife, if she was his wife; Lucivee was the only one he dared to trust."

Miss Rondel poured herself the last inch of water from the pitcher. "As to that story about Elva's having kept Jean-Luc's cyanide pill, it's pure spite and nonsense. The last thing Jean-Luc would have wanted was any reminder of what he'd gone through in Europe, and particularly not a deadly poison that one of his family might get hold of by accident. His whole heart and soul were with Elva and the children. They were his life, his one real hope of immortality."

Her voice was shaking a little by now, it was the first sign of weakness that Peter had seen in her. "I am very upset over this affair. My inclination is to unburden myself to the state police, but they'd ask for more tangible evidence and as yet, I have none to give. So I suppose the only thing for me to do is stay home and tend to my weaving and wait for the next bomb to drop. Well, that's enough doom and gloom for today. I'll tell the artist about the potato bugs and wait for your call in the morning."

Chapter 14

"What a day!" Helen flopped back against the car's upholstery and made fanning motions with her hands. "I feel as if I've been wrung out and hung up to dry. Those incredible paintings, then water from the sacred spring with the high priestess. Am I being perhaps a bit fanciful?"

Peter finished sorting through his key ring and stuck the right one in the ignition. "How am I supposed to know? I thought librarians were up on this stuff."

"So did I, but that lady is something else. Have you any idea how old she is?"

"M'well, she went to school with Mrs. Bright's grandmother."

"Mrs. Bright being the innkeeper?"

"Correct. According to Withington, Mrs. Bright, who's really Madame something French, aristocratic, and too lengthy to be practical, married a hero of the French Resistance who'd been smuggled out of France after having been captured, tortured, and left a physical wreck by the Nazis. This, presumably, would have been sometime around 1945, she being then

159

sweet sixteen and he twenty years older or thereabout and eager to make up for lost time. Their first child was born a few months prematurely, in a manner of speaking, but it worked out all right. Jean-Luc, as he seems to have been generally known, turned out to have a noble nature, an inherited income and a keen business sense. He was devoted to his wife and their two daughters. If I've got my numbers straight, Michele, the elder daughter, must be in her own forties by now and her mother, who looks about forty, is at least sixty. So Miss Rondel has to be pretty well along toward the big one, wouldn't you think?"

"I must say I have a hard time thinking of her as being any age at all," Helen replied. "She gives the impression of having always been there, like the everlasting rock. But she carries herself so straight, and her movements are so vigorous, a person might take her for somewhere between sixty and seventy herself, if it weren't for that feeling she projects of being Mother Earth incarnate. How in the world do you suppose they do it?"

"By keeping busy and interested and choosing the right genes, is the best I can offer. Incidentally, Miss Rondel's a weaver by profession."

"I should have known at a glance. How could she not be a weaver? Or at least a spinner?"

"Or Atropos who chops off the thread?"

"Miss Rondel never would, she's much too nice. What sort of weaving does she do?"

"The sort that she taught Michele, who has a shop in the village that sells the weaving they weave to which I'm already bespoken to take you tomorrow morning, as if we hadn't spent enough money already this trip."

"Bah, humbug. You know you love to make an occasional

lordly gesture. Besides, we'll be splitting the cost of the paint-ings fifty-fifty."

"Says who?"

"Says I, that's who. I'm not sure, now that I think about it, that we shouldn't have asked about the portrait of Miss Rondel."

"What portrait of Miss Rondel?"

"Darling, you stared at it for about ten minutes without blinking. The small canvas that has the twisted old cedar tree growing out of the rock."

"That was a portrait of Miss Rondel?"

"Of course. It's exactly like her. The real her, I mean, not just what she looks like. I was going to say something to that effect when we were in the dining room but it seemed a bit too personal. Miss Rondel may not want to part with that one, or the artist mightn't. I certainly wouldn't, if it were mine."

"If you're really that taken with it, we might at least ask, when we go back tomorrow. Maybe she'll let us chalk up another potato bug on the slate." Peter glanced at the clock on the dashboard. "Good Lord, is that the right time? I hadn't realized we'd stayed so long, you must be starved."

"Oh, I'll try to hang on till we get to the inn. Do we change for dinner, by the way?"

"Into what, for instance? Did you remember to pack your feed cap and a clean flannel shirt?"

"Shucks, I plumb forgot. Are they de rigueur?"

"Not altogether. Mrs. Bright's fairly broad-minded about the dress code. Her granddaughter who waits on table wears those skinny pants and floppy tops. What you might call the Prince Valiant look, depending on how chivalrous you happen to be feeling. I don't know what the world's coming to, we're all going to hell in a handcart."

161

"Who cares? What was good enough for Marie Antoinette is good enough for me. Is the granddaughter pretty?"

"All young girls are pretty, no matter how idiotically they dress. Thurzella, her name is. Judge for yourself when you see her."

"Yes, your worship. Will I have time for a quick shower? I feel ooky after that long ride, and the clam tacos and all."

"Egad, woman, we can't have you bursting upon the assembled multitudes in an advanced state of ookiness. If we had a laundry basket aboard this craft, I could smuggle you up to our room in it. Want to scooch down and lurk in the car till I can run in and borrow one?"

"No, I most emphatically do not. That thing Cat drives is as close to a laundry basket as I ever intend to get. I'll just adjust my yashmak over my face and make a quick dash for the stairs. You did remember to switch my overnight bag from Cat's car to ours?"

"I did and it's in the trunk, and I'll carry it up for you. How's that for husbandly devotion?"

"As good as I can reasonably expect and possibly even a little better. I do like that blue shirt on you, Peter. How are you fixed for clean clothes, by the way? Shall I rinse out a few oddments for you after we've eaten? They ought to dry overnight in this weather."

"What's the point, if we're going home tomorrow?"

"Good question. What's the answer?"

"Why don't we wait till tomorrow and see what develops?"

"Uh-huh. All right, I'll wash your shirts. Thank the Lord for drip-drys. What's our room number?"

"Three. Up the stairs and turn left to the end of the hall. Here's the key."

Helen darted ahead. Peter unlocked the trunk, made sure

no harm had come to his lupine seeds, and took out his wife's overnight bag. This was a flowered tapestry satchel about the size of the handbags many women carried as a matter of course. In it she would have packed her nightgown, robe, slippers, a change of underwear, her cosmetics and toiletries, a casual skirt and blouse, a simple but attractive dress with shoes that matched it, and quite likely an evening gown and an ostrich feather boa just in case. Everything would emerge crisp and clean and ready for business. Helen Marsh Shandy was by all odds the most organized packer in Balaclava County and possibly in the world, though she did have an advantage in the fact that all her clothes came in small sizes.

Helen had left the door ajar for Peter and was already half undressed when he handed her the bag. "Oh, good. This is obviously not the kind of place where they give you a free shower cap. Luckily I brought one, just in case. Go on down to the dining room if you want. I'll be along."

"Nay, mine own. I shall abide by thy right side; at least I should if that shower stall were big enough for more than one average-sized person and a small frog to get into at the same time. Being as how Bright's Inn doesn't have a liquor license, I might as well beguile the interval with a small preprandial libation from my private stock. Want a snort?"

"Not now. I'll be right out."

Helen was as efficient in her bathing and dressing as in her packing. She was clean, combed, made up, and dressed in a travel-proof cream-and-taupe shirtwaist and bone-colored leather sandals by the time Peter had finished his drink and ruminated a short while over the events of the day, notably that odd conversation with Miss Rondel.

It was not a likely occurrence for a woman of her caliber to open up as she'd done to a couple from away, one of whom she'd never so much as laid eyes on before this afternoon. Of course it would have told in Helen's favor that she was a long-time friend of Catriona McBogle, to whom Miss Rondel was somehow connected. Now that Catriona had returned from years of wandering and settled in the old family place at Sasquamahoc, the two were evidently seeing a fair amount of each other. After that adventure on the whale-watching trip, Catriona could hardly have avoided telling Miss Rondel about the Shandys; the Maine papers and television news programs had been full of it. There was a great deal more that Cat could have told, and it was not to be supposed that a professional storyteller would have skimped on the telling.

So Frances Hodgson Rondel must, one way and another, have got quite an earful about Professor Shandy's strange avocation. Today's confession that she'd come upon a local situation with which she couldn't cope had been, whether Miss Rondel realized it or not, a plea for help. Maybe she'd been taken aback to hear her own voice spilling her trouble to strangers. Maybe she had felt rebuffed when Peter hadn't hurled himself immediately into the breach. Whatever the reason, she'd been awfully quick to slam the door that she herself had opened.

Peter didn't know what to think, he wasn't at all sure he cared. Dragon-slaying was not his profession. He was just another middle-aged academic, tired from yet another year of teaching; he felt no great yearning to grab a spear and charge into somebody else's war. Nevertheless, Peter had to concede that the situation at Rondel's Head presented an interesting conundrum. He rinsed out his whiskey glass, left it on the inadequate shelf above the copper-streaked porcelain sink, and squired his wife down to the dining room.

Business must have been brisk a while ago. As he'd feared,

they were late arriving and not many others were still eating. Claridge Withington was alone at his corner table. Evander Wye was alone in the opposite corner, sitting with his back to the room. A couple whom Peter vaguely recalled having seen here before were just leaving, a party of tourists were tackling boiled lobsters with varying degrees of ineptitude. They all had red-and-white-checkered cloth napkins tied around their necks, Elva Bright was not the kind of innkeeper who'd stoop to the modern gaucherie of paper or, God forbid, plastic bibs. Thurzella was scooting around with a big aluminum tray, whisking used dishes off recently vacated tables. She was only too pleased to park her burden and usher the Shandys to a freshly reset table.

"It's nice you could come, Mrs. Shandy. Too bad you weren't here a little earlier. The lobsters are all gone, but there's still some great lamb curry left. It's a recipe my great-grandmother got off a cook from a clipper ship who'd learned to make it on a voyage to India. Or my grandmother could broil you a nice tinker mackerel if you're scared to try the curry."

"We're not the least bit afraid of your grandmother's curry," Helen assured her. "At least I'm not. What about you, Peter?"

"Nothing ventured, nothing gained. Except perhaps a few gas pains and an extra roll of fat around the waist. By all means let's have the curry with a green salad if you have any, and I'd like iced tea with my meal. Does that sound all right to you, Helen?"

"Exactly right. There'll be lemon with the tea, I assume. It's not presweetened, is it?"

"Oh, no! Gram wouldn't dream of such a thing, she makes it fresh and you doctor it to suit yourself. I'll be right back as soon as I dump these dishes."

"She's a cutie," Helen remarked after the swinging door to the kitchen had flapped shut. "Is that Thurzella?"

"None other than."

"And that man in the corner trying to catch your eye is Mr. Withington the oracle?"

"It is indeed. And the chap with his back to us is Iolanthe's brother-in-law, Evander, either sulking or giving her and Fred an evening to themselves. Usually he sits where he can glower at me, or did until last night when their cousin Schuyler Tilkey, that fellow I picked up along the road, asked me to sit with them. Ah, here comes our curry. Thank you, Thurzella, this smells like the start of something beautiful."

"Believe me, Professor, it is. Bon appetit, as my grandfather used to say. At least my mother says he did. This sticky stuff in the little bowl is Mum's homemade mango chutney. She's got jars of it for sale at the shop, Mrs. Shandy, in case you want some to take home. Holler if you want me, I've got to finish setting up the tables for breakfast."

"We'll manage," said Helen. "Would you please pass me the chutney, Peter?"

Elva Bright's lamb curry was first-rate, toned down enough for Occidental tastes without sacrificing any of the flavor. Michele's mango chutney added exactly the right fillip. Comparative quiet settled over the dining room. The sated lobster eaters were washing off the butter, rubbing away the fishiness on the slices of lemon that floated in their green glass finger bowls, asking each other whether they still had room for dessert or if they'd better get back on the road before it got too dark to find their motel. The wily Thurzella solved their dilemma by wishing them bon voyage, as her late grandfather would doubtless have done, and handing them half a dozen sugar

166

cookies in a plastic bag to eat on their way back with the compliments of Bright's Inn.

Evander Wye waited till the outlanders were gone, then laid money on his table and shambled toward the door, combining a brief glower with a curt nod as he passed the Shandys' table. They replied with smiles and nods; whether he noticed these small courtesies was open to question. He was in no great hurry, he still hadn't reached the door when Lucivee Flodge barged in.

Peter assumed the widow would go over to sit with Claridge Withington, then he noticed that Withington had brought a book to the table tonight and buried his nose in it before the now unwelcome late arriver could get to him. Peter half expected Lucivee to whip the book out of Withington's hands and demand his full attention, but she stopped halfway across the room and sat down at one of the clean tables that Thurzella had just finished setting for the breakfast crowd.

The widow was dressed tonight in the trim black suit she'd had on the first night she'd appeared at the inn. The same leather briefcase was in her hand. Peter deduced that she'd spent the day in Portland or Augusta on business connected with the estate that she still seemed determined to believe Jasper Flodge had left her. When Thurzella came back for another load of dishes, Lucivee signaled for attention.

"Bring me a menu, can't you?"

Thurzella shook her head. "No sense in that, all we have left is lamb curry. Unless you'd like grilled mackerel."

"That the best you can do? What about those lobster shells over there? Somebody else had lobster, why can't I?"

"Because you didn't phone in advance, the way those other people did, and tell us you wanted one and how soon you'd be here to eat it. It's too late now anyway, my grandmother's already cleaning the kitchen and making the rolls for breakfast."

"Oh, for God's sake. All right, bring me the curry. Boy, will I be glad to get back to Portland."

"Her and me both," Thurzella muttered as she refilled the Shandys' iced-tea glasses. "She'd better not pull another of her stunts tonight, my grandmother's about ready to land her one with a frying pan. Gram's awfully embarrassed about what's been going on here the past couple of nights. She's never had anything like this before."

"But it's not her fault," said Helen. "Peter, do you think you ought to go and talk to Mrs. Bright?"

"And get beaned with a skillet? My own grandmother always waxed pretty testy if anybody came pestering her while she was putting her dough to rise."

"I didn't mean right now, silly. Anyway, I don't suppose we'll see much in the way of histrionics tonight. We're not a big-enough audience."

Chapter 15

Elva Bright must have finished her rolls. She'd taken the time to smooth her hair, remove her apron, and put on her wide gold wedding band, and another ring with a diamond the size of a large pea in a massive gold setting. She made an impressive figure in her plain white dress as she came through the swinging door and over to the Shandys' table.

"Thurzella says you want to speak to me, Professor."

Peter hadn't reckoned on this. Lucivee Flodge was taking a keen interest in the innkeeper's appearance, now was not the time to bring up delicate subjects. He pushed back his chair and stood up.

"I wanted you to meet my wife. Helen, this is Mrs. Bright, who's been making my stay so pleasant."

"How do you do, Mrs. Shandy? I'm glad the professor's found our place to his liking. It's nice to have you with us, too bad you can't stay longer. I understand you're a friend of Catriona McBogle's."

"Yes, Cat and I go back a good deal further than we're admitting to these days. She's just been down visiting me in

169

Massachusetts, as my husband may have told you. That was a lovely curry you served us, by the way."

"I'm glad you enjoyed it, I expect Thurzella told you it's an old family recipe. Maybe you'd like a scoop of my lemon sherbet to cool it down."

"That sounds marvelous. And you make everything yourself?"

"I or my helper, who lives down the road. And Thurzella's not a bad little cook when she puts her mind to it. Bright's Inn has been a family business ever since my grandparents' day."

"I don't suppose you've ever thought of retiring."

"Lord, no. I wouldn't know what to do with myself. I was born right here in this inn, I expect I'll die here one of these days. I'll get your sherbet."

"Wait a second, Elva." Lucivee Flodge was on her feet, taking something out of her briefcase, darting over to where Mrs. Bright was still standing beside the Shandys' table. "I've got something to show you."

It was a black-and-white snapshot, dog-eared and yellowed with age, showing a boy and girl on a dirt road. He was swinging a few books on a leather strap, she had a small wicker basket over her arm.

"Oh, for goodness' sake, wherever did you find that?" said the innkeeper. "That's Jasper and me coming home from school when we were about twelve years old. He used to walk me home and carry my books because he knew my mother would have something good waiting. One thing about Jasper, he always knew how to get his share of whatever pickings were going around. And your share, too, if you didn't keep a pretty sharp eye on him. Jasper never changed much, did he?"

"You ought to know," Lucivee answered. "You and he were pretty well acquainted there for a while."

"Jasper and I were acquainted all our lives, as you ought to know. I'm not so sure about the 'well.' If you're trying to get at me for some reason, Lucy Veronica, or whatever you want to call yourself, you just spit it out right here and now. I'm sick and tired of your theatrics. Go on, say it and be done with it."

"Oh, it's no big deal. I just thought your friends here might like to see how much Thurzella takes after her grandfather."

"How would you know? You never met her grandfather."

"Like hell I didn't. I married him. Come on, Elva, be real. Everybody knows why your parents were so damned quick to marry you off to that doddering wreck of a Frenchman. Had a little something in the oven, didn't you? And poor old Jean-Luc sure as hell wasn't the guy who—"

"Get out of here!"

The crack of Elva Bright's hand against Lucivee Flodge's face was quite likely heard in Sasquamahoc. A few drops of blood trickled from a scratch left by Elva's heavy rings. Lucivee stood stunned for a second or two, then raced for the telephone that stood next to the cash register.

"I'm calling the state police!"

"Call whoever you want to, but not on my phone. You get out of my house this instant and don't you ever come back."

"Try to keep me out. I'll make damned good and sure you lose your victualler's license."

"Go."

"You others are all witnesses!"

"Go."

Elva Bright was walking toward Jasper Flodge's widow with a look on her face that could have routed an army. Peter,

Helen, and Thurzella were right behind her. Withington was pulling himself half-upright, pawing around for his cane. Lucivee went.

"I don't know what came over me."

Now that the moment of truth had passed, Elva Bright was slumped into one of the dining-room chairs, her elbows on the table, her head in her hands. "What in God's name would Jean-Luc have thought?"

"Thurzella," Peter said quietly, "is there anything alcoholic in the kitchen? Brandy, cooking sherry, liqueur?"

"I know. Just a second. Oh, hi, Evander."

Thurzella was off and back with a tiny glass and a bottle of Grand Marnier before the swinging door to the kitchen had quit swinging. Peter took the liqueur bottle from her and poured out a healthy tot; Helen picked up the glass and held it to the innkeeper's lips.

"Here, take a sip. It will do you good."

Mrs. Bright sipped, coughed, picked up a clean napkin and wiped her face with it, took another sip and coughed again. "Pour me a glass of water like a good girl, Thurzella. What was that you were saying about Evander Wye?"

"Nothing special, Gram. I just caught sight of him coming in and then he disappeared. Maybe he's using the pay phone. Shall I go and see?"

"It wouldn't hurt any. You know what he's like when he gets into one of his moods. I've had about as much as I can put up with for one night."

"I'll go," said Peter. He reconnoitered, but found nobody.

"Thank you, Professor," said Elva. "I'm sorry I've let you in for all this. But to hear that she-devil talking about my husband as if he'd been less than a man, trying to make out that I'd ever have let Jasper Flodge so much as—oh, I don't know what I'm saying. Jean-Luc Mercier de L'Avestant-Portallier never needed any defending from me nor anybody else. He was the best husband a woman could ever want, and a wonderful father to his own two begotten daughters for as long as he was spared to us, as they themselves would be the first to tell you. Thurzella does take after her grandfather, I'm proud to say, and so does her mother. My other daughter favors my side of the family, but you can't hang her for that. Victualler's license or none, if that harridan ever tries to set foot in this inn again, she'll darn soon wish she hadn't. Are you sure you saw Evander, Thurzella?"

"Either him or his ghost."

"Now, don't start on that nonsense. I've got troubles enough without Claridge here spreading some yarn about the inn being haunted."

Withington had hauled himself out of his corner and across the room. He was standing braced against the front counter looking wounded. "Elva, how can you say that? I'd never do such a thing."

"Oh yes, you would, if you took the notion. And I'd know right where it came from, so just you watch that tongue of yours, mister. Furthermore, I can't say I greatly relish having my family's personal business spread the length and breadth of Rondel County; so why don't you go to your own bedroom for a change and read a book or watch your television instead of watching to grab the first poor fish who walks in the door and give him an earful about Lucivee Flodge's latest piece of viciousness? I'll bring you an eggnog when I get around to it."

"A man in my condition has to be humbly grateful for small favors. Thank you, therefore, Elva, and good evening to you all."

It was not an elegant leavetaking. Withington's way of

moving along was neither so swift as a crab's nor so graceful. By tacit accord, the other four stayed in the dining room until he might reasonably be expected to have got himself tucked away. Thurzella, with great presence of mind, went back to the kitchen for a couple more liqueur glasses.

"Have a little, Mrs. Shandy, it'll help take the taste away. Here's yours, Professor. Mind if I take a sip, Gram?"

"No, go ahead. Just don't think you can make it a habit."

"I know, liquor's a good servant but a bad master."

"And don't get carried away with your own cleverness. Go clear out the dishwasher if you're still hankering for something to do."

"Will that mean I get to turn up late tomorrow morning?"

"I expect likely I can manage by myself an extra hour if you want to sleep in. You've been a pretty good girl, all things considered. I hope I wasn't too hard on poor Claridge just now, but he does get my goat sometimes. I must be getting crabby in my old age. Well, where do you suppose all those policemen are that Lucivee said she'd send to drag me off to jail?"

"I expect she was just blowing off steam." Helen always knew when troubled waters could use some oil. "Tell me about your husband, Mrs. Bright. He must have been a truly remarkable person."

"Oh yes, he was."

Tactfully drawn out, the innkeeper chatted on, easing her mind of the painful confrontation that had led her, for the first time in her life, to assault a patron of the inn. She talked of her beloved Jean-Luc, of his care for her and their two precious daughters, of the good men they'd married, of the grandchildren in whom her heroic husband lived on although he had never got to see them in the flesh. She spoke of his benefactions to the town, of the lives he'd enriched by the example he had

set. By the time Constable Frank showed up with a couple of
state troopers in tow, the four in the dining room had forgotten
all about Lucivee's threat to call out the troops.

"Understand you've had a little foofaraw around here tonight, Elva," said the constable. "Mind tellin' us what happened?"

"Not at all. What it boils down to is that Lucivee Flodge,
as she claims to be nowadays, called me a whore and I slapped
her face."

"Called you a—I never heard such a spout o' bilge! Was she
drunk?"

"Don't ask me, Frank. If she was, she didn't buy it here, as
you well know. Last evening she blew in with two bottles of
champagne, all dressed up like a hog going to market, and
tried to throw a party to celebrate Jasper's funeral, but she
didn't get many takers. She may have been haired up because
I made it pretty plain that I didn't care for such goings-on in
my dining room. But I don't know, she's been acting pretty
strange ever since she blew into town."

"Which was when, Mrs. Bright?" said one of the state
troopers whose name was Gilbert and whose Uncle Evon did
odd jobs around the inn when the spirit moved him.

"Day before yesterday, sometime in the midst of dinner is
the best I can tell you, though she may have been around for
a while before she came here. Claridge Withington probably
knows, he's in his room if you want to talk to him."

"Maybe in a little while," said Sergeant Gilbert. "Just to
get things straight, this Jasper you've mentioned, he's the man
who bit into a cyanide pill and died here in the dining room,
right?"

"Yes. He'd been sitting at that table right over there. Frank
knows all that. Can't we get on to what you came for?"

"Oh, sure. You're probably tired. Why don't you just tell how the—er—incident came about?"

"Well, Lucivee—it's Lucy Veronica, but that's what she calls herself—came in here a while ago, loaded for bear. She'd come across an old snapshot while she was rooting around Jasper's house, which she's claiming is hers, trying to find all the money and securities she's bound and determined he must have had hidden away someplace. The snapshot showed Jasper and myself walking home from school. I must have been about twelve years old at the time."

Elva Bright drew a long breath. "As I tried to tell her then and as I'm telling you now, the only reason Jasper ever bothered to pay me any attention was that it gave him an excuse to bum a nice snack off my mother when we got here. He knew he wouldn't get much at his own house but a drink of water and maybe a piece of bread and molasses if his own mother happened to be in a generous mood, which she generally wasn't, and who could blame her? Old Flodge was generally at one racetrack or another, trying to palm off a broken-down nag on some poor fool who had no more sense than to trust him. And getting away with it, often as not; Jasper didn't get his conniving ways from anybody strange. But you don't want to hear all this."

"It's interesting," said the other state trooper, whose name was Armand and whose cousin Lurline sometimes helped out at Michele's shop, "but we're running sort of late. What was Mrs. Flodge trying to make out of this snapshot, Mrs. Bright?"

"A darn sight more than she had any business to. Thurzella, Michele's youngest, you know her—was here setting up the tables for breakfast and Lucivee started comparing her to the snapshot, making out she was the image of Jasper when he was a young fellow which was nonsense. Then didn't that hussy

176

tell me to my own face that everybody in Pickwance knew my parents had married me off to the first sucker who came along because I was already carrying Jasper's child and they didn't want a scandal."

"But I've always heard your husband was some kind of a nobleman or something."

"He was noble in every sense of the word. I'm not saying Jean-Luc and I didn't jump the gun a little because we did and I've never been one bit ashamed of it. But for that wretch to come up with such a blatant yarn after all these years—I couldn't take that, I just hauled off and landed her one to shut her lying mouth. If you want to arrest me for that, you go right ahead."

"According to what Mrs. Flodge said when she phoned the station, you'd slashed her face with some kind of weapon and she was losing blood."

"That so?" Elva held up her left hand, with her heavy gold wedding band and her impressive diamond engagement ring in a handsome though somewhat cumbrous Belcher setting. "I'm left-handed, as Frank can tell you. These are the rings my husband gave me when we were married, I seldom take them off unless I happen to be kneading dough or gutting fish. As you see, this is a fairly good-sized stone and right now the ring's a little bit loose on my finger. I expect what happened was that the diamond swiveled around toward my palm and scratched her on the cheek."

"But it was no more than a scratch," Helen insisted. "My husband and I were right here when it happened. We noticed a drop or two of blood, but that was all."

"So that's how it was, Mr. —er?"

"Shandy," said Peter. "I've been here since Sunday night. My wife just arrived today and Mrs. Bright had come out of the kitchen to welcome her to the inn. We were exchanging a few pleasantries when Mrs. Flodge barged in on us with that snapshot in her hand and started making offensive remarks, as Mrs. Bright has just told you. This was the third time since Flodge's death that Mrs. Flodge has made a major nuisance of herself here at the inn, I expect tonight's episode was simply one too many for Mrs. Bright. I felt like swatting the woman myself, if you want to know. So would you, if you'd been subjected to her goings-on.".

"But you took no active part in the swatting tonight?"

"Of course not. The whole incident was over within a matter of seconds. Mrs. Bright had been goaded into reacting and was shocked that she'd done so. There was no question of a—er—slugging match."

"Do you agree with that, Mrs. Shandy?"

"I certainly do. As my husband says, it was merely an instant's flare-up. Mrs. Flodge had behaved unpardonably. She should have been apologizing to Mrs. Bright, rather than trying to set the police on her."

"But she didn't. So then what happened?"

"Mrs. Bright told Mrs. Flodge to leave the inn and never come back."

"Did she yell at her, try to shove her out the door, anything like that?"

"Not at all. Mrs. Bright had herself under perfect command by then, she simply told Mrs. Flodge to go. Mrs. Flodge shouted a threat about having the inn's victualling license taken away. Mrs. Bright said 'Go' again, and this time Mrs. Flodge went."

"Were you two the only witnesses?"

"No," said Peter. "Thurzella was still here and so was Claridge Withington, whom you may know. I understand he's been a regular summer boarder here for—how many years is it, Mrs. Bright?"

"Too many, I'm beginning to think. I'd have to look it up in the old registration ledgers. Claridge wasn't in very good shape when he first came, he's a little worse every year, and has come to expect more attention than I have time or staff to give him. The upshot is that he tends to involve himself with other people's affairs more intimately than some of us appreciate. I may as well tell you that he got huffy with me tonight after Lucivee went."

"Why was that?" asked Armand.

"Because I warned him that I didn't much care for his habit of broadcasting my personal affairs to every Tom, Dick, and Harry who'll stop to listen. I further told him I'd just as soon he went to his room, which didn't set any too well, I don't suppose. Which reminds me, I did say I'd bring him an egg-nog. Maybe I'd better go fix it while you three are here. You can watch and make sure I don't slip in any cyanide pills."

Chapter 16

"Don't suppose you'd be fixin' to warm up the coffeepot while we're in the kitchen?"

Constable Frank, who'd been lounging in one of the dining-room chairs with the brim of his cap pulled down over his eyes so that it was impossible to tell whether he was awake or dozing, was now sitting up and taking notice. "Might kind o' sharpen our minds a little."

Elva Bright's mind was already sharp, and so was her tongue. "I wish to goodness you folks could get the matter settled once and for all so that I can sleep of nights. I've said before and I'll say again that I don't for one minute believe Jasper Flodge would ever have committed suicide no matter what kind of fix he was in. He was too fond of his own skin for that. Further-more, he'd been lying his way out of one scrape after another ever since he stole my slate pencil our first day in school and claimed I'd poked it down a chink in the floor. He'd have trusted his luck to come through again, no matter how big a mess he'd got himself into."

She headed for the kitchen. "Come on, I'll make the coffee.

181

You and Mrs. Shandy come too, Professor, if you're not too tired."

Both the Shandys realized that Mrs. Bright must be thinking she'd feel more comfortable having witnesses along who were unequivocally on her side. How could they not go?

The kitchen was clean as a whistle. Thurzella was nowhere to be seen. A note on the scrubbed counter said "See you in the morning, Gram. I took two doughnuts for Daddy's lunch box."

"Bless the child. Here, Mrs. Shandy, take this stool, it's all there is to sit on. I don't suppose you'd want a doughnut, this time of night. There's a little of that lemon sherbet left, and some madeleines. I learned to make them for my husband."

"I'd love a madeleine, thank you."

Peter took one too, but the other men all opted for doughnuts. Constable Frank was wide awake by now, and ready to pick a bone with the innkeeper.

"I don't see why you're so hell-bent and determined to make out that Jasper was murdered, Elva. Seems to me it would be a damn sight more to your advantage if you went along with what they're sayin' about suicide."

Sergeant Gilbert nodded agreement. "Mrs. Flodge makes out a reasonable case. According to her, Flodge got himself involved in some shady real estate deal, tried to outsmart the wrong people, lost all his money, and got in serious trouble with the mob. She maintains that he knew he was a goner and decided he might as well take his own way out before some gunman caught up with him, giving himself one last kick by doing her out of the insurance policy she'd been paying on ever since they split."

Elva still wasn't biting. "You don't have to remind me. The

182

first thing Lucivee did after she hit town was barge into my dining room and make a big scene over the way Jasper had cheated her. If she's so bound and determined to make everybody believe Jasper died penniless, why's she so busy rooting around after whatever she thinks he's got squirreled away? Would you kindly and gently answer me that?"

"That's an interesting question, Mrs. Bright," said Sergeant Armand, "but it's not what we're here about this time. I guess what we'd better do now, Frank, is see what Mr. Withington has to say, then go take a look at Mrs. Flodge's awful mutilations. She'll be staying here in Pickwance for the night, will she?"

"I should think so," Elva replied. "She does have a flat in Portland, I believe, but it hardly seems likely she'd have gone there tonight, specially now that she's found another excuse to make trouble up here. Most likely she's at Jasper's, just over on the next street. Frank can show you where. She claims the place is hers now, not that it's anything to brag about. Will you be coming back here after you've seen her?"

"That depends, I guess," said Gilbert. "Look, Mrs. Bright, if I were you, I'd get hold of my lawyer first thing in the morning. I expect what Mrs. Flodge is angling for is an opening to sue you for damages. Considering the way you say she's been acting in your dining room, I shouldn't be surprised if you could bring a countersuit against her for defamation of character, disturbing the peace, and a few other things. It mightn't be a bad idea for your lawyer to write her a pretty stiff letter, then you just wait and see what develops. Chances are she'll back down in a hurry, otherwise she could find herself in a mess of trouble."

"Rather she than I. I suppose I'd better make that eggnog,

seeing as how it's what we're here for. You watch me, now, I wasn't joking about Claridge Withington. He's quite capable of pulling some stunt just to keep the pot boiling."

She beat an egg, added milk, nutmeg, and a tablespoon of cooking sherry. "Well, poor soul, I suppose he has to get his fun one way or another. Here, you take this eggnog in to him. I'm not feeling any too sociable right now. Good night, Mrs. Shandy. You too, Professor. I'll see you in the morning, if the posse here hasn't carried me away."

"She's quite a person, isn't she?"

Helen hadn't taken time before dinner to do more than unpack her all-purpose dress and shoes. She was finishing the small task now, putting the hangables on hangers, hooking them over the rod hidden behind a chintz curtain that did duty as a closet, laying her underthings in a drawer, setting out her comb and cosmetics on the embroidered dresser scarf.

"There we are. Now where's the stuff I was going to wash?"

Peter was regarding his wife with amusement. "I thought you wanted to leave tomorrow."

"Did I?" Helen rooted in the suitcase that Peter had by degrees been turning into a hamper and began to fill the bathroom sink. "Give me that shirt, for goodness' sake. It looks as if you've been wearing it all week."

"Only since yesterday. I meant to borrow one of Guthrie's."

"His shirts would swim on you. Bless that woman, she's put a folding laundry rack in here. You weren't planning to take a shower tonight, were you?"

"Am I to deduce from your query that the clothes rack is in the shower stall?"

"You're so clever, dear. I've missed you."

184

"M'well, we might play duets if you'd thought to pack us a couple of pianos."

"So we might, I knew there was something I'd meant to put in. What have you done with your other sock?"

"Helen, is that sock germane to the topic under discussion?"

"It's germane to the fact that you're going to feel awfully silly tomorrow morning going down to breakfast with one foot covered and the other one bare if we don't find it."

"Do you honestly think so? Am I so abject a slave to fashion? Is it my life's crowning ambition to become known as the Beau Brummell of Pickwance? I suppose you'll be nagging at me to buy myself a feed cap next. One with velveteen antlers sticking up out of it and a slogan across the front that says 'The Moose Is Loose,' perchance? Here's your dratted sock. I seem to have been using it as a bookmark, for some reason that escapes me at the moment. What in Sam Hill is going on down there?"

Perhaps because it had once been a pesthouse, if Withington's history could be trusted, the squarish, two-storied, gambrel-roofed gray clapboard building that had been known for the past half-century and more as Bright's Inn was set off a little from the other buildings along the main street. The three broad slabs of granite that served as its front steps came right out to the edge of the sidewalk, as was to be expected in a latitude where snow fell thick and often in the wintertime and nobody wanted to do any more shoveling than necessary. At each side, however, a strip of land about six feet wide had been left bare beside the foundation, and a paved alleyway broad enough for two cars to pass, unless one of them was a truck, led around behind the inn to a parking lot big enough to hold as many as twenty vehicles.

These side strips, and the narrower ones that ran along the

185

front from the alleyways to the steps, had been filled in with a deep mulch of beach stones about the size of eggs, tumbled smooth by the in-and-out of countless tides, kept in place by a white-painted wooden picket fence about a foot high. The noise that Peter and Helen were hearing was of footsteps rattling over the stones.

"Sounds as if the constable's dropped his car keys," Helen giggled. "Do you think we should go down and help him hunt for them?"

"I think you should eschew frivolous remarks and either put your dress back on or take off the redundancies. My own inclination is toward—"

"Sh-h! I think they're saying something about asking the professor. Why don't you poke your head out and see what's going on? Can you raise the screen?"

"It seems to be fastened on with rusty hooks and eyes. Drat, they're stiff as—ah, here we go. Long as I don't drop the thing and brain the constable. These old wooden frames are heavy."

Having checked to make sure the hooks at the top were still secure and could serve as hinges, Peter eased the lower part of the screen far enough out so that he could see what the commotion was about. The state police cruiser was still parked at the curb, Sergeant Gilbert was sitting in the driver's seat with the door open, talking into a hand-held microphone. Frank was patrolling the sidewalk, shooing away pedestrians who wanted to stop and see what was going on. Sergeant Armand was inside the picket fence. He appeared to be standing guard over something black that was sprawled over the stones just around the right-hand corner of the building. As Frank waved a car on by, its headlights picked up a flash of red against the black. Peter pulled in his head and hooked the screen.

"You'd better get dressed, Helen. I think it's Lucivee Flodge."

"Peter, no! You mean she's—"

"She's something. Passed out, maybe. Mrs. Bright mentioned that she'd been drinking a lot."

Helen didn't believe this. Peter didn't either. A drunk with a nearby home to go to would mean nothing worse than a distasteful task for the constable or some helpful neighbor who knew where her door key was hidden. A state policeman sending a radio message meant a situation that he and his partner either couldn't or shouldn't try to handle by themselves. Such as a bad accident or a case of homicide.

Since Helen had already put his shirt to soak, Peter pulled on a light sweater over his undershirt. "I'm going down."

"Then so am I. Do you have the room key with you?"

"Yes, in my pocket. You'd better bring your handbag, though. Will you be warm enough in case we have to go someplace?"

"Where, for instance?"

"God knows."

Helen took out the pale-blue cardigan that she'd so recently put in the dresser drawer, picked up her handbag as bidden, and gave Peter a kiss. "Poor Mrs. Bright! I do hope it's not something awful."

That would depend on how one defined awful, Peter supposed. The front door was ajar, they stepped out on the top step. Gilbert motioned for them not to go any farther and kept on nodding into the microphone. As their eyes adjusted to the moonlight, they could see Lucivee well enough. There was no pool of blood around her, no knife protruding from her back, no obvious sign of a bullet hole or even of a struggle. The woman who had so viciously baited Elva Bright not much over an hour ago seemed now to be resting quite comfortably on the stones. Her good black suit wasn't torn or rumpled, her hair not even mussed. The briefcase she'd been carrying lay close to her left hand, still fastened. She had fallen face down, all they could see was part of her left cheek, with a large, ugly abrasion on the temple.

"Ugh!" Helen drew her cardigan close around her. "It took more than Mrs. Bright's diamond to do that."

What about an embattled Mrs. Bright with a rock in her hand? Peter had a hunch the others were thinking what he was thinking; he wished he weren't. "Where's Mrs. Bright?" he asked.

Gilbert, who'd finished his call and come back out on the sidewalk, told him. "She's in the lobby with Mr. Withington. We'd be grateful if you and Mrs. Shandy would go inside and stay there with them. We're not supposed to let anybody in or out until the homicide squad gets here."

"Homicide squad?"

Well, yes, they'd have to. Lucivee must surely be dead, and there was that call she'd made claiming grievous bodily assault. Peter and Helen went dutifully back into the lobby. There was no fire in the grate tonight, Elva Bright and her out-of-favor boarder were sitting as far apart as the space would allow, in two of the wicker chairs. Mrs. Bright was still in her white cotton dress. Withington had put on a heavy woolen robe and house slippers but retained his socks and trousers. For once, the oracle wasn't saying a word; but he perked up a little when the Shandys sat down together on the love seat.

"This is indeed a shocking development. After we—ah—parted company, I watched television for a little while. Then, much to my surprise, I had a short visit with Frank Webber

188

and two nice young chaps from the state police. I'm afraid they found me a dull witness."

That could have gone without saying, Peter thought. He pulled Helen a little closer and prepared to endure what couldn't be avoided. Withington worked his way syllable by syllable through his dull witnessing, then back to the tube.

"I was trying to find something worth watching—I have one of those remote-control gadgets, so I'm able to manage easily enough—when, lo and behold, the boys were back in my room wanting to know whether I'd happened to hear anybody prowling around outside while they were in the kitchen with you and our kind hostess."

He shot a slightly acrimonious glance at Mrs. Bright. "I explained that I wouldn't have heard because my television was on. I wear earphones, you know, so that the noise won't bother anybody else. I do try to be as considerate a resident as my infirmities will allow me to be," he added with another side-long glance, which was a waste of effort because Mrs. Bright wasn't looking. "Please excuse my attire, Mrs. Shandy. The policemen were quite insistent that I stay here with Mrs. Bright where she can keep an eye on me. It's quite a change for a physical wreck such as I to be treated as a suspicious character."

That got a rise out of Mrs. Bright. "Don't start giving yourself airs, Claridge. You're here to make sure I don't try to sneak away, and well you know it. What's going on out there, Professor?"

"M'well, we're not quite sure yet. Sergeant Gilbert was on the car radio last I knew. I assume he was calling for an ambulance and—er—whatever else they do in such cases. Helen and I got shooed in here to await further developments. Is that what happened to you?"

189

"Pretty much. I was still in the kitchen puttering around. There's always some little last-minute thing to do about breakfast, it seems. I was in the pantry hunting for a spare jug of maple syrup that I'd hidden away and forgot where I put it when Jemmy Gilbert came galloping in as though the devil was after him, wanting to know if I'd seen or heard anybody run down the driveway and out through the parking lot. I said I probably wouldn't have paid any attention if I did. Joggers often cut through there. Anyway, I wouldn't have heard them from inside the pantry. So I asked Jemmy what the trouble was and he told me there was a woman lying up near the corner of the driveway and would I come and have a look at her?"

"That must have been a shock," said Helen.

"It was one too many for me, I can tell you that. I suspected right away that it might be Lucivee Flodge. I figured she'd gone home, taken a few quick drinks, and decided to come back and fight another round but had had one too many and passed out before she quite made it to the inn door."

"Would that be possible? Does she live that close to here?"

"Oh yes, just the next street over, practically back-to-back with the inn. All she'd have had to do was cross her own backyard and cut through the parking lot. So anyway, Jemmy Gilbert wanted me to go out with him and have a look, and sure enough, it was Lucivee. She still had on that black suit with the red collar and cuffs that you saw her in. I wanted Jemmy and Armand to turn her over so that I could get a proper look at her face but they said it was against the rules and they'd have to call for instructions. So Jemmy marched me back in and brought Claridge to guard me, and here we are. What's the matter with Lucivee, Professor? Hasn't she come to yet?"

Chapter 17

By brute force, Peter kept himself from glancing at Helen. "They wouldn't let us any farther than the doorstep, Mrs. Bright. It was hard to see. Would you mind if I lit the fire? My wife is shivering."

It might not have been on account of the after-dark cooling, but Helen played up. "I should have known enough to bring something warmer than this thin cardigan. Peter's been telling me about the lovely hand-wovens your daughter has for sale, he's promised to take me to her shop tomorrow."

Sweet are the uses of small talk in an emergency situation that one can't do anything about; Mrs. Bright pounced gratefully on Michele's hand-weaving. They whiled away the time not too unpleasantly with the help of the multicolored driftwood blaze, until the sound of a siren and the flashing of blue lights brought back the fear. It was impossible then to stay away from the windows, although Mrs. Bright did do what Peter's mother would surely have done, drawing the curtains across the windows for decency's sake but leaving a narrow slit to peek through.

Lucivee Flodge was dead. Nobody could doubt that now, not when they'd watched her body being encased in a long plastic bag and slid on a stretcher through the open back doors of the police ambulance. As the doors were shut and the ambulance eased itself away from the curb, Peter heard the innkeeper murmur "God be merciful." He took her by the arm, steered her back to the chair she'd been sitting in, and laid another stick of driftwood on the fire.

Then came more waiting while the men outside poked around among the rocks with no apparent result. It might not have been more than fifteen minutes, but it felt like an eternity before Jemmy Gilbert reentered the lobby.

"Mrs. Bright, would you mind coming into the kitchen with me for a minute or two?"

She minded, all right, though she put a brave face on it. "What for, Jemmy? Surely you're not hungry again already?"

"Not yet." He was at least as nervous as the innkeeper was, and not covering it up half so adroitly. "It's just that the . . . the officer in charge"—he was trying not to say "homicide"— "thought we ought to double-check that bit about somebody being able to run through the alley without being heard."

"I told you I was in the pantry."

"Yes, I know you did. You and I are supposed to go into the pantry together and you sort of do what you were doing before while I listen."

"Well, that's pretty dumb. All they'd have to do would be take off their shoes and run in their socks."

"That's what I said, but Detective Blake said what if they didn't have time to take off their shoes? We're supposed to think of it as part of the investigative process."

"Does it make any difference what I think of the investigative process? Come along, then, let's do it and get it over with."

Claridge Withington was not taking kindly to his assigned role as passive listener, he cleared his throat with a loud "Ahem! What would you like the rest of us to do, officer?"

"I'd like you all to stay right where you are for the time being. Somebody will be in here shortly to take your statements."

"Ah yes, our statements. That ought to be an interesting experience, don't you think, Professor?"

Withington was all set to elaborate, but Jemmy Gilbert wasn't stopping to hear. He and Elva Bright were on their way to the pantry before Withington could clear his throat again. Peter held up a shushing hand.

"Hadn't we better keep quiet and listen for the footsteps?"

He didn't know why they should, particularly, but it was one way of getting that old nuisance to shut his mouth for a while. Now that Mrs. Bright wasn't around to maintain decorum, they might as well see what was going on outside. Peter shamelessly pulled back the curtain at the side window and turned out the lamp on the table so that their eyes could adjust to the darkness.

It wasn't much of a show. First on the program was a fine figure of a sergeant in regulation boots, making enough of a clatter as he ran to be heard up and down the road. Next came another who'd changed into jogging sneakers. His footsteps were audible but not noticeably so, they could easily have failed to catch the attention of an innkeeper working in the pantry with maple syrup on her mind. The last man in was a brave soul wearing thin black socks and nothing over them. He'd have stood a fair chance of not being heard if he hadn't stubbed his toe and said "Ouch."

So much for the investigative process. Peter hastily rearranged the curtain the way Elva Bright had fixed it, switched on the lamp, and went back to the love seat to comfort his wife, contemplate the fire, and wonder why he hadn't thought to bring back an armload or two of driftwood from Rondel's Head. There'd been plenty of it strewn around the rocks. He could have left an envelope on the table so that Miss Rondel wouldn't think he was trying to take advantage of their brief acquaintance to swipe her flotsam.

It was boring, just sitting here wondering when the hell those myrmidons of the law were going to quit horsing around out there and get on with the grilling. Helen had fallen asleep with her head against his shoulder, Peter was glad that she was able to snatch a little rest.

She'd had far too long and exhausting a day, starting out from Balaclava Junction before the early birds had got fairly started on the worms, driving so long a distance with only an occasional pit stop to work out the kinks, picnicking with Catriona and Guthrie, coming at last to Pickwance and being plunged forthwith into a maelstrom. She ought to be upstairs in bed by now.

And he ought to be up there with her, drat it! How the flaming perdition had he manged to get them into this mess? He tried to think of some way he could hold Catriona McBogle responsible but that was hardly fair, he might as well chalk it up to Kismet. Things happened because they happened. Even Withington was nodding now. Peter didn't recall having shut his own eyes but all of a sudden Elva Bright was back in the chair where she'd been sitting before Gilbert came to get her and a tall man who oozed authority was pulling up a straight chair to the edge of the circle so that he could face them all as he spoke.

"Sorry I had to keep you waiting, folks. I guess you all

know by now that we've got a pretty serious problem on our hands here."

No, he didn't have to tell them, but not even Withington said so. "I'm Detective Drake of the state police, in case you're wondering. According to certain identification we found in the briefcase she was carrying, the woman whom Sergeants Gilbert and Armand found on the inn premises a little while ago was one Lucy V. Lach, attorney, of 1037 Robinwood Road in Portland. Can anybody confirm that? Mrs. Bright?"

The innkeeper jerked as if she'd received a galvanic shock, but answered calmly and coherently. "I don't know the address, but I expect the Portland telephone book will have it. There's one at the front desk over there. The V's for Veronica, I know that, not that it matters much, I don't suppose. Lach may be her real name, but she's been calling herself Lucivee Flodge."

"Why Flodge? Was she connected in some way with the Jasper Flodge who died here this past Tuesday?"

" 'In some way' is about right. About six years ago, I think it was, she started coming up here just about every weekend, staying at Jasper's house, which is just behind the inn. They'd come in here to eat now and then, but I can't say I paid much attention to her. Jasper always had some woman on the string, there've been a few more since her. This one lasted about a year and that was the last I remember of her until she blew in here Tuesday evening claiming to be Jasper's legally married widow. Do you want me to get you the phone book?"

"No, sit still. I just want to be sure we're talking about the right person. When she came in here the other night, did you recognize her as the same woman who'd been staying with Mr. Flodge six years ago?"

"Oh yes, Lucivee hadn't changed any to speak of, and she wasn't the sort of person you'd be likely to mistake for anybody else. I was busy in the kitchen when she came in, but I heard somebody out here braying like a donkey and recognized the voice, so I peeked out to make sure. She had on that same black-and-red outfit she was wearing tonight. She always wore black a lot."

"What became of her handbag?"

"I don't think she had one with her. All I saw was a briefcase, or what looked like a briefcase. It might have been a handbag, I suppose. Mr. Withington would know better than I, he's good at remembering things. What did she die from, were the ambulance crew able to make out?"

"I expect you're the one who can best answer that, Mrs. Bright."

The multicolored flames were still dancing behind the fire screen but the temperature in the room seemed to have plunged about twenty degrees. "Just what do you mean by that?"

"Okay, Mrs. Bright. According to information received, you subjected Mrs. Flodge to bodily assault with an undisclosed weapon earlier this evening and ejected her from these premises by use of force."

"The information received was a telephone call from Mrs. Flodge herself, wasn't it?"

"That was the name given by the caller."

"And what signs of bodily assault did you find when you turned her over? Was there a very small scratch on her right cheek?"

"There may have been. There was also a massive wound on the left temple which appears to have been caused by one of the stones you have lying around the foundation here. We think we've found the one she was hit with, but we'll know better after the stone's been analyzed for blood, hair, and tissue. And fingerprints, of course. We'll be wanting yours."

"Take all you please. You're saying it was the blow on the temple that killed her?"

"We'll know better when we get the autopsy report."

"I see. Would you mind telling me how big that stone was?"

"I'm the one who's supposed to be asking the questions, Mrs. Bright."

"Then I'd suggest you ask these people here what really happened. They were in the dining room at the time, they saw what I did to Lucivee Flodge and why I did it; and they've been right here with me ever since."

Withington's throat-clearing was getting monotonous. "Excuse me, Elva. I was dismissed from the group, as you may recall."

"Not until after Lucivee had left the inn, you weren't. Thurzella was still here then, and so were Professor and Mrs. Shandy."

"Who's Thurzella?" asked the detective.

"And how do you spell it?" asked Armand who'd been taking notes in the background.

"It's spelled the way it's pronounced," Mrs. Bright replied pretty crisply, "and Thurzella's my granddaughter, Detective Drake. She's waiting tables this summer."

"Does she live here at the inn?"

"No, just down the road, in that big white house next to the church. My daughter Michele is married to Bob Cluny, who manages the lumber mill. I sent Thurzella home a few minutes after Lucivee flounced out, mad as a wet hen and threatening to put me out of business, which she'd have had as much chance of doing as I would of being elected Pope of

Rome. Not that I'd care much anyway, the way things have been going lately."

"How do you know Mrs. Flodge would have lost her case? Weren't you at risk of losing your livelihood?"

"Oh, I don't think so. I expect I'd be able to keep body and soul together one way or another." Mrs. Bright moved her left hand just enough for the big diamond to catch the firelight and send a dazzle of light in the detective's direction. "The inn's my hobby, not my life. Getting back to Thurzella, I went out the front door with her and stood watching on the steps till I'd made sure she was safe home. There certainly wasn't any corpse by the alleyway then, she'd have had to pass it and neither of us could have missed seeing it. Thurzella's not one to miss much."

"Why did you send her away at that time?"

"Because she'd finished her work and her parents wanted her home at a reasonable hour. You would yourself, I daresay, if she'd happened to be your daughter instead of theirs."

"Um. You also sent Mr. Withington away."

"I told him he'd better go to his room. You might bear in mind that I'm not exactly a spring chicken and I've had a fairly trying week of it, what with Jasper Flodge dying in my dining room and that so-called wife of his putting on her performances ever since. And now here she was again, traducing myself and my daughters in my own house, right to my face, bold as brass. I know Claridge Withington of old, I was fully aware that he'd been soaking up this last piece of slander like a sponge and was itching to spill it all to the first person who'd stop to listen."

"That's unfair, Elva!"

"No, it isn't. I'm sorry, Claridge, I know it's not very nice of me to speak out like this in front of strangers, but I'm sick and tired of the way you've been blabbing my family business ever since you first started coming here, and you might as well know it."

Withington whipped out a nicely ironed white handkerchief and made a big production of blowing his nose. "Thank you for telling me, Elva. I had no idea you found me so offensive to have around. I'd been foolish enough to believe that, after all these years, I'd become almost a member of the family."

"Don't you start in on that wounded and abused act of yours, Claridge Withington. My husband was in a darned sight worse condition from the moment I met him than you ever were or will be. He never traded on his infirmities, not that you'd know because he was dead before you ever started coming here, much as you like to let on that you and he were the best of friends. As long as you're so ready to bask in his glory, you might care to start profiting from the example he set."

"Oh, but I have profited in a number of ways, though this hardly seems the time to go into particulars. Since you're the one who's asking the questions, Detective Drake, is there any way I can help you?"

"I don't know yet." The detective sounded a bit fed up also. "I'd like to get Mrs. Bright's sworn statement down first, for the record. You'll be asked to sign this, Mrs. Bright, so I hope you'll try to be as accurate and specific as possible. Would you mind coming into the dining room with me and Sergeant Gilbert? The rest of you please wait here until you're called. Sergeant Armand will be right at the door in case any problems should come up."

Her lips in a straight line, Elva Bright followed Detective Drake into her dining room. Peter glanced over at Armand, shrugged, and put some more driftwood on the fire.

199

Chapter 18

Whatever went on in the dining room didn't take very long. Elva Bright came out as stony-faced as she'd gone in.

"They want you next, Mrs. Shandy."

That was all the innkeeper said. Helen raised her eyebrows, straightened her skirt, and went into what had become the interrogation chamber. Considering that she'd arrived only late that afternoon, there wasn't a great deal she could say and she obviously wasted few words in saying it. She was out in just under ten minutes.

"Would you please go in, Mr. Withington?"

"Really? I expected to be last on the agenda."

Notwithstanding his demurrer, Withington had had his cane braced for the effort of rising ever since Elva Bright went into the dining room. He hauled himself out of his chair more expeditiously than usual and made what haste he could manage through the dining-room door.

Either the women had been cautioned not to talk or else they had nothing left to say. Helen patted Mrs. Bright's hand and gave her a companionable smile. The innkeeper managed to return the smile, but it was an effort. She leaned back in her wicker armchair and shut her eyes; she must be worn to a frazzle.

It was not to be expected that Withington would be done talking soon. Peter resigned himself to a long stretch of further boredom but the wait was less tedious than he had anticipated, mainly because he dozed off for ten minutes or so. The self-styled oracle managed to wear out his welcome in twenty-two minutes and thirteen seconds. He came out looking smug and went around the corner into his bedroom without wishing anybody good night.

That left only Peter Shandy. He knew pretty much what Drake would ask, he had his answers ready. Naturally the interrogation didn't go at all as he'd expected but the gist of it was easy enough to cope with. As bidden, he explained why he'd happened to come to Pickwance and what he'd been doing here. Peter saw no reason to mention the paintings that he and Helen were hoping to buy, but he did go on at some length about the lupine seed he'd gathered at Miss Rondel's and what he hoped would come of it in the experimental greenhouses at Balaclava Agricultural College.

His bona fides established, he was taken over the circumstances of Jasper Flodge's death, the subsequent appearance of the woman who had claimed to be Flodge's lawful wedded wife, the disgusting show she had put on here on the night of the funeral, and the unprovoked and unfounded attack she had made on Elva Bright so short a time before her own death tonight.

"That's the part I just can't see," said Drake. "Why do you think Mrs. Flodge acted up the way she did tonight, Professor Shandy? Was she just sore because her party had fallen flat?

"I think it was a good deal more than that," Peter replied.

"Mrs. Flodge might have been a capable lawyer, I wouldn't know about that, but she seemed to be a fairly scatterbrained thinker. That first night, for example, she boasted to Withington, as he may have told you, that she was now the heiress to Jasper Flodge's house and all his other assets. A few minutes later, she was standing up, bellowing to the whole restaurant that Jasper Flodge had committed suicide in the presence of witnesses for the sole purpose of cheating her out of a big insurance policy on which she'd been paying, apparently in the fond hope that somebody would bump him off before she got too old to enjoy the money. He must have been a good bit older than she, by the way, though I don't suppose that's particularly germane to the issue."

"You never can tell," said the detective. "Did she say why he'd committed suicide?"

"Her claim was that he'd got into trouble with what she referred to as the mob. He'd lost all his money in some shady enterprise or other and was going to be rubbed out for not being able to pay what he presumably owed. I don't know whether there was any truth in her story or not. Since then, she'd apparently continued to root around in the hope of discovering some hidden assets but didn't seem to be happy about the results. My guess, for whatever it's worth, is that by tonight she'd been forced to accept the fact that Flodge had in fact died broke and decided to make up the deficit by a spot of blackmail."

"Against Mrs. Bright? What could she have hoped to get out of her?"

"Quite a lot, if Withington's tale is even halfway true. According to him, the late Jean-Luc Mercier de L'Avestant-Portallier, which is Mrs. Bright's actual married name although she understandably continues to use the old family name for business reasons, was a man of means. He not only had an income of some sort from France, where he'd played a heroic part in World War Two, but was so shrewd an investor in the stock market that he and his wife were soon able to buy out her parents and turn the inn into a very successful enterprise."

"How come? His wife said he was badly disabled."

"There was nothing wrong with his mind. He knew he wasn't likely to make old bones, so he concentrated on building up a substantial legacy for his wife and their two daughters. Both the girls married well, have nice children and interesting careers. I don't suppose either of them will care to keep the inn going. Some of the grandchildren might, I suppose, but that's irrelevant. The point I meant to make is that Mrs. Bright was most likely telling the simple truth when she said that, at this stage of life, the inn is only her hobby."

"Why did you mention blackmail?"

"I mentioned it because it was so obviously what Lucivee Flodge had in mind. I'm sure Mrs. Bright must have explained to you why she slapped the woman's face."

"She said it was because Mrs. Flodge was flashing a photograph around and claiming it proved that Mrs. Flodge's own alleged husband was the father of Mrs. Bright's kids. Does that add up to blackmail?"

"The only two explanations I could think of were either that Mrs. Flodge had gone completely around the bend or else that she thought she could bully Mrs. Bright into paying her off to avoid a scandal."

"Do you think Mrs. Bright would have committed murder rather than pay up?"

"I think nothing of the sort and you damned well ought to know it. There was nothing to make a scandal out of. Mrs.

Bright's not one whit ashamed of the fact that she was already pregnant when she and her husband got married. From what I've heard, it was a genuine love match and stayed that way. He was a fine husband and father and a respected member of the community and it's too bad there aren't a lot more like him."

"But she keeps this guy Withington hanging around."

"He occupies one of her rooms for a few months each year as a paying guest. That's what inns are for, you know. I have a hunch she took him in the first place because having a handicapped man at the inn may have seemed a little bit like having Jean-Luc back. Unfortunately, Withington's not the stuff that heroes are made of and seems not to have improved with age and increasing infirmity. I suppose it's hard for a good-hearted woman to refuse a room to a longtime regular patron just because he's become such a pest that she can't stand having him around any longer. I doubt very much that she'll poison Withington's soup to get rid of him. As for that yarn about Jasper Flodge's having sired Elva Bright's daughters and Lucivee's trying to use Thurzella Cluny as proof, it's just not true."

Drake was not too happy with the turn this interview was taking. "What makes you so sure of that, Professor Shandy? As I understand it, you only saw him with his face in a plateful of chicken pot pie."

"On the contrary, I happened to be sitting opposite him at a nearby table, where I could watch him eat. It was such an arresting spectacle that I couldn't keep my eyes away. I'm sure Flodge didn't notice me gawking, he was too busy wolfing down his food. I'd never seen anybody eat so much so fast. When he fell forward, I assumed he'd choked but he wasn't making any sound. Thurzella, who happened to be clearing a table nearby, took hold of his hair to pull him up, but the hair turned out to be a toupee. That was more than she could handle, so I straightened him up and tried to mop off the gravy. That was when I realized he was dead."

"Then what happened?"

"Mrs. Bright called the local constable and an ambulance. Withington and I stayed with the body until it arrived. That gave me ample opportunity to study Flodge's facial structure. It was in no way similar to Thurzella's. Or her mother's, for that matter; the mother and daughter could pass for twins. I'm sure Mrs. Bright must have photographs of her husband, she says Michele and Thurzella take after him. Jean-Luc, as she calls him, is said to have been a handsome man, even in his mutilated condition."

"All right, Professor, we can check on that. How long did it take the ambulance to show up?"

"A good deal longer than I'd bargained for. At least half an hour, probably more. Mrs. Bright made a second call to see what was keeping them."

"Did she stay with you the whole time?"

"No, she walked Thurzella home and stayed long enough to tell the girl's parents what had happened. She was back here a good while before the ambulance showed up, though."

"M'h. How do you think Flodge got the cyanide?

Peter shook his head. "I'll pass on that one, if you don't mind. Were you aware, by the way, that Flodge was in the habit of drinking almond extract?"

"Huh? What the hell for?"

"For the purpose of keeping a buzz on, according to both Mrs. Bright and the ambulance driver. They claim he'd been hauled in for drunk driving so many times that he'd been threatened with a stiff jail term and permanent loss of his license unless he went on the wagon and stayed there. He seems to have struck a viable compromise by carrying a small bottle of almond extract around with him and taking a quick nip every so often when he thought nobody was looking."

"Why almond, I wonder? It's usually vanilla or lemon they go for."

"Flodge happened to be an almond freak. Mrs. Bright said he'd eat almonds in any form: plain, on pastries, cutesied up as marzipan rutabagas, you name it. After we'd detected the almond odor on his breath, I did make a quick search of his pockets and, sure enough, there was the almond extract, about an inch left in the bottle. I didn't touch the glass and left it where it was. I assume it was analyzed in the police laboratory but of course I have no way of knowing."

"I'll have somebody check on it," said Drake. "I doubt if they'd have found anything but almond extract, though. Cyanide works so fast that he'd hardly have had time to recap the bottle and get it back into his pocket. And it apparently wasn't in the chicken pie."

"Not to my knowledge. Flodge had the last piece in the pan. I ate the next-to-last one myself, with no ill effects."

"Okay, then, Professor. I guess that does it for now. Say, don't I know you from somewhere?"

"I believe we—er—met briefly in Hocasquam a year or so ago."

"Oh hell, yes. You're that friend of Guthrie Fingal's who helped him get back the college weather vane.*"

"I was just one more face in the crowd," Peter replied modestly.

"That's not what Guthrie says. Your wife and the McBogle

---

*Vane Pursuit

207

woman who writes those crazy books were in on it too, as I recall."

"Yes, they were. Catriona's been visiting us, she and my wife just drove back to Maine today. Helen and I were planning to leave for home tomorrow, but I expect that's not going to happen, is it?"

"I'd just as soon you stuck around, if it won't inconvenience you too much."

"No, not if we can be of any use to you. We'll just phone home and let the neighbor who's minding our cat know that we're staying on another day or two."

"It might be more than a day or two," Drake cautioned. "Seeing as how you're a friend of Guthrie's, I don't mind telling you I'm none too happy about this situation. Two deaths in one week in the same place are kind of hard to swallow, even if one was a suicide and the other could have been an accident, or been made to look like one. Kids are pretty crazy these days, some of them. Like tonight, Theresa, was it?"

"Thurzella."

"Okay, Thurzella. She could have run back here after her grandmother came inside, and lammed Mrs. Flodge with a rock for calling her mother a bastard."

"I doubt that very much," said Peter. "I doubt still more that Mrs. Bright had any hand in either of the killings."

"What makes you so sure, Professor?"

"Instinct, I suppose. I'm not saying she couldn't kill somebody under certain circumstances, say if some thug with a knife was threatening to rape her granddaughter. But for her to sneak poison into food that she'd prepared herself and was about to serve to a patron in her own dining room would have been not only wicked but also stupid. Mrs. Bright is neither one."

"She attacked Mrs. Flodge, though."

" 'Attack' is far too strong a word. She slapped Mrs. Flodge's face for good and sufficient reason. If anybody ever asked for a backhander, that floozy surely did. As my wife must have told you, and as you must have seen for yourself, the bloody assault that Mrs. Flodge was raving about when she phoned your station was nothing more than a practically invisible scratch caused by the stone in Mrs. Bright's ring. That's a common occurrence, my wife says. People's fingers do tend to swell or shrink very slightly, depending on what they're doing, what they've eaten, what time of day it happens to be, whether it's the full of the moon, I don't know. I suppose it's more notice-able in women because they're more apt than men to be wearing rings. Anyway, a ring that fits too perfectly may be hard to get off if the finger happens to swell the least bit, so most people would as soon wear them a trifle loose. That's how Mrs. Flodge's face got scratched."

"Very scientific, Professor. But what about the rock that killed her?"

Chapter 19

"Now, that's another story," said Peter. "You're quite sure the wound that caused Mrs. Flodge's death was on the left side of the head?"

"Yes, of course."

"And the scratch caused by the ring was on the right cheek?"

"So?"

"So Mrs. Bright happens to be left-handed. That's how the ring came into play. Wedding and engagement rings are customarily worn on the left hand, as I'm sure I don't have to tell you. Mrs. Bright was facing Mrs. Flodge when she struck, so the scratch naturally appeared on the right cheek. In order for Mrs. Bright to have inflicted the fatal blow holding the rock in her hand, she'd have had to be standing either behind Mrs. Flodge or at her right side."

"She could have thrown the rock."

"Assuming that she'd happened to see Mrs. Flodge standing outside the inn, had a rock handy in the house, unhooked the window screen without being detected, and thrown the rock

211

accurately enough to hit her target on the crucial spot in very dim light."

Drake started to say something more, but Peter cut him off. "Moreover, Mrs. Bright's own immediate reaction to the slap was one of acute embarrassment and humiliation at having committed so gross a breach of civilized conduct. Even if she had found a way to slip out and pound Mrs. Flodge with a rock, I cannot for the life of me visualize her lowering herself to do it. She's just too much of a lady."

"Well, damn it, the Flodge woman's dead. Somebody must have killed her."

"Oh yes, I certainly can't quarrel with you there. I do think however, that there are other avenues to be explored."

"Such as what?"

"Well, for one thing, has anybody else happened to mention a small incident that occurred just after Mrs. Flodge had left the inn in high dudgeon but with all parts in working condition? As I mentioned, Mrs. Bright was in a bit of a state by then. The inn doesn't have a liquor license, but I figured there must be some cooking sherry or liqueur in the kitchen for culinary purposes, so I asked Thurzella to go get her grandmother a drink. As she turned toward the kitchen, she happened to glance out into the lobby and said 'Oh, hi, Evander.' "

"Evander? You don't by any chance mean Evander Wye, Fred's brother who works at the tourmaline mine?"

"That's the only Evander I know of. He's a regular patron here in the dining room."

"He's been an occasional patron of the county lockup too, in case you hadn't heard. What was he doing?"

"I don't know. Mrs. Bright said something about going to see what he wanted, so I went out into the lobby but nobody was around. The door to the upstairs was shut and it shrieks like a soul in torment when I open it to go to my room, so I doubt very much that he could have gone upstairs without my hearing him. It's possible Thurzella was hallucinating, I suppose, or that the inn is haunted by the ghost of Evander's great-grandfather who died in the pesthouse, assuming he did. If it really was Evander Wye, he must be pretty nippy on his pins to have skinned off before I could catch him. I did look around behind the desk, check the phone booth, and all that, because Mrs. Bright acted concerned over his coming in after the dining room was closed for the night."

"I can see where she might," said the detective. "I used to hear stories about that guy when I was riding a cruiser. He'd get kind of playful sometimes when he'd had a few too many. Is there any other way than by the front door that he could have got out?"

"Not through the kitchen, anyway. He'd have had to come through the dining room and we'd have seen him. I don't know the inn all that well, though. Withington has a downstairs room, but I doubt whether it has an outside door. Of course Wye could have jumped out a window easily enough, they're not that high off the ground. But he'd have had to unhook the screen and leave it flapping, and he'd surely have rattled a few stones when he landed. If he really was here, he must have left by the front door."

Drake nodded. "That's something none of the others mentioned. I guess we'll have to talk to Thurzella. I don't suppose Bob Cluny would take it very kindly if I barged in there now and woke her up. Will she be here tomorrow morning?"

"I expect so, but I can't tell you when. Her grandmother gave her permission to sleep in to make up for the rough time she got tonight. Around half past nine should be a good time to catch her, the breakfast crowd's usually cleared out by then. That's assuming there'll be one. I don't know what effect Mrs. Flodge's murder is going to have on Mrs. Bright's business. Oddly enough, it was Mrs. Flodge's antics that saved the bacon after Flodge cashed in his chips."

"You don't say? How did that happen?"

"M'well, the day after he died, I went off to collect lupine seed at Rondel's Head, as I believe I mentioned to you earlier. I got back around suppertime, cleaned up a little, came down here, and discovered that I was the only customer in the place, except for Withington. At first I thought I'd misread my watch and got here too late or something, but I hadn't. Normally that would have been the busiest time of the evening, so of course I realized there was trouble. Poor Thurzella was practically in tears when she took my order. Then Lucivee Flodge blew in, just back from Portland, or so she said, and sat down jabbering with Withington. One or two people started drifting in off the street out of curiosity, and pretty soon the place was packed as usual. That was when Mrs. Flodge stood up and delivered her spiel about Jasper's having got in trouble with the mob and killed himself in front of witnesses as a way to spite her out of the insurance money."

"Those two must have been quite a pair," said Drake. "Flodge sounds like a good guy to stay away from."

"Oh, Flodge was all that and then some, judging from what I've been hearing the last couple of days. Guthrie Fingal told me about a rotten trick Flodge pulled on him some years ago, and we had a real melodrama played out here last night, stemming from one of the filthiest scams ever pulled on an innocent woman. That one involves a case of grand larceny which never got reported to the police, you may be interested

214

to know. It's too late tonight to go into the particulars, but we could talk about it tomorrow if you want."

"You bet I want. Was Mrs. Bright in any way involved in either of those cases?"

"Only to the extent that last night's event took place here in this dining room and Mrs. Bright came out of the kitchen to help celebrate the happy ending."

"So you wouldn't advise us to take her in as a material witness?"

"I think you'd be making a serious mistake if you tried. Mrs. Bright's a woman very much looked up to in this town. You don't have a single damned thing to pin her with, and you'd be lucky to escape a lawsuit after you'd been forced to let her go. My suggestion would be for you to leave a guard on duty here tonight and get on with the investigation when there's daylight to see by."

The detective sighed. "I just wish we knew where to investigate next. At least we don't have to worry about how Flodge died, that part's all sewed up. This afternoon, for your private information, Mrs. Flodge turned over to our lieutenant some letters and a diary that she'd found among her husband's effects. They established beyond any possible doubt that Flodge had in fact been wiped out financially, was being pressured for money he had no way to pay, and was definitely planning to kill himself rather than sit around waiting for some hired gun to mosey along and do it for him."

"That's very interesting," said Peter. "Who wrote up the diary?"

"Oh, he did. It was just one of those little day-at-a-glance things that you jot down appointments and whatnot in. Mrs. Flodge identified his handwriting. She also verified his signa-

215

ture on a couple of letters he'd written to her and on their wedding certificate."

"Then there's where you start investigating. I strongly suggest that you take all the material Mrs. Flodge gave you, particularly the handwritten diary, out to Rondel's Head and show it to Miss Frances Rondel."

"You mean that old lady who raises the big lupines? What's she got to do with Flodge?"

"She told my wife and me yesterday afternoon that she'd had Jasper in her third-grade class when he was a kid. He was evidently smart enough in some ways, but he could never learn either to read or to write. He was either hopelessly dyslexic or else too lazy to apply himself; he squeaked through on a superlative memory, a wide streak of cunning, and a glib tongue. His wife claimed she'd been handling his paperwork for some years, even after she'd got fed up with having to cook breakfast for the lady friends he used to bring home nights, and moved back to Portland."

"Godfrey mighty! Then the diary and letters were nothing but out-and-out forgeries?"

"I'm reasonably sure that both Miss Rondel and any competent handwriting expert will tell you so," Peter replied. "Mrs. Flodge must have spent the bulk of the time since her husband died cooking you up a nice bunch of evidence. I doubt very much whether she herself had any inkling that she might be in danger. She struck me as being much like her husband, crafty and cocky but nowhere near so smart as she thought she was. It wouldn't surprise me if you found out that they'd both been taking their orders from a third party who was clever enough to stay out of sight, coach them to perform as directed, and scoop the lion's share of the profits as his or her reward for doing all the heavy thinking. I'm only guessing about that, of course. I do think I'm on firm ground in saying that I don't believe there's one iota of truth in that tale Mrs. Flodge spun about the mob."

"What makes you so sure, Professor?"

"The pattern. The modus operandi, if you want to get fancy. Guthrie Fingal told me about some of Flodge's scams. The one with the Wyes that came to a head last night here at the inn, and Mrs. Flodge's abortive attempt to shake down Mrs. Bright this evening were along the same lines. Both involved situations where there was a goodly chunk of family money that could be got at through one vulnerable person. Whether Mrs. Flodge bungled her boss's instructions, entertained a mistaken notion that she could handle Mrs. Bright on her own, or was deliberately set up to be killed because she was getting out of hand is moot now, of course. The fact remains, however, that somebody was right on the spot to shut her up as soon as she either came back or was lured back to the inn. Why a rock was used as a weapon is for you and your colleagues to decide."

"Right now I'm in no shape to decide anything," Detective Drake groaned. "Cripes, I can't even think straight. Any more murders you want to tell me about?"

"Yes, Jasper Flodge's. If that man committed suicide, I'm Count Dracula's grandmother. He came swaggering into this dining room all togged out like the Lord Duke of Magurriwock as if he owned the place, and started hectoring Thurzella about what was on the menu. This was quite late for the inn to be serving, they'd evidently had a slew of customers and the kitchen was pretty well cleaned out by then. He rather snooted the chicken pot pie until Thurzella told him there was only one piece left and she wanted it for herself. Then he insisted on having it."

"Nice guy."

217

"You can say that again. Incidentally, Guthrie mentioned later that Flodge had won a number of pie-eating contests at the county fairs. That's hardly the sort of hobby one associates with a master criminal, I shouldn't think. Flodge might have been playing Russian roulette with a cyanide pill, but he didn't show any sign of it that I could see."

"That's interesting." The detective's observation was blurred by a yawn of impressive proportions, Peter knew just how he felt.

"Look, Detective Drake, I'm sorry I seem to have blown your case for suicide, but I'm in about the same shape as you are and my wife's been traveling since before dawn. I've got to get her to bed."

"I told Mrs. Shandy she was free to go upstairs if she wanted," Drake retorted in a put-upon tone.

"She wouldn't have felt right leaving Mrs. Bright without some moral support. And you know as well as I do that Mrs. Bright isn't going to call it quits until the last gun's fired and the smoke cleared away."

"No, I suppose not. Poor woman, it's a hell of a fix for her to be in, not that I'm supposed to feel sorry for the suspects, but even a cop can't help it sometimes. Do you have any plans made for tomorrow?"

"I promised I'd take my wife to Michele Cluny's weaving shop in the morning and we're invited to tea with Fred Wye and his wife later on. We're also hoping to see Miss Rondel sometime during the day, but we can adjust our visit so it won't conflict with yours."

"You're all heart, Professor. See you in the morning, maybe."

Chapter 20

Everything must have been running late at the inn the next morning. Peter and Helen both woke early, as was their custom, both pretended they hadn't so as not to disturb the other and drifted back into a series of catnaps until it got to be ridiculous. They didn't get down to the dining room until after nine o'clock, they were surprised when Elva Bright herself came to take their orders. She was wearing her professional innkeeper's smile but it looked a bit frazzled around the edges.

"Morning, folks. I guess you managed to get some sleep. My helper, Gladys, is the cook today in case you're wondering what I'm doing on this side of the door."

"What happened to your pretty granddaughter?" Helen asked.

"Jeanine went back to Portland yesterday afternoon. Her parents came and picked her up, which was a relief to me as things turned out. I'm just sorry Thurzella didn't go with her, it would have saved my other son-in-law a trip. Bob and Michele thought Thurzella ought to be out of the way till this latest mess gets settled, for which I certainly can't blame them.

I'd go myself if I could. But that's no skin off your noses. Can I interest you in buckwheat cakes with my special blueberry syrup? It's just blueberries stewed with a slice of lemon and a dash of cinnamon. If you want it sweet, you can add a little maple syrup."

"Sounds good to me," said Peter. "What about you, Helen?"

"Oh, my. Are they big pancakes or little ones?"

"That's up to you. We flop 'em any size you want 'em." This must have been a standard quip, the smile that went with it was turned on automatically and shut off just as fast.

"Two small ones, then, with orange juice and coffee, please."

"And sausages? We grind our own sausage meat."

"Just one, then. You're a hard woman to resist, Mrs. Bright. Peter, while we're waiting for our pancakes, don't you think we ought to give Miss Rondel a ring? She must be waiting to hear from us."

"Good thinking. I'll go. Biggish pancakes for me, Mrs. Bright, and sausage by all means. Don't worry, Helen, we'll work it off climbing that precipice she calls her driveway."

On her way to the kitchen, Mrs. Bright hesitated. "I'd better warn you, Professor, that you're apt to get waylaid in the lobby. We've had a slew of reporters here this morning, as I suppose we should have expected. They began coming about six o'clock. I wasn't even dressed, I had to open the front window and holler down that they'd have to wait and they needn't expect free breakfasts. Then I phoned over to Gladys. She came right away, bless her heart. We did give them coffee once Gladys had it made, but I was darned if I'd let them pester me with a lot of fool questions. Luckily, Claridge heard the commotion and got himself up. He's been a real help, I have to give him credit for the way he took over with the reporters. I expect he's still at it out there. The Lord only knows what he's telling them by now, but I'm long past caring."

There were still a few people, all strangers, all from the media, sitting around the dining-room tables. Some were eating breakfasts that Mrs. Bright was going to make them pay for, the rest were just drinking her free coffee. Peter found himself thinking that the dining room seemed empty without the Wye brothers.

Withington was in his glory, however, sitting in one of the wicker chairs. A small table was drawn up to it with a tray holding the remains of breakfast. A young woman sat next to him with a notebook on her lap, while a photographer poked a camera at his face. He was making great play with an early-morning newspaper, calling attention to a headline that proclaimed NEW EPIDEMIC HITS FORMER PESTHOUSE, TWO DEAD IN ONE WEEK. That should be great for business, Peter thought cynically.

The uniformed guard at the front door was refusing to let anybody in without a police badge or a press card, the gawkers on the sidewalk were having plenty to say about that. Elva Bright's business had been saved the first time by Lucivee Flodge's unexpected histrionics, she would hardly strike it lucky twice in a row, not with Lucivee herself the second victim. Two macabre deaths so close together would be enough to put even the most dedicated patrons off their feed.

By a mixture of stealth and luck, Peter managed to slip across the lobby and into the phone booth without getting nabbed by either the reporter or the photographer. Miss Rondel had indeed been waiting for Professor Shandy's call and sounded a tad acerbic about his having left it so late. Peter apologized, giving as his excuse the fact that he and Helen hadn't got to bed until the small hours. Perhaps Miss Rondel was not aware that Jasper Flodge's widow had been killed last night just outside the inn.

She took the news with relative calm. "Oh dear, what a time poor Elva's having. If it isn't one thing, it's another. That silly, silly woman! Some people simply will not learn. Would you please tell Elva for me that I'll do what I can? Where is Thurzella?"

"In Portland, staying with her cousin. Her father drove her down last night."

"Bob Cluny is a sensible man. An adolescent girl does not need to have her mind cluttered with horrors. Neither do the rest of us, I suppose, but at least we're more inured to them. Were you and Mrs. Shandy still planning to come over here today?"

"If you're willing to have us."

"Oh yes, it's all arranged. I've obtained verbal permission from the artist to proceed with the transaction. I believe there ought to be a bill of sale, or something of the sort, shouldn't there? I can ask Michele, she knows what to do. She hasn't gone to Portland too, has she?"

"Mrs. Bright didn't say so. I have the impression that the family are trying to play things down as far as possible. I was planning to take my wife to the weaving shop this morning. It hadn't occurred to me that Mrs. Cluny might not be open for business."

"I doubt whether it's occurred to Michele either," Miss Rondel replied rather dryly. "She knows better than to attach undue importance to an occurrence that, while of course regrettable, involves the Bright family only coincidentally."

That was stretching coincidence pretty far, Peter thought,

but he wasn't about to argue the matter with Miss Rondel. "What time would you like us to come?" seemed the most sensible thing to say at this point.

"Would noontime be convenient for you? I thought I might offer you a light lunch, if you think Mrs. Shandy would be agreeable?"

"I'm sure she will, and so am I. I might mention that Mrs. Bright's helper is just now cooking breakfast for us, so please don't go to the bother of preparing a big meal."

"I never prepare big meals. Do give my love to Michele when you see her. Tell her I have that last lot of stoles ready whenever she wants to pick them up. Until noontime, then."

Miss Rondel hung up without wasting time on good-byes. Peter reconnoitered from inside the phone booth and saw to his horror that Withington was pointing him out to the photographer. There was nothing for it but to look preoccupied and keep walking once he'd left the booth.

It didn't work out that simply, of course. The photographer was right there when Peter stepped out, with the camera lens about ten inches from his nose and the reporter shrilling rapid-fire questions into his ear. Peter had been through this sort of hectoring too many times before. He knew better than to employ strong-arm tactics, or even to show annoyance. The only thing to do was to lose neither his temper nor his impetus.

"Sorry, miss, I'm just here about the lupines. Mr. Withington knows all about everything, he can fill you in far better than I. My wife and my breakfast are waiting for me in the dining room, so you'll have to excuse me."

The officer on duty was understanding about letting Peter inside and keeping the others out. Mrs. Bright must have been peeking through the kitchen door. As soon as she spied him coming, she was there with the buckwheat cakes; small ones for Helen, big ones for him as ordered, with a pitcherful of dark-purple syrup and a refill of coffee for both.

"This looks great, but we probably shouldn't have ordered it," Peter remarked as he sat down. "Miss Rondel's invited us to lunch."

The innkeeper's lips twitched. "Don't worry. Miss Fran's not one to go in for heavy meals. You'll be lucky to get a dandelion salad and a glass of water. Speaking of which, could I prevail on you to have her refill my jugs for me, Professor? If it's not too much trouble?"

"No trouble at all, Mrs. Bright. We had some of her water yesterday. I was telling Helen on the way back about the hidden spring Miss Rondel has on her property. Too bad you couldn't have the water piped down here to the inn, Mrs. Bright."

"Huh. Don't talk to me about that, Professor, and for goodness' sake don't so much as breathe a word of it to Miss Fran. One of the good things about Jasper Flodge being taken is that he won't be pestering her any longer about selling out to him."

"Good Lord! Why would she want to do that?"

"That's just the point, she wouldn't. But he'd got this great bee in his bonnet about tearing down the old farmhouse and building a big resort at Rondel's Head. What they call a health spa. Of course that would have meant us townfolks losing our spring to a pack of strangers, but that wouldn't have cut any ice with Jasper. It's an awful thing to have known somebody your whole life long and tried to make allowances, and then to hear all this awful talk coming out and have to face the fact that he was plain rotten clear through and never been anything else. But you don't want to hear all this. I'd better get back to the kitchen and help Gladys get ready for the dinner crowd, if there's going to be any. Will you two be eating here to-night?"

"My vote is yes," said Helen. "I'm going to be ready for an early bedtime, but right now I'm itching to get to your daughter's shop. Peter tells me it's full of wonderful things."

"That reminds me," said Peter. "I'm supposed to let Mrs. Cluny know that Miss Rondel has a bunch of stoles ready for her to pick up. I didn't offer to bring the stoles back because I didn't know what—er—arrangements they have between them."

"No reason why you should," Mrs. Bright replied. "Anyway, Michele would rather go herself. She loves to sit down with Miss Fran and talk weaving, always has. Ever since she was old enough to ride up there on her bicycle, she'd be at Miss Fran's every chance she got, pouring herself a drink of water out of that old yellow pitcher. Some think the benefit was in the pitcher, which would surely have been one big joke on Jasper Flodge if he'd ever got what he was after, but—" She caught herself in mid-sentence. "Look at me, jabbering away like a flock of sparrows when there's a day's work to be done. You sure I can't get you anything else?"

"Not a thing," said Helen. "That was a lovely breakfast, now we'd better go brush our teeth before we leave. Do you remember Mrs. Goose and the Black Cat from Green Street when they ate the blueberry slump?"

Helen had a knack for striking a chord. For a moment, Mrs. Bright's face lived up to her name. "Oh, my, yes. My husband used to read Mrs. Goose to our girls when they were little, first in English, then in French. They were crazy about Madame l'Oie. Thanks to him, they're both completely bilingual. And they've passed it on to their children, I'm happy to say. I was never much of a hand at French myself, but Jean-Luc and I

225

understood each other well enough. No, Professor, put that money away. This meal's with the compliments of the house. You folks have a nice day and I'll see you when you get here."

"Fairly spoken and thank you very much," Peter replied. "I hope it's safe by now to wish you a good day too. It's high time you had one."

"Hope's about all I have to fall back on right now, it seems. Why such things have to happen is beyond me, but maybe we'll understand it better by-and-by, as the old hymn says. My aunt Verbena used to play that on the melodeon for us every time we went there to visit. She had a voice like a train whistle, but she loved to sing and we never tried to stop her. Not that we'd have been able to anyway. Aunt Verbena wasn't one to give up without a fight."

"And neither are you," said Helen. "We'll see you tonight, then."

The media people had all cleared out by now. Withington sat alone in the lobby waiting patiently as a blue heron for the next poor fish to come within reach of his beak. The Shandys could not be uncivil enough to pass him by without a few minutes' chat and a little greasing of the ego about how deftly he'd handled the briefing session. They then pleaded blue teeth and urgent business elsewhere and got away from him without much trouble. When they came down again, brushed and flossed and ready to smile, Withington appeared to be asleep in his chair. They didn't wake him up to say good-bye.

When Peter and Helen walked into Michele's shop, they found the master weaver busy with a customer. She gave them the ritual nod and smile and left them to poke among the racks. Helen wished no greater bliss, she lost little time in picking out a handsome tie for Peter, a set of place mats for the Stotts, and a wondrous garment that was either a jacket, a waistcoat, or something in the nature of what Peter's grand-mother would have called a wrapper for Catriona. These were only the tip of the iceberg. As the pile on the counter rose ever higher and Michele Cluny's smile grew broader, Peter's patience began to decline.

"What in Sam Hill are you planning to do with all that stuff?"

"I'm doing our Christmas shopping, dear. Do you think your niece Alice would like this angora scarf? It's lovely and soft, but angora fuzz does tend to come off on things."

"With six Chihuahuas in the house, Alice can use a little extra fuzz," said Peter. "Go ahead and buy the scarf. Aren't you going to get anything for yourself?"

"Need you ask? Hold my handbag for me, will you? I'm going to try on this heavenly suit. I've never seen such exquisite blending in a heather mixture. Did you do this, Mrs. Cluny?"

"Miss Fran wove the fabric, I made the suit. If this one doesn't fit, I could make another to your measurements. Unless you see something else that you'd like better."

There was nothing that Helen liked better, the suit fit slick as a whistle, obviously it had been meant for her and nobody else. Far was it from Peter Shandy to come between his wife and her credit card, he even suggested she take the handsome scarf and hat that went with the suit. Those could be her presents for next Groundhog Day.

"How very thoughtful of you, dear. They'll be just perfect to wear to the bonfire. Groundhog Day is a major event at Balaclava," Helen explained to Michele Cluny, who was look-ing a trifle nonplussed, as vendors were wont to do when the Shandys got thoroughly involved in one of their fortunately infrequent shopping sprees.

For some reason, the word "groundhog" joggled Peter's

memory. "I'm supposed to tell you, Mrs. Cluny, that Miss Rondel has some stoles ready for you to pick up at your convenience. Helen and I are lunching with her and she's asked us to arrive around noontime. So I'd suggest, my love, that we settle up here and get cracking because it's already half past eleven."

Chapter 21

"It's a good thing you didn't get carried away in there," Peter remarked as he moved his hard-won lupine seed to the farthest reach of the car's trunk to make room for Helen's deluge of parcels. "By the time we get the paintings in with all this other stuff, we're going to have quite a cargo aboard."

"Don't worry, dear. Practically everything I bought is squashable except my suit, and we can lay that on top after the paintings are in. Michele Cluny certainly knows how to charge, but this suit's worth every penny. It's the sort of thing a person can wear forever and never get tired of."

Helen would probably do just that, she didn't even consider a garment properly broken in until she'd had two or three years' wear out of it. At the moment, though, her mind was not running on clothes.

"Peter, what do you suppose Mrs. Bright meant this morning about the benefit being in the pitcher?"

"I was wondering when you'd get around to asking me that. How old would you say Mrs. Bright is?"

"I really don't know. If I hadn't seen her daughter just now,

I'd have said Mrs. Bright couldn't be more than forty. If I didn't know Thurzella, I'd swear Mrs. Cluny was about twenty-three. Do they marry straight out of eighth grade around here, or what?"

"According to Withington, Mrs. Bright was married at sixteen for—m' er—technical reasons; but I understand both her daughters went to college, so they probably didn't marry until they were twenty or more. Just to make it more interesting, Mrs. Bright told me that Miss Rondel was in school with her grandmother."

"She must have been joking."

"She wouldn't joke about Miss Rondel. By the most conservative estimate, Miss Rondel must surely be ninety or more by now; but look at her. Spry as a cat and blooming like the rose."

"I assume you're talking about those little old bush roses whose petals come out faded and wrinkled. But they smell far sweeter than the new hybrids, and they do go on forever. When do we get to the pitcher? Hasn't your pal Withington given you a rundown on its history?"

"No, oddly enough, that's one subject on which Withington hasn't uttered so much as a yip. Of my own knowlege, however, I find it safe to say that the pitcher was an artifact of ordinary yellow earthenware with brown stripes such as could have been found years ago in your average New England farmhouse. I happened to see the shards of one on Miss Rondel's kitchen table the day I went to collect the lupine seeds. When I mentioned that fact to Mrs. Cluny on Wednesday, she lost her composure."

"Peter Shandy, I do not believe for one second that Mrs. Cluny lost her composure. That woman was born composed."

"All right then, she didn't lose her composure. But it wobbled a little. You'll grant me a wobble, I trust?"

"Yes, dear, you may consider the wobble granted. So what you've been leading up to in this unnecessarily circumlocutory way is that the pitcher had been used to carry water from the hidden spring, thus imparting to the water, as Mrs. Cluny apparently believes, and her mother doesn't, certain mystical powers comparable to those that Ponce de León never found because he wasn't looking in the right place. One is reminded of Kipling."

"One is?"

"Certainly one is. Haven't you ever read 'Venus Annodomini'?"

"Oddly enough, I have. You refer, perhaps, to the sentence 'Youth had been a habit of hers for so long that she could not part with it.' "

"One might also cite 'She was as immutable as the Hills. But not quite so green,' " Helen suggested. "That would explain why Mrs. Bright stays so young looking but doesn't buy into the theory that it's the container and not the water itself that does the job. She's old enough to know better. How do you feel about that?"

"M'well, if the pitcher was in fact enchanted, I've wasted seventy-five dollars plus tax on the disenchanted one that I bought Miss Rondel to replace it; so I'm rooting for the water. You know, Helen, it's by no means an untenable premise that the spring at Rondel's Head does have a high concentration of minerals conducive to strong growth and extended longevity. That could explain why people around here all look so healthy, why Miss Rondel is able to raise those enormous lupines in a location where it's theoretically next to impossible for them to grow at all, and even why her hens lay ostrich eggs. No wonder she looked mildly amused when I took soil samples without thinking to test the water. Your old man's a dunderhead, macushla."

"If you say so, dear. Personally, I think you're rather cute. What do you suppose she'll give us for lunch?"

"A lettuce leaf and a black-eyed pea."

"That sounds about right, I have a premonition that Mrs. Wye may be planning to lay on a fairly impressive high tea. Imagine her having lived right across the Crescent from us all this time, and we never knew who she was."

"Algernon's going to miss her," said Peter.

"And she him, no doubt, but think how happy Iolanthe must be to get back into her own kitchen, after all she's been through. Can you imagine the sort of childhood she must have had, growing up with that hypocritical ghoul of a father pouring brimstone and ice water on her head every step of the way? He *stole* from her, Peter! It's not only that inheritance he kept her from getting; it's her whole life he tried to rob her of. He's as big a thief as Jasper Flodge ever dared to be."

"He deserves to be preached to death by wild curates."

"Don't you go quoting Sydney Smith at me when I've got a good mad worked up, Peter Shandy. That man's a beast."

"The woods are full of them, my love."

"What's that supposed to mean? You don't think Fred Wye's going to turn on his wife again?"

"No, I don't think Fred Wye will do anything of the sort. He must know by now that it's not safe to rush into hasty judgments. Try me on Evander."

"That's the brother who gets drunk and picks fights?"

"There are just the two brothers, as far as I know. I don't know the specifics, but the word around town is that Evander

Wye in a snit is not a man to be taken lightly. I haven't mentioned this to anybody else, Helen, and I hope you won't, but I witnessed an odd little circumstance Tuesday morning when I went to Rondel's Head to gather the seed. I'd parked my car down below the path, there was a blue pickup truck parked a little farther up. As I passed it, I heard a man's voice up above, yelling 'I'll do it and you won't like it.' "

"Oh, my."

"Then something came whizzing past my ear and lammed into a yellow birch tree. Not caring to get in the way of the man's target practice, I stepped behind that big boulder you may have noticed yesterday and waited till he'd gone by. As he passed the boulder, I got a look at him and realized he was somebody I'd seen at breakfast in the dining room. Once he was well away, I went over and took a look at the yellow birch. There was the pebble, a smooth piece of granite about the size of a walnut, embedded so deeply in the tree that I couldn't prise it out without breaking the blade of my jackknife."

"Oh Peter! He must have put terrific force into his throw. But he wasn't necessarily taking deliberate aim at the tree, was he?"

"Considering that I heard a second thud right after the first, and that, on my way back to the car later on, I found another tree with a rock in it just as deep and just the same height from the ground, I'm inclined to believe he was. I'll show you the two trees when we get there, if you want."

"And Thurzella caught a glimpse of Evander in the lobby right after that Flodge woman had had her run-in with Mrs. Bright and been ordered to leave. And not long after that, Mrs. Flodge was killed by a stone not much bigger than a walnut. Doesn't it make you wonder, Peter?"

"How can I help wondering? I've even wondered whether I

233

might be keeping pertinent information from the police by not telling them. But I'd eaten dinner with the Wyes Wednesday night. I'd seen Evander the first of the three men to speak up in Iolanthe's defense. Then he and Fred and their cousin and I went to shoot a few rounds of pool and, well, we got to be sort of buddies. The mere fact that a man can throw straight doesn't necessarily make him a murderer. Drat it, Helen, I could have hit that tree. I suppose I could have hit Lucivee Flodge if she'd happened to get in my line of fire at the wrong moment. So could any kid who's ever played a game of catch. Even a person who couldn't hit a barn door on purpose might do it by accident. I can't go running to the police with a story like that."

"I understand, dear. But don't you think you might at least mention the incident to Miss Rondel when you get a chance? She seems to be the real power around here, from what little I've seen."

"I'll think about it. Let's not say anything until after we've got squared away about the paintings."

"And eaten our black-eyed pea. It's your decision, dear. I feel funny, not bringing anything for the hostess. Except a bagful of money."

Peter began to laugh, Helen joined in. They were both still laughing when they tackled the horrible path, not taking time to look for embedded pebbles in the birch trees because they were barely on time as it was. Miss Rondel met them at the top of the path, put down the hen she'd been carrying, and ushered them into the house.

"Right on the dot, I see. Now, are you people very sure that you wish to proceed with this transaction?"

"Yes," said Peter, "we are. Helen, I believe you've brought the necessary?"

"I have ten certified checks, each in the amount of a thousand dollars. That seemed the easiest and safest way to handle the money. All I have to do is sign them in your presence, Miss Rondel, then you can either cash them yourself or endorse them over to the artist. If our bill runs over ten thousand, we'll just have to scratch around for the rest."

"If your purchases ran any higher than that, I expect the person for whom I'm negotiating would die of shock." Miss Rondel didn't commit the solecism of laughing at her own quip, but there was gladness in her voice. "You two have no idea of the marvel you've worked by your spontaneous show of admiration for an unknown artist's work, and the price you're willing to pay for the pleasure of having it in your house. The cash itself is the least part of the bargain. It's the fact that you were willing to spend so much that gave such a tremendous lift to someone who's been burdened for a long time by depression and self-doubt. Money does talk, you know, and yours shouted loud enough to reach an ego that needed a good, swift kick to get it going."

This time, Miss Rondel did laugh. "I seem to have scrambled my metaphor there, but I trust you get the drift. Now, as to the payment. I'm instructed to say that your offer is too large and that you may have the four paintings you selected for a flat five thousand dollars, which still seems a great deal to me. I strongly advise you to accept the offer without quibbling, for everyone's sake, mine included. I find that being put in the position of an artist's agent is not a job that I care to keep. Now, why don't we go into the dining room? I thought you might want to eat your lunch among the paintings."

"What a wonderful idea, and what a beautiful table!" Helen exclaimed. "I love your china dishes."

"Early Sears Roebuck. Sit here, Professor, so that you can see your special favorite."

The meal was a little less austere than Elva Bright had predicted. Peter found it somewhat awesome to be eating half a deviled egg on a bed of assorted greens in the midst of such glory. Not that the egg itself wasn't awesome in its way; he doubted whether he could have managed the other half. Those super-hens of Miss Rondel's certainly kept their minds on their job.

Miss Rondel had mashed up the yolks with finely chopped fresh chives and a touch of lemon balm and moistened them with the same kind of boiled dressing Peter's grandmother used to make. There were slices of home-baked whole-wheat bread and tumblers full of water from the hypothetically miraculous spring. Peter could think of nothing he'd rather be eating.

Facing his own painting, the one that would truly be his once Helen had finished her deviled roc's egg and got around to signing the checks, he felt like a proud father about to bring his firstborn home from the hospital. At least he thought he did. Actually, it was more the way he'd felt when, after long, long months of nursing turnip seedlings to their ultimate fruition, he had produced the primordial *Brassica napobrassica balaclaviensis*, the Balaclava Buster, that mega-rutabaga which by now had fed millions of bovines and bipeds wherever rutabagas are known and loved, or even moderately liked. Peter was in no rush for the meal to end. He sensed that Helen was feeling the same as he, and that Miss Rondel was not displeased to have their company.

"I was thinking, Miss Rondel," Helen remarked when it seemed the right time to do so, "now that a sale has been made, your artist friend may be more amenable to having his

236

or her work shown through a reputable gallery. Catriona has friends who own a gallery, maybe you all could get together and find out how the system works. Cat was saying on the way up that she wants to visit you before she starts her new book."

"I shall be pleased to see her. I do think this sale is already effecting a change in the artist's attitude about showing the work, which I intend to encourage. The sooner I'm shut of the whole business, the happier I shall be. Michele and I have some new ideas we want to try out and we'll need this room for work space. Now, why don't we get our bit of business taken care of? Did you happen to bring something to wrap the paintings in?"

"Unfortunately, it didn't occur to me," said Helen. "Driving up with Cat was a last-minute decision, I didn't dream at the time that we'd be buying a painting."

"No matter, I have some old sheets from the inn that Elva gave me. Michele and I use them in the workroom for dust covers. You can borrow a couple and bring them back on your next visit, which I hope will be soon."

"How kind of you to say so."

Helen was already signing the checks. Miss Rondel accepted them with a nod and went to get the sheets while Helen cleared the table and Peter took down their selected paintings from the wall. Miss Rondel reappeared with the sheets over her arm, took full charge of the wrapping, and made a neat job of it, as was only to be expected.

"And now, I want you to tell me precisely what's been happening down in Pickwance. I understand that Iolanthe Wye is back where she belongs. That father of hers ought to be locked up. And you people are going to tea with her and Fred this afternoon."

"Yes. I believe she wants us there about three o'clock."

"Good, that gives us plenty of time. Come into the kitchen so that I can wash the dishes while we talk. And, no, I don't want any help, thank you. This was my mother's china. If any of it's going to get chipped or broken, I'd just as soon the blame fell on myself."

Chapter 22

Miss Rondel was a relentless questioner, the story took a fair while in the telling. By the time the luncheon dishes were done, the paintings stowed in the Shandys' trunk, and the hostess's curiosity satisfied, it was half past two and a little beyond. When Helen and Peter began to repeat their thanks and say their good-byes, Miss Rondel demurred.

"Oh no, I'm coming with you. Why don't you and I sit together in the back seat so we can talk, Helen?" She was using their first names by now, although they knew better than to use hers. "Peter can drive. I expect I'll stay to dinner at Elva's. Somebody will drive me home."

Her object being, of course, to show the townsfolk that it was still as safe as ever to eat at Bright's Inn. Miss Rondel wasn't bothering to change her faded cotton dress, to tidy her hair, to do any of the small things women generally do when they go out in society. Why should she? She was who she was, and that was enough. She did pick up a handwoven tote bag and lock the door in case of wandering tourists.

"Time was when nobody around here ever locked a door,"

she remarked, "but these days, one never knows. Sometimes I get to feeling I've lived too long and might as well quit, but there's always something that needs to be done first. Now, Helen, I want you to tell me about your work on the Buggins Family archive. I had a great-uncle who married a Buggins. Bethseda, her name was."

"Bethseda Elvira." Helen knew all there was to know about Bethseda's antecedents but little about her married life; she and Miss Rondel talked genealogies until they'd got down into Pickwance and up the hill to the Wye mansion. Both Iolanthe and Fred were on the front veranda waiting to greet the Shandys, they were surprised but visibly honored to see Miss Rondel.

"Miss Fran, how dear of you to come!"

Iolanthe Wye had shed another five years or so by now. Her hair was softly curled, her face lightly made up. She had on a frilly pink dress that must be one of those which she'd left behind when she fled and Jasper Flodge hadn't bothered to steal. On her ring finger, left hand, was a clear pink tourmaline set in gold. She noticed Helen's admiring glance and smiled.

"Fred gave me this on our first anniversary. I just found it an hour or so ago, when I was trying to straighten out the pantry. I'd taken it off that morning because I was rolling out biscuits, and dropped it in an empty jelly tumbler for safekeeping. And here it was three years later, still waiting for me to put it back on."

"She's going to have a real nice one soon as we have decided on what she'd like," said Fred.

"I don't need another ring, darling. This one's too precious."

Iolanthe might perhaps have enjoyed a quiet sniffle about then but she was, after all, the hostess. "I've got iced tea all made. If anybody'd rather have hot, I can boil the kettle in a jiffy. Fred and I thought you might like to sit out here on the veranda, it's such a beautiful day. And besides, I haven't had a chance to put the front parlor back in shape yet. It's going to take a month of Sundays to fix up this house the way it ought to be. I don't know what this big lummox was doing all the time I was gone."

"Waiting for you to come home." Fred Wye bestowed a somewhat indecorous caress on his wife, caught Miss Rondel's eye, and reddened. "Guess I'm supposed to wheel out the tea cart about now. Eh, boss?"

"Want some help?" Peter was beginning to feel awkward standing here doing nothing.

"Sure, Pete, come ahead. You can pick up what I break."

"Bring out the big armchair for Miss Fran," Iolanthe called after the men.

"No, please," Miss Rondel protested. "I much prefer a cane rocker. I remember sitting in this same chair on an afternoon like this, back when Fred was one of my pupils and his mother was still alive."

"Telling her all the awful things I'd been doing at school, I bet." Fred was in great form. "Come on, Pete, before these women gang up on us."

He and Peter went into the house. Iolanthe managed to drag her eyes away from her husband and back to Miss Rondel. "Was he really awful, Miss Fran?"

"Frightful! Fred was the only child I ever had in my class with whom I could not cope. I can't begin to tell you what a scamp he was. He'd wait till my back was turned, then pull some foolish trick that got the whole class laughing. When I turned around, he'd be sitting up all innocence. I could almost see the angel's wings sprouting out of his shoulders. I think it

241

was the day Fred brought a long-haired hamster to school and set it loose on the floor just as the principal walked into the room with the county superintendent that I decided it was high time for me to retire from teaching."

"Do you ever regret your decision?" Helen asked.

"Never. I'd been wanting more time to devote to my weaving and I'm glad I made the move when I did, so I suppose I ought to feel grateful to Fred for spurring me on to do it. If he'd been more like his elder brother, I don't suppose I'd have had the heart to leave. Where is Evander today, Iolanthe?"

"Working at the mine. He'll be sorry he missed seeing you. It's funny, I can't picture Fred being the bad boy and Evander the star pupil."

"I can see why you might wonder. I can assure you, however, that Fred was an imp and Evander was pure joy."

Helen Shandy was surprised. This didn't fit in with what Peter had told her about the man who drilled holes in trees with rocks. "He didn't bring a hamster to school?"

"If he had, he'd have taught it first to stand at attention and salute the flag," Miss Rondel answered. "Evander was far and away the most intelligent child I ever had the privilege of teaching. He genuinely loved to learn. I had to keep thinking up special projects to keep him interested. Which turned out, I'm sad to say, to be the worst mistake I ever made."

"But why?"

"Well, you know how children are. The others noticed that I was, as they saw it, playing favorites. They didn't dare say anything to me, of course, but they taunted Evander outside the classroom, calling him sissy and teacher's pet. The boys were less vocal because they knew Evander Wye could lick the lot of them if it came to a fight, but the girls were simply dreadful. Mainly, I suspect, because he was too far ahead of them mentally to be attracted physically. Words can be cruel weapons, however, and Evander was too sensitive not to be terribly hurt. He became increasingly antisocial and more—I believe these days they call it macho. The upshot was that he dropped out of school, went to work in the mine, and spends his evenings at the pool hall. A terrible waste of a brilliant mind. But please don't mention this to Fred. He loves his brother and it hurts him to see Evander making so little use of his abilities."

A jingle of silver against glassware and a mild curse or two heralded the approach of the tea cart, an impressive vehicle of carved mahogany that some collector of Victoriana would have given an eyetooth for. Peter and Fred lifted it over the threshold without visible scathe and Iolanthe poised herself to do the honors.

Along with a mammoth cut-glass pitcher full of iced tea, there were fat strawberries with their stems on and a bowl of brown sugar to dip them in, hot buttermilk biscuits, pats of sweet butter with little daisies imprinted on them, and two kinds of jam in glass cups set into a pierced silver holder with a handle in the middle for easy passing. There were tiny sponge cakes with dabs of lemon curd inside, there was a wondrously elegant chocolate layer cake covered with mocha icing and walnut halves. Nobody was likely to go away hungry.

Fred unfolded a nest of small side tables and set them around at strategic points. Iolanthe dealt out the lavishly gilded and painted bone-china plates, the embroidered linen napkins, the polished silver dessert forks, the long-handled spoons and the crystal goblets for the iced tea, with a sprig of mint and a slice of lemon perching at the lip of each glass. Fred came around with the huge pitcher and poured the tea because he didn't want Iolanthe straining herself. Peter, as he helped himself from the wagon to strawberries, a biscuit, and a sponge cake, couldn't help thinking what a pity it was that the late Dr. Samuel Johnson couldn't have been of the company. This was definitely a tea to invite a man to.

As the tea cart circulated, conversation became desultory and mostly confined to pleasant nothing-muches like "What a beautiful day!" "These strawberries are the best I've tasted this year." "How on earth do you get your biscuits so light, Iolanthe?" and "I know I'm making an awful pig of myself, but would you mind passing me another sponge cake?" When it came to cutting the chocolate mocha walnut cake, not even Miss Rondel could refuse a wee sliver.

A tree sparrow and a catbird came to check out the menu and were treated to half a biscuit that somebody hadn't been able to find room for. There were desultory offers of further refreshment but no takers. There was a general breathing of contented sighs, there was loosening of belts among those who had belts to loosen. There was talk of strolling around the yard to shake down the carbohydrates but nobody cared to set the example. This was a magic time, it would be a crying shame to break the spell. Nobody was much pleased to see a long, shiny, aggressively opulent-looking black sedan slow down at the end of the driveway and turn up toward the house. Fred Wye was downright miffed.

"Now who the hell is that coming? Somebody about the mine, I suppose. I suppose I ought to straighten up some of this mess."

"I'll take care of it," said Iolanthe. "You go see who it is."

"Why don't you let Peter and me—"

That was as far as Helen Shandy got. The car put on a burst of speed and pulled up at the steps in a shower of gravel. The driver erupted like a blazing fury.

"Oh, my God!" Iolanthe groaned. "It's Father."

Fred advanced to the head of the stairs and stood there, legs wide, arms folded, like Horatius guarding the bridge. He uttered no word, he wouldn't have been heard if he'd tried.

Iolanthe's father was a big man, tall and broad, with a voice to match. He was in full spate, making little sense but an astounding volume of noise, brandishing a piece of paper in front of his son-in-law's nose. Fred was not backing off an inch. As soon as he could get a word in edgewise, he roared right back.

"Are you going to shut your mouth and get off my property or do I call the police and have you arrested?"

"You dare! You actually dare to talk to me like that? To ME? What is the meaning of this preposterous piece of effrontery? Answer me that, if you dare!"

"Oh, I dare all right. If that's the letter Matt Barrett sent you at my instruction, I expect he got it all down plain enough. Iolanthe is suing you for misappropriation of funds bequeathed to her by her great-aunt, which is what you must have bought that boat you're driving with some of, unless you've swindled somebody else in the meantime. We're both charging you with cruel and abusive treatment toward your daughter, deprivation of our connubial rights, and every other damned thing Matt can think of for the way you colluded with that other damned crook, Jasper Flodge, to embezzle our joint funds and break up our marriage. And damned near succeeded, damn you!"

"I was performing my duty as a careful father and a devoted pastor, attempting to snatch my daughter away from a licentious sinner that she might avoid the flames of hell."

"You're the one who put her through hell, you vicious old bastard. You brainwashed her from the day she was born, you damned near drove her into a nervous breakdown, you stole

245

her money and didn't give a damn if she starved to death for lack of it. That's how careful and devoted a father you've been, you rotten old whited sepulchre! Did I get it right, Iolanthe?"

"You certainly did, Fred. I'm ashamed to call this disgusting hypocrite my father."

"Judge not, daughter, lest ye also be judged."

"You're the one who's going to be judged, Father, and juried too. You've put Fred and me through three years of hell and now you're going to get a taste of what it feels like to have the ground pulled out from under you. Fred's right, isn't he? You have been dipping into Aunt Prunella's money."

"As executor, I am entitled to a yearly stipend."

"The hell you are," said Fred. "You're not entitled to one red cent, and haven't been since Iolanthe's twenty-first birthday. That's when your executorship ran out, but you never did get around to mentioning that little detail to her, did you?"

"I was only doing my duty as I saw it. She would not have understood. Woman's intellect is too frail to apprehend the intricacies of finance."

This was too much for Miss Rondel to swallow. "On the contrary, Mr. Bliven. Woman's intellect is quite as capable as man's, not only of grasping the intricacies of finance but also of unraveling the machinations of a swindler. If I have the opportunity of testifying against you at the trial, I shall be more than willing to do so. I do not hold with petty revenge as a rule, but a scoundrel who passes himself off as a man of God while trafficking with the Devil must reap what he has sown."

"This to me, Miss Rondel? To me, a man of the cloth?"

"To you, a hypocrite and a villain. Why, when your daughter's husband was away on a camping trip, did you conspire with Jasper Flodge to break up their marriage? The conspiracy, I assume, was prompted by the fact that you had been growing steadily more uneasy about the tenuous hold you had thus far been able to maintain over Iolanthe's inheritance. Fred Wye is a good businessman, it was only a matter of time before he would inquire into the terms of the legacy and find out that you had for some time been defrauding your daughter of the money due her. Once he knew the facts, you would not only lose all control of her fortune, you'd be lucky if you escaped being sent to jail."

"Ridiculous!"

"Oh no, not at all. You are a vain and selfish man, Mr. Bliven, and a tyrant to boot. You couldn't bear the thought of your daughter's having all that money and yourself having to scrape by on a pittance since you were asked to vacate your pulpit and can't get another because of your ranting and bullying. Being also a rather stupid man, you couldn't see any way out of the pit you'd dug yourself into until you happened to fall in with Jasper Flodge. Everybody in the county was aware of Jasper's talent for underhanded dealing, you probably considered him an answer to your prayers. So, to make a long story short, you came to an arrangement. In return for helping you pry Iolanthe loose from her husband so that you could bamboozle her out of her great-aunt's legacy once and for all, Jasper was to keep whatever pickings he could get his hands on before Fred came back, and lay the blame on Iolanthe. Isn't that how you worked it out?"

"I see no reason to defend myself against so palpably false an accusation from a senile old busybody."

"Calling names isn't going to get you anywhere, Mr. Bliven. I myself see no reason to believe that such a smoothly orchestrated operation as has been described to me could have been the result of anything but a great deal of careful planning between two wolves in sheep's clothing."

"Miss Rondel, you go too far. I defy you to prove that."

"Oh fiddlesticks. Don't try to humbug me. Your role was to poison Iolanthe's mind against Fred by reading her several letters purporting to prove that he'd impregnated nine mythical teenaged girls and been blackguard enough to desert them all, and their nine mythical illegitimate infants into the bargain. You wrote those letters yourself, needless to say."

"I did no such thing. They came in the mail."

"All nine of them in a bunch on the same day? Don't try to pretend that Jasper wrote them for you. Jasper could neither write nor read."

"He—"

She'd taken the wind out of Bliven's sails. Perhaps for the first time in his career, he could think of nothing to say. Miss Rondel pressed her advantage.

"You then proceeded, as planned, to rant and rave and browbeat your daughter until you'd driven her into hysterics and rendered her so distraught that she was only too ready to capitulate when Jasper Flodge came along with his spurious assurances of protection and help in getting away from her wicked young husband and starting a new life. Once Jasper had secured Iolanthe's signature on a forged power of attorney and gained possession of her bankbook and her door key, he dumped her in a Portland rooming house and came back here to steal her jewelry."

She paused for comment, none came. "I wonder, Mr. Bliven, if you've ever realized how well your accomplice made out on his share of the deal? Was it because you'd finally discovered what his profit had been, or was it because he'd started to blackmail you for more, that you somehow contrived to poison Jasper Flodge?"

Chapter 23

"I did not poison Jasper Flodge!"

Bliven was sweating now, his starched white collar wilted, his hands and his voice beginning to shake. "I refuse to continue this unwarranted inquisition. Iolanthe, you are no longer a daughter of mine."

"That's the nicest thing you've ever said to me. I only wish it were the truth."

Iolanthe turned her back on her father and began stacking sticky plates on the tea cart. Fred and the Shandys rushed to help her. Miss Rondel just stood there looking until, totally deflated, the unmasked rogue slouched down the veranda stairs and got back into the expensive car that he'd paid for with funds stolen from the legacy of which he had been so false a steward. Flushed and dejected, Iolanthe looked up at her guests.

"I'm terribly sorry to have let you in for this."

"Don't be," said Peter. "We're glad we were here to back you up. Something was bound to happen, you know, and the sooner the better. Now you won't have to go through another confrontation scene."

"Until the trial." Fred slid his arms around his wife. "Come on, honey, smile. I guess you won't mind me telling Matt Barrett to swear out a warrant."

"Not a bit. You go right ahead, dear. I'd just as soon tell Matt myself, for that matter."

"Then we'll tell him together. Anybody want another piece of this cake before I wheel it back to the kitchen?"

Helen Shandy was first to speak. "I wish I could, but I'd need to be wheeled out myself if I took another bite. Besides, Mrs. Bright is expecting us back at the inn for dinner. How we're ever going to eat it is more than I can figure out right now, but this is our last night and we'd hate to disappoint her."

"I do wish you were staying longer," said Iolanthe.

"Oh, we'll be back. We're going to show Catriona McBogle our great find on the way home, and that should set off some fireworks. You won't mind, Miss Rondel?"

"It's not for me to say, Helen. The paintings are yours now. I'm glad somebody appreciates them and it's high time they got looked at. I don't know what else pictures are good for."

"Who painted them, Helen?" Fred asked.

"Miss Rondel could tell you better than I, though I'm not sure she wants to right now, Fred. All I can tell you is that somebody in these parts is an artist of the first rank and Peter and I have been lucky enough to buy four absolutely magnificent paintings at a ridiculously low price."

"That so? Not to be nosy, but would you mind giving us an idea of what you paid for them?"

"Fred!" gasped his wife. "That's rude."

"I'm just curious. I've never known anybody who bought a painting. What do they go for, roughly speaking?"

"Anywhere from a few dollars to several million, depending on how good they are and what people are willing to pay. There are lots of paintings in museums and private collections that I personally wouldn't give a nickel for, but these are—I can't begin to tell you. Peter was the one who spotted them and recognized how great they are, and he's not even interested in art as a rule. We'd gladly have paid much more than we did, but the artist thought our offer was too high, if you can believe it. The upshot was that we got all four for just five thousand dollars."

"You call that cheap?"

"In this case, dirt cheap. Once the artist gets tied in with a gallery, I'll be very surprised if the prices aren't at least doubled. When the New York dealers get wind of a new talent like this, goodness knows what might happen."

"Well, I'll be damned. Want to give me a hand over the doorstep with this contraption, Pete? If you're not too high-falutin' now that you're an art collector. Wait till they hear about this down at the poolroom."

"Cut it out, Fred. They'll think I'm a sissy."

"Like hell they will. They'll all be bustin' their britches to grab one for themselves before the price goes up. Me included. You wouldn't happen to have the pictures with you?"

"Yes, but they're all wrapped up and buried under Helen's Christmas shopping; it would take a day and a half to get them out and pack them back in again. You'll have a chance to see them when you come to visit us. I know the Enderbles must be missing Iolanthe and I expect she'd be glad to see them and the critters, long as she doesn't have to clean up after Algernon.

251

By the way, Fred, not to change back to a less pleasant subject, there's one thing that I thought your ex-father-in-law, as I presume he now is, was telling the truth about, and it puzzles me a good deal."

"It would sure puzzle me if that old buzzard ever told the truth about anything. What was it he said?"

"It was in regard to those letters about your—er—alleged derelictions that Jasper Flodge was so careful to take away and destroy once they'd served their purpose. I don't know whether Iolanthe was in any shape to study them herself during the interval after her father had left and before Jasper Flodge blew in but there was always the chance that she might. The notes would have had to be hand-written, of course. Jasper couldn't write them because he didn't know how. Bliven wouldn't have dared; his daughter would have been sure to recognize her own father's handwriting no matter how hard he tried to disguise it. People think they can do that but it almost never works, particularly if the writer's a middle-aged man trying to pass himself off as nine different unwed teenaged mothers."

"What about Flodge's wife?"

"She might have written one or two of the letters, I suppose. She was living here in Pickwance with Jasper at the time, I believe, though she spent most of the week in Portland. I don't doubt for one minute that she was the one who faked up the power of attorney that Jasper used to clean out your and Iolanthe's bank account. I doubt if Mrs. Flodge could have written all the letters, though. She was such a flamboyant personality that she'd have had an awful struggle trying to tone down her handwriting."

"So what you're saying is that a fourth person was most likely involved, right?"

"That's what it looks like to me, Fred. Regardless of what

252

Miss Rondel thinks, I can't see how in Sam Hill Mr. Bliven could have got cyanide into Jasper Flodge. I was there in the dining room when Flodge died, as you probably know; I had a ringside seat for the whole performance. It's conceivable, I suppose, that Bliven could have found some mad dentist to anesthetize Flodge and fit him with a hollow tooth programmed to squirt out a lethal dose of cyanide when he got well into his chicken pot pie, but I can't say I'm sold on the notion. I'd help you put this stuff away if I knew where anything was intended to go."

"Don't sweat it, Pete. Iolanthe'll be here in a minute to find out what's taking us so long. So where does that leave us?"

"It leaves me right where I've been for the past three days, wondering who killed Jasper Flodge. Are you really serious about slapping a warrant on Iolanthe's father?"

"If we have to. It's not so much the money, Pete, it's what he did to Iolanthe that I can't stomach. Though I can't say I'd mind getting back some of the money I spent trying to trace her after Jasper Flodge showed up a few months later with another woman on the string. Old bastard, sixty years old and still tomcatting around. If he'd been twenty years younger, I'd have beaten the bejesus out of him. Claimed all he'd done was give Iolanthe a ride to the Portland Airport so she could fly to Boston with her cousin Willie. She never had a cousin Willie and she'd have been scared to death to fly. Jasper knew he was lying and so did I, but that didn't cut any ice."

Fred Wye snorted like a wild bronco. "I even tried to get some sense out of my father-in-law, which was the dumbest thing I ever did. He lit into me about being a child molester and threatened to set the police on me. I had to get out of there or I'd have killed him with my bare hands. Anyway he didn't know where she was and didn't want to, or said he didn't, which I can well believe. I hired detectives and they were no more good to me than he was. I put one on Jasper's tail for a while but all it came to was another hole in my bank account. I tell you, Pete, if it hadn't been for Evander holding me together, I'd have either gone crazy or killed myself. Ah, what the hell, it's over now and we're back together. And she'll be wondering what's keeping us. Damn, I wish you folks weren't leaving tomorrow. Ah, here's the old woman now, right on deck."

And there she was, giving her husband a tug on the ear and a peck on the cheek. "What's been keeping you two? We thought you must have got lost on your way to the kitchen. I hate to interrupt a stag party, but Miss Rondel's getting fidgety."

"I believe she wants to stop at the inn and say hello to Mrs. Bright before she goes home," Peter explained. "Fred and I were saying we'll have to get together in Balaclava Junction before too long. Algernon must be missing you, Iolanthe."

"Sweet old bunny. I do want to stay in touch with the Enderbles. You'll like them, Fred. They were so good to me."

Sensing that an intimate moment was about to occur, Peter went back to the veranda and assured Miss Rondel that he was ready to roll as soon as their host and hostess got untangled and came out to say good-bye. They did come, slightly flushed and disheveled and not altogether reluctant to speed their parting guests. Everyone was firm in the opinion that it had been a lovely afternoon and they must do it again, then Miss Rondel took a firm and determined step toward the Shandys' car and the tea party was over.

"Well, that was delightful." Miss Rondel spoke for them all. "I do hope Fred and Iolanthe have a child fairly soon, I hate to see the old families dying out. Iolanthe was just a little thing when her mother died. Claire Howard, she'd been. Claire's sister Margery came to help out, but once she realized what she'd let herself in for, she eloped with an encyclopedia salesman. Absalom's sister Virginia had been living with them right along; she took decent enough care of Iolanthe, but then another traveling salesman came to town. By that time Iolanthe was almost through high school and Virginia was fed to the gills with Absalom's bullying, so off she went and nobody blamed her a whit."

"That left Iolanthe stuck there alone with her father, then?" said Helen.

"Yes, but she'd always spent a good deal of time with her great-aunt. Prunella had been married to a plumbing-supply magnate who'd left her wealthy as Croesus's widow with no children of her own. Absalom would have been only too happy to pray Prunella into her grave, but she couldn't stand him and wouldn't have him in the house. She knew better than to give Iolanthe any money while she was still alive, but she used to send away for pretty clothes out of mail-order catalogs. Left to her father's tender mercies, Iolanthe would have grown up wearing sackcloth and ashes. Thanks to Prunella she was the best-dressed girl in her class."

"And the prettiest, I'll bet."

"Without question. All the boys would have run after her if they'd been given the chance. Needless to say, Absalom chased them off. He had a husband all picked out for Iolanthe, a piece of chewed string named Heber something—nobody ever remembered Heber's last name, he was that sort of fellow—who made ghastly noises on the broken-down old church organ and worshiped at his beloved pastor's feet. Absalom's expectation seems to have been that his daughter and her apology for a husband would stay meekly in the house and do

255

all the work while he swanked around on the money he was vain enough to think he'd inherit from Prunella. But some dear soul dragged Fred Wye to a church supper one night when Iolanthe was waiting tables, and that was that."

Helen smiled. "How long was it before Fred proposed?"

"I don't know the precise moment, but three weeks later she was wearing his ring and within six months they were married. If Fred had had his way, the wedding would have been even sooner. However, Prunella, who'd been ailing for a long time, died only a few days after she'd sent the engagement announcement to the newspapers and given a lovely party to which she'd invited both Margery and Virginia to make sure that Absalom wouldn't come. Naturally Iolanthe wanted to honor her great-aunt's memory with a decent period of mourning and also, I suspect, to get her trousseau together. They worked the same stunt at the wedding, Virginia was matron of honor and Margery's husband gave Iolanthe away. The wedding took place right there in the house with the Methodist minister officiating. I just wanted to give you a little background because I can see that you and the Wyes are going to be friends and you might as well have the straight story before you hear too many variations. I hope I live long enough to see their baby."

Considering the mean rate of longevity around here, not factoring in the homicides, Peter didn't see any great need for the Wyes to rush headlong into parenthood, but it was time he said something.

"Maybe they ought to start drinking your magic spring water."

He wished he'd picked something less provocative to say, but Miss Rondel took no umbrage. "A very sensible suggestion, Peter. I'll see to it that Iolanthe gets a jugful tomorrow.

Not that I claim any special curative properties for my spring, mind you; though there are some who do, or pretend to. I hope Elva isn't expecting me to stay for dinner."

They'd reached the inn by now, Peter pulled up at the front door. "Why don't you two hop out here? I'll drive the car around back."

"No," said Miss Rondel. "We'll go around with you and in through the kitchen door. I do want to see Elva, but I don't want anything to eat after that enormous tea. Furthermore, Claridge Withington's bound to be either in the lobby or in the dining room and I refuse to get involved with him."

"Can't say I blame you," Peter grunted. "He's about as much fun as a toothache."

"He's a good deal worse than that. He did something once that I've never forgiven him for."

"Good Lord! He didn't—er—" Peter floundered. The thought of Miss Rondel in the lustful embrace of Claridge Withington was mind-boggling and then some. But worse was to come.

"You may think I'm foolish, but it was the most—oh dear, I'm no good at this sort of thing. Anyway, Michele had brought me some supplies I needed—this was some years ago—and Claridge came along for the ride. He was better able to walk then, and he wanted to see the lupines. I set up a lawn chair for him a little down the slope, and he seemed quite content to sit there while Michele and I went inside and took care of our business. After a while I thought it would be only courteous to take Claridge a drink of water, so I started down the hill with the tumbler in my hand. And there he was, with an elastic band twisted around his fingers, ripping seeds out of the lupine pods and snapping them at the butterflies. I saw two mourning cloaks, a beautiful yellow swallowtail, a monarch, and a spangled fritillary, all lying dead on the ground."

Peter almost wrecked the car.

The wrapping-up process was, on the whole, rather dull. Withington couldn't run, of course. Neither could he explain away the very workmanlike slingshot, the small heap of egg-sized pebbles, or the cellular phone via which a neighbor trying to reach her husband at the pool hall had, by some technological quirk, overheard that old coot from the inn coaxing some married woman to meet him outside the inn, on the dark side of the drive. This happened to be the side toward which Withington's bedroom windows faced. Seeing so many cops around all of a sudden, the neighbor had thought maybe they'd like to know.

Even more interesting were the architect's rendering of the spa that Withington was intending to build at Rondel's Head once he'd disposed of Miss Rondel and the careful notes he'd made of the steps by which he had meant to hasten her demise; not to mention the will that would reveal his true identity as her only living relative, hence her lawful heir. The will would be discovered on the afternoon of the third day after the funeral, under the winter underwear in her bottom left-hand dresser drawer. A master criminal left nothing to chance.

The novel that Withington had been writing about a master criminal who wove his sinister webs far and wide while posing as a nice old gaffer to whom everybody came for advice and comfort was so excruciatingly dull that the detectives and handwriting experts assigned to study it would most likely have to be shaken awake and refueled with black coffee at frequent intervals. A quick riffle through the hand-written text revealed, however, that the meat of the matter was all there, from the master criminal's early attempt at ruining Guthrie Fingal just for practice to the far more expertly plotted scam that had worked so well on Fred and Iolanthe Wye until the necessary removal of a rebellious henchman had so regrettably brought them back together. The master criminal could at least congratulate himself on the cool finesse with which he'd projected the cyanide pill smack into the midst of Jasper's chicken pot pie.

Withington had projected further travails for the belea-guered pair, but had not got much done about it by the time Constable Frank and a contingent from the state police got the evidence neatly packed together and escorted the master criminal to a quaint little cell at the county lockup until something more permanent could be arranged.

Withington was still cocky when they carted him away. He must either be plotting a dramatic getaway or else psyching himself up to stun the bewildered prosecutor with the bril-liance of his self-defense and leave the courtroom free as a butterfly, surrounded by worshiping jurors, beautiful adven-turesses bent on tucking their telephone numbers in his breast pocket, and media people waving microphones in his face and urging him, quite unnecessarily, to talk.

Luckily for those others involved in the case, the process of the law had taken a remarkably short time, considering. Tomorrow morning, Peter, Helen, Miss Rondel, Mrs. Bright, and Thurzella would all be asked to show up at the state police station and give their formal statements. Right now it was still a few minutes short of eight o'clock and all of them, even Miss Rondel, were avid for the dinner that Elva Bright had saved for them. Understandably, they took a table as far as

possible from the one in the far corner where Claridge Withington had been for so long a fixture.

Once the food was ready to serve, Elva herself came out of
the kitchen and joined the rest at the table. Thurzella got a
kick out of waiting on her grandmother as if she were a tourist.
The innkeeper was ready to drop, but no end relieved to have
her own most worrisome mystery solved.

"At least now we know how that cyanide pill got into
Jasper's chicken pot pie. Imagine Claridge Withington just
sitting there in his corner, cool as a cucumber, popping it
across the room with an elastic for a slingshot! Anyway, maybe
I'll feel able to put chicken pie back on the menu one of these
days without having to wonder whether I'll wind up with
another corpse on my hands. I hope to goodness there aren't
any more mysteries floating around."

"Er—" Peter glanced uneasily from the innkeeper to Miss
Rondel. "There is one thing that's been puzzling me, though
I expect it's none of my business."

Elva Bright sighed. "Go ahead, Professor. Spill it and get
it over with."

"M'well, it happened the morning I went to pick lupine
seeds. As I was walking up toward the house, Evander Wye
came storming down the path, shouting back over his shoulder 'I'll do it, and you won't like it.' He sounded a trifle—
er—"

Miss Rondel only smiled. "Evander can be somewhat intim-
idating on first acquaintance. I'd suggested that he write me
a paper about his school days. Busybody that I am, I thought
it might prove a form of catharsis, get some of the anger out
of his system. However, he'd already found a different way to
work off steam."

"Throwing rocks at trees?"

"Oh, dear, is he at that again? I've told him and told him—Elva, I believe you have a customer."

The innkeeper didn't even turn around. "Thurzella, go tell whoever it is that we're closed.

Her granddaughter giggled. "It's Evander Wye."

"Speak of the devil! Come on, Evander, haul up and set. Have you had your supper?"

He shook his head. "I ate at the house. I just wanted to—ah, hell. Here."

Peter and Helen were sitting side by side, Evander laid a rectangular object about the size of a novel on the table between them. A piece of white paper, the remains of a doughnut bag, was wrapped around it. When Helen slipped off the improvised wrapping, she uncovered a deep shadow-box frame, with a piece of plastic wrap stretched over it to protect a small miracle. The paint was still wet, the subject was nothing but a few inches of dirt road, a lichen-covered granite boulder, and a blur of something that might be anything.

"Yet it's all here," Helen marveled, "the sea, the spring, the cliff, Miss Rondel, the house, the hens—and Peter. He's in it too. And so are you, Evander."

Even librarians get carried away sometimes. Helen pushed back her chair, flung her arms around the grinning, blushing artist, and planted a kiss on his chin because she couldn't reach any higher. Immediately, she apologized.

"I'm sorry. I don't usually get so familiar on such short acquaintance."

"Heck," said Evander, "I don't mind a bit. Come on, Miss Fran, I'll run you home and pick up those other canvases you've been itching to get rid of. Iolanthe claims she's going to hang one in the front parlor. There's a hole in the plaster that wants covering up."

"Well, that's how it is when you're rich and famous," said Peter. "Thanks for the painting."

"Thanks for the business. Let me know next time you're coming and I'll teach you how to play pool."

"You and who else? Don't worry, Evander, we'll be seeing you soon. We're coming to fill up our water jugs, if Miss Fran has no objection."

"None whatsoever." Frances Rondel smiled, and the face Peter Shandy saw was that of a young woman in the prime of her health and beauty. "Just so you don't tell anybody where the water comes from. People do get the oddest notions."